MW00352260

Until the Darkness Goes
A Novel

RENÉE EBERT

Until The Darkness Goes. Print Edition Copyright © 2013 by Renée Ebert. Cover by Rob Ebert and by Bart Palamaro of Dark Horse Productions. All rights reserved. This book or any portion thereof may not be reproduced or used in any manner whatsoever without the express written permission of the author except for the use of brief quotations in critical articles or reviews.

Until The Darkness Goes
ISBN-13: 978-1-946229-40-3
ISBN-10: 1-946229-40-7

Published by arrangement with the author,
who is solely responsible for its content.
Dark Horse Productions, Bath, PA. 18014
Distributed by Bublish

ACKNOWLEDGMENTS

Above all, I owe heartfelt thanks to my editor, Noreen Ayres for her professional honesty and acute literary eye. I feel very fortunate that this award-winning novelist took time from her own work to offer her insights and edits.

Thanks to Barbara's Writers Group -- both past and present members -- for their valuable suggestions.

Great appreciation goes to Bart Palamaro for his magnificent powers of observation and excellent formatting of the text. Thanks also to Rob Ebert -- a veritable poet of the camera -- for tracking down the best cover photo to mirror the mood of the book.

Part One

The Beginning

Outside the sun beat down on concrete and occasionally a car passed by. But for the most part stillness and a silence prevailed. It was the dead of summer, the Santa Ana winds blasted through the Long Beach 'hood and everyone moved slower for it. On a Sunday afternoon like this you could hear the Mariachi pouring out of radios, but today it was as if the energy of the music robbed every one of their last vestige of strength just to listen. The children were all quiet; Molly Morris peeked out between the slats of the blinds to see them listless on the steps in front of her building. They were all intent on sucking the sweet juices from their popsicles before they dripped onto their already sticky fingers. She watched the rainbow of colors as they quickly disappeared. Hector had a red one, Amelia a green and Ramon what looked like a pale yellow. That would be lemon.

Molly stepped back away from the blinds adjusting them to keep the sun's rays from slanting onto the crib. Stella was fretful but Molly avoided picking her up because she feared the heat from her own body would make it worse. She rinsed out a wash cloth in cool water and wrung it almost dry; just wet enough to bring the infant some relief as she placed it slowly, gently on the baby's naked back.

Javier was stirring in the other room. His late shift last night gave them the extra income they needed while Molly was on leave from her teaching position. At least he was inside, air-conditioned. He was a good man, proud of his gringo girlfriend and their baby.

Stella's tiny body relaxed as her mother ran her soft hand over the baby's head. The cool cloth reduced some of the heat from her body. Molly rinsed another cloth and replaced the old with the new. Javier shuffled into the room, his face flushed with sleep and the unremitting heat.

"Querida. I should buy a fan." He looked with worry toward Stella.

"She's okay. It's close to her feeding time again." Molly explained Stella's fussing to him, and he seemed comforted to know all was well. She unbuttoned her blouse and settled into the rocker with Stella who quickly grabbed hold of the nipple and began to suckle. There was a momentary pinprick of pain that eased as Molly felt the milk flow from her. Her love for this perfect little girl overwhelmed her and tears stood in her eyes as the baby's fingers held on to her pinkie. Getting pregnant had been almost too easy but at forty-one, almost forty-two, Molly cherished the happy accident even more so.

While Stella suckled vigorously Molly revisited her concerns about her mother's impending visit. Stella was just three months old and Molly still held her mother off because she knew Esther's will would prevail.

At least she gave me a few weeks' notice to prepare, she thought. She held the baby and rubbed her back to express any air out of her tiny belly. She didn't care what the doctor and La Leche League said, even babies that nursed gulped and needed to be burped. The baby had a dreamy look on her placid face. She was almost halfway to a nap when Molly placed her on her side, propped with a receiving blanket. She marveled at this little miracle. Her hair was darkening yet her eyes looked like they were turning green, almost like her own. She shrugged; maybe Javier's Spanish side had some Anglo to it.

The phone rang at exactly 1:00 pm.

"Hi, Mom."

"You picked up on the first ring?"

"I didn't want the phone to wake Stella."

"She should get used to noises, you know. Otherwise you'll be tiptoeing around the rest of her life."

Molly bit her lip to keep back a snorting laugh, thinking of the noise that penetrated their lives daily; fire engines, fly-bys and drive-byes a street away, and the inevitable LAX traffic as the planes headed toward Inglewood and barely missed the freeway.

"What?" Esther's antennae were up and in fine form.

"Nothing, Mom."

"Well, I wanted to give you my itinerary. I'll be leaving from JFK at 1:20 and will arrive at Los Angeles at 5:00 pm. Still don't understand how that happens with the time change."

"The date. What day are you flying?"

There was some fumbling and rattling of papers. She knew her mother made her reservations through Uncle Sol, and was probably going to be the only person on the plane with a paper ticket in its proper blue United Airways folder.

"May fifth. Uncle Sol got me a good deal for arrival on a Sunday."

There was a pause as Molly let go of the desire to ask her when she would be returning. Her mother could not conceive that Molly would ask. She wondered how it would all play out. Her mother and Javier in the same space. She could even see Esther leave and stay in a motel. Maybe she should start looking for a place nearby, like Hermosa or over on Warner Avenue in Huntington Beach.

"Now where did you say you'd be? I don't want to get lost or anything."

"We'll be near the gate as you come out. Security won't let us get any closer. Just look for a Mexican and his gringa girlfriend and half-breed baby."

Silence pervaded the space between her ear and her mother's lips. "You're not married." It was a statement, maybe an expectation, possibly a demand.

"Hey Mom, we'll be there." Molly hunched her shoulders to relieve the tension, and said good-bye.

* * *

Molly surveyed the room with Esther's eyes and was glad for a new coat of paint in all the rooms. But that wasn't going to assuage her mother whose big unanswered questions seemed to always be on the tip of her tongue whenever she called. Who was Javier? Where had she met him? What was she thinking to have started up with a Mexican, a guy who worked in a body shop? How could she answer these questions sufficiently for herself let alone her mother, who never recovered from her disappointment when her daughter graduated and left Boston College and with it, the Resident in Orthopedics, her mother's idea of a perfect match?

She walked quietly from the room where her baby slept and stepped out onto the back porch of the apartment house. It was a quiet enough neighborhood, although mostly a barrio close to but not in the gentrified section of Long Beach. The more expensive shops down near Ocean Avenue were only minutes away, but she admitted that you had to pass through "the 'hood" to get there. Which begged the question, why she was here and with Javier. She lived in Long Beach because it was cheaper and because she couldn't stand Orange County with its overly tanned white-bread communities measuring their own worth by the year and model of their Mercedes or BMWs. That part she could defend, she chose to live here before Javier came into her life.

Leaning against the railing, she remembered how Javier's cousin Theresa introduced him to her just a little over a year ago. Molly noticed him hanging around the outside of Theresa's Hair Salon while Molly lingered after the last customer, helping Theresa close up for the night. It was the least she could do for such a great highlighting job and for so little. Besides, she liked Theresa; the two shared their lives with one another. To Molly's way of thinking, Theresa had more to share. All Molly could relate to Theresa were her academic credentials and a guy her mother wanted her to marry.

She glanced again at her image in the mirror; the blonde streaks were subtle and Molly felt they took years off her appearance, something she gave more thought to than she'd ever admit.

"There's some guy out there. I'll stay with you until you lock up."

"That's my cousin, Javier." Theresa nodded toward the young man as she wiped her hands on a towel and opened the door to speak with him. Molly stood to one side looking between the slats on the blind. He was tall and angular for a Mexican, maybe it was the Spanish side or some Apache wandered down south of the border. She glanced at herself in the mirror and pushed her long hair away from her temples. She felt flushed; her skin had more color than usual.

"Javier wants to meet you." Theresa's voice had a heightened sound to it. Molly heard her jesting with customers, teasing their secrets out of them. This sound was not unlike that. Theresa hinted once in a while that some of her boy cousins would really like to meet a nice gringa. She wondered vaguely whether she was being set up.

Molly looked again into the mirror nearby and stood taller, tightening her tummy muscles. She walked toward him and extended her hand perhaps a little too eagerly. "Hi, Javier. Mucho gusto."

"The simpleton. He was afraid to come in because a woman customer was still here." Theresa playfully shoved Javier toward Molly which almost sent him crashing into her.

Javier held Molly's hand in both of his. His hands were warm, big and the palms were calloused. He spoke in a soft and low voice. "Hello, Molly. My cousin can be foolish with her jokes."

"See how pretty her hair looks?" Proud of her work, Theresa rearranged a strand of Molly's newly shaped coif. "Too nice to waste on a Saturday night alone. Eh?" Theresa and Javier spoke quietly for a few minutes while Molly tugged her arms into her jacket, trying not to listen closely although they resorted to a rapid, staccato Spanish she could not understand. It was evident that their chat had to do with her. Javier occasionally looked in her direction. Although, she told herself, they could just as easily be talking about some old neighbor who died last week.

"Molly, would you like to come to my brother's party? We're going there now. You can leave your car here, and it will be safe, and you can drive with me." He spoke in short halting sentences. He spoke shyly and his color heightened too.

"But that's a family party. I don't know anyone…I am not invited."

"We both want you to come. You won't be crashing anything. We don't send out invitations. Nothing formal. Just Enrico's new business but in this family there's never much of a reason to have a party, so we just have them."

So that was it? She accepted an invitation to a party, and then proceeded to have a baby? Would Esther make that connection? If anything had driven her to accept, it was the night before which was so frustrating. The blind date with Howard Spellmann.

Her friend Sarah assured her, "You'll like him, he's from

North Jersey."

To Sarah that was sufficient explanation for a date — Howard grew up thirty miles from the Bronx. Maybe Sarah saw a connection to Molly's Masters in History at UCLA with Howard's job and his degree in accounting at UCLA's Extramural Fund Management. So she was ready for Sarah's call this morning, eager to hear how well it all went off.

"What can I say? He's a nice guy if you like guys who spend half an hour cutting the skin off the pickled crab apple that was meant for presentation."

" He really is a nice guy who doesn't know too many people. I thought you two would get along. He's always so accommodating at Agape meetings." Sarah was talking about her half-baked religious conversion, half Christian, one-third Judeo-Christian mix and some sprinklings of Eastern enlightenment for good measure.

"I know, I know." Molly smiled at the thought. "Remember me, I'm the one you took with you as a guest?"

"What? You didn't like the singing? I know you liked the singing."

Friday night dates are only good when you already know the person, when it's something done among friends in Westwood or Santa Monica where you celebrated the advent of a weekend. Instead it was an evening of tiresome conversation spent with a passionless but well-meaning guy. And all it did for me, she thought, was set me up and leave me vulnerable to the attentions of the first dark and handsome guy that came along.

And Javier was handsome, all that dark hair, the dark brown leather jacket and the very white tee shirt, and the way he filled it out. She didn't need to mention the way his jeans fit. She admitted she liked living in the semi-barrio among the people there. It reminded her of home in the Bronx, the mix of so many cultures up and down Fordham Road, the smells of tropical foods on one floor of her mother's apartment house, Middle Eastern on the next and all that eastern European cuisine on her mother's fourth floor.

Molly felt the need for a cigarette, something she and Javier had forsaken from her pregnancy till this very minute. Yet the desire for a drag and a glass of wine or beer were strong. She left the back porch for the kitchen where she poured herself a lemonade and thought again of their first meeting.

That night she rode with Javier as Theresa suggested. They were both quiet, she looked over at his profile from time to time. He would look toward her, the sun was setting and they could see in the half-light. He didn't smile. The cars ahead suddenly began to slow down, the freeway accordion effect. It was happening too fast and Javier swerved to the left to avoid hitting the car in front of him. There was the thick smell of burning rubber tires as a line of cars all screeched to a dead stop. Javier instinctively put his arm out to prevent her from lurching forward and bumped against her breast. A practical man, his face registered more concern for her physical welfare than embarrassment. And she did something she would always remember; she reached out and held his arm to her, saying, "I'm okay Javier." He took her hand for the time they sat in the traffic near El Segundo just below LAX, and held it until the traffic began to pick up and he had to shift gears.

* * *

They arrived at the party. Enrico lived in a neighborhood just off the freeway on the ocean side. The house had a small front lawn with a porch painted in white and yellow. The side yard was ample, with people everywhere. Molly and Javier parked the car down the street. He came to her side of the car and took her hand to help her out, and he kissed her, just a light, furtive kiss, but it was enough. She looked around self-consciously, sure others would notice the heat of him and her heat throughout the evening.

Theresa was sitting on the porch, a bottle of Corona in her hand. She was quick to see their hand holding and as quick to wipe the smile off her face. "Took you long enough." She paused. "To get here, I mean." She handed her beer to Molly. "I'll get another."

"What about me?"

"You can take care of yourself."

His smile was different with Theresa and the others she met that night. It was full and open, and she compared it to her life in the Bronx, where her mother kept a lock on how much fun anyone was having on any given day.

Fuck it, she thought. Maybe that was it, maybe fuck it was what propelled her closer to Javier and the life she entered from the time she moved to Long Beach.

Javier stopped to speak to an old person there, a very frail and thin-boned woman who had to be ninety.

"Tía Consuelo, ésta es mi molly del amiga." He said this as he tugged on Molly's resistant hand. She understood his words as they were spoken slowly for the old woman who seemed hard of hearing. Aunt Consuelo's eyes glistened as she looked up at Molly, and Molly wondered what she must think of the gringa.

"Es un placir, senora." Molly stumbled through the language. The aunt smiled and patted her hand, speaking to both of them, but her words were lost on Molly.

As they walked around he introduced her to this one, the brother of that one, the cousin of the next one. They all laughed, the men gave her an appraising eye, and then looked a bit closer at their cousin. She never felt this good, that she looked good, that her life was worth a positive appraisal from the men and welcome from the women.

They were both quiet on the way back down to Long Beach, she in her reverie of the evening and how much she liked everyone and liked how they assumed she belonged to Javier. Beyond handsome, he was kind and observant. More than once he helped her through the conversations that whirled around her in rapid Mexican, and stayed near her side. She liked his physical closeness. She could smell his soap and water clean skin, the casual elegance of his dark brown leather jacket and jeans. He looked like a fucking movie star.

What did he think of her? Why had this happened?

She turned to him now as he drove south on the 405 and asked. "Javier, why did you ask me to come to the party?"

She trembled because she knew his answer would tell her everything. She chided herself for being so adolescent.

His silence was disquieting, it felt like a goddamned eternity before he responded.

"You are wonderful, mi muchacha querida." His hand had been resting on the shift, and now he slid it onto her bare arm in a whisper of a caress.

He slowed the car to a respectable seventy-five miles an hour and took quick and frequent looks at her. She saw an expression of sincerity and warmth. Yes, she understood the words, though she noted that from now on, she would be translating a lot of words on Babelfish from English to Spanish and back.

"You don't know me, Javier. You may not even understand all of what I am about to say. I am a tired and lonely person. I don't feel like I have a home, like I ever really had a home."

"I understand." He was saying this as he put her hand to his lips.

There would be opportunity for her to ask him later and many times what he understood that night. As her Spanish and his English improved, she would see herself through his eyes. Tonight he gave her a hint. He would tell her he wanted a woman who was smart, and a woman who was wild and pretty, and he found her to be all of that. She would ask him why smart and he simply said, to have smart children you need a smart woman.

He parked his Camaro at the curb and walked her up the backstairs to her apartment. "I see you many times at Theresa's," he confessed.

"How many?" She asked. Her voice was playful.

"You are so beautiful, so different." He fingered her hair, pulling it close to his face, bringing her closer too. They were on the landing in front of her door. She fumbled for her key and he took it from her, leading her into the darkened apartment. He undressed her by the time they reached her big brass bed. His movements were deliberate, slow, someone who could control his own desire and fan the flame for her in the process.

He stroked her body in long and slow movements that had her almost out of her skin. She fought the climax that wanted to explode, until he entered her. His movements were deep and yet very gentle as he plunged again and again. When she finally released herself, so did he. He lay next to her and she gently pushed his hair away from his forehead. She examined his body as he had hers. She noted every little nick or scar, asking him for an explanation as if it were all a road map to his life, which in many ways it was.

"What is this from?" She rubbed the short scar on his forehead.

"Enrico hit me with a heavy metal object." He laughed.

"What?"

"My father bought a horse," he hesitated, "small, metal

statue." The words came to him. "Enrico picked it up and hit me as I napped."

"Was that here or in Mexico?"

"No, not here." He breathed deeply in memory of some other place. "It was home. In Mexico." He pronounced it in Mexican and in a loving way that told her he missed his home there. They napped on and off and then, revived, they made love again.

There was too much fervor to call it sex. It was truly tender and ardently genuine love making.

* * *

Now, all these months later, over a year, Molly thought most about that. He loved her that night, maybe before that night and for sure every night since. And what about her? Was her ardor cooled? Did she still hunger for him? While she knew the answer to that question, she couldn't be as quick to call it love. She wandered around the quiet apartment, the place that became home for her, for him, and for this wonderful little girl they shared. No, she decided, I love him. And Esther? Somehow, for the moment, Esther didn't matter.

She's Gone

An eternity passed while Molly waited for Esther to pick up the phone. Her mother's voice came from the three thousand miles distance. It was expectant, expectant as though Esther was waiting for her call.

"Mom, something happened." In speaking the words, she realized she would relive the horror of it all over again. Her words pushed out in gasps as she walked through the moments of her discovery, when she woke, at dawn, knowing something had to be wrong. Stella did not cry out for her feeding, the cool breeze on her breast as it wept the milk awakened her.

"Mom," she started again. "Mom, Stella stopped breathing. Sometime during the night, after her ten o'clock feeding, she went right back to sleep and then when I woke to feed her this morning she was gone."

She expected wailing or recrimination, but Esther went inside herself as she did when Molly's father died. "Did you call emergency paramedics?" Mercifully Esther was asking questions, leaving Molly to answer monosyllabically. She answered alternatively, yes she had or, no they could not resuscitate her or yes, they thought it was SIDS. She didn't tell her that she refused to let them take her baby away, that it took three strong men besides Javier before she relinquished her daughter. That for a while, they let her sit rocking Stella, bundled in the softest of her blankets, that she crooned to her over and over, my pretty girl, my pretty girl until there was no breath left in her either. She didn't tell Esther that she let her go only after they agreed to her written conditions for an autopsy on the forms and initialed them; that the coroner would look at all other means to a diagnosis, would take blood and other samples to arrive at what seemed obvious, then and only then would she let them take her away.

"Where did they take her?" Esther wanted to know, and Molly explained. And the inevitable and wholly predictable, be sure she is buried tomorrow. Molly could not speak further, other than to lie.

"Don't worry, Mom," she cried. "It will all be done right." Javier stood beside her with tears in his eyes. She felt the warmth and weight of his hand on her thin shoulder that now rose and fell with her sobs, and she could not explain because he could never understand the Jewish tradition and Esther's demand to have their child buried as soon as possible, tomorrow.

"Mom, please don't misunderstand, but hold onto your tickets. Don't come now. Wait till it's all over and things are quiet. I can't..." She stopped. She wanted to say, "I can't have you here, I don't have strength to comfort you. Who will comfort me, she thought angrily? Who will be here for me?"

"Will your mother come here for the church?" In his grief as when he was fatigued, English eluded Javier, but she understood.

"She will come later." She wanted to tell him there was no need. That Esther was not the kind of mother to be a comfort the way his family, who were now arriving from Los Angeles and the San Joaquin Valley, could be. As their apartment filled with noise and genuine grief from the women and stolid strong faces of the men, she found it a respite in which she could hide away from her own grief. She let Javier's mother weep for her. The tiny dark woman was very wise. Molly knew she saw through it all to where Molly really was. She placed a loving arm around her and hugged Molly to her warm, soft body, and spoke loving words in Spanish, as though she were rocking the infant who was now so absent from the room.

Something cold crept into Molly as she thought how it remained her little secret, because Esther was too far away to intervene and to know that Stella would be buried a Catholic instead of a Jew. There was time for Esther's discovery and the consequent tirade that only Esther could whip up. More anger built in Molly with each new thought.

She looked at her watch, just after three. The phone had rung ceaselessly. She remembered to call her friends, Sarah and

Helena. They called her school for her. She forgot it was a weekday, it felt almost celebratory, a Sunday, with the food, the surreptitious bottles of wine that quickly became Sangria. She drank the wine fragrant with fresh orange slices and sweet strawberries; the bold burgundy held up under all of it but did not touch her body much less her heart. The heaviness of the day progressed into a headache, allowing her to beg off and retire to her bedroom so that she could get away from the constant barrage of offers to eat something.

The bedroom still held the baby smell of her little girl, more so in the sheeting of her crib. She placed her hand flat on the mattress and it was cold, no sign of the miracle that so recently inhabited this space in the universe. She tore at the crib sheet and found under it a textured cloth meant to capture baby drool, and she inhaled Stella's milky smell. How could this be and not Stella? How? Molly lay down on the bed and closed her eyes.

The door opened quietly and Javier sat down next to her on the bed. They remained still, as if they could reclaim their lives by doing so. She got up and sat in the rocking chair, her arms felt so empty. He passed his cigarette to her, a breach, already, from their agreement to never smoke in the house with the baby. She took a long drag and filled her lungs with the nicotine, felt her heart race because she was not used to its effect. But it was marijuana and as soon as she knew, she held it deep inside feeling her head swim, her body soften and relax.

"Querida. Go slow. Go mellow." He spoke to her in a singsong fashion. And she did what he suggested and the day and the world began to fade away.

13

Ritual

Ritual alone seemed to get Molly through those first days after Stella died. The Mexican women who lived in the apartments below and alongside her were genuine in their outpouring of food and condolences; some attended the small funeral Mass. Others brought well-meaning Mass cards because they didn't know she was Jewish. It was easier not to correct their assumption.

Molly would wake up at 6:00 am, her breasts seeping milk because the pills had not yet dried her up. She'd pull off her gown and step into the shower, letting the hot water stream down her body. She would soap up her legs and thighs and swollen breasts and shampoo her hair that became even more blonde streaked from walks on the beach. She would stand there, not moving until the water washed all but the grief away.

Afterwards, after the toweling and wrapping of hair, she'd start the coffee, rummage for some fruit in the fridge, and wait while the coffee dripped slowly filling the pot with the liquid and the apartment with the aroma. Each day she began the same way, after her breakfast and her third cup of coffee she'd invariably light a cigarette and take out a yellow legal pad, and slowly write her thoughts down. Sometimes her hand glided across the page, as a conduit to the sorrow of the lost child. At other times her pen was all jerky motion as she vented her anger, until it became near rage at whatever god had taken her sweet infant daughter from her.

More and more her pen described her utter loss and loneliness, her musings at what it would have been like when Stella was two or in kindergarten or when she read for the first time. After this Molly glanced once at what she wrote and tore the page. Long vertical tears from top to bottom, then across before she deposited the pieces into her kitchen garbage can along with the orange peels and coffee grounds.

This life could not go on because her leave from school was soon over. Her friend Sarah was gentle about it, suggesting that she might find work to salve some of her wounds. She didn't say it quite that way, but it meant the same. "Molly, you have to work through this. I know you'd like to stay home a little longer. You may feel differently when you get back to school."

Molly liked Sarah. She was a good friend, fun to be with, intelligent and truthful. No bullshit about Sarah. They became fast friends while working on graduate school projects together at UCLA when Sarah helped remove a student, tossed out of their group for not holding up her end. Sarah was fearless.

Molly did try. Her first day back at school was the hardest because everyone didn't say how sorry they were though their eyes betrayed them. She began the day reading over the lengthy notes the substitute teacher left for her. They told less of what she taught and more of who provoked whom into a fight in class, which kid resented the way their text depicted the Civil War, and how many tardy slips she handed out. The kids were the least problem for Molly. She opened the door to the same rowdy bunch whose voices spilled out in a cacophony she could hear down the hall.

"Hey guys! Let's quiet down." She could tell they were slightly deferential which meant some other teacher, maybe the sub, lectured them about being nice to Ms. Morris. But it didn't last long because the first hand that shot up was Dewain Thompson. "Hey, Mrs. Morris, can I go to the boys' room?"

She leveled him with one look and dropped her papers on the desk. "You're getting off easy today folks because I want to do some catching up. I have a long letter from Mrs. Beacham. Anyone care to comment?" The long pause in sound was broken by Arista slowly raising her hand.

"Mrs. Beacham didn't teach your way, you know. She read the book and asked the questions the book has, so's we never got to the truth."

It seemed to go well from then on, the rhythm she once had with them came back, yet she caught herself feeling her heart like an empty valve pumping nothing.

She thought it was going to be okay, the short drive home to the apartment gave her the brief respite between her day and her night, and she stopped at the supermarket on the way. It wasn't her usual store so it took a little longer to shop for the things she needed. She found herself going up and down some of the same aisles looking for coffee and syrup. She turned down the next aisle to find it was baby food, Pampers, formula. She stopped and picked up a pink container of baby bath soap and flipped open the top and breathed the subtle sweet smell of the soap, recalling the way Stella smelled when she swathed her in soft towels after her bath. Stella, all wrapped up after a bath smiled her first smile. And, she remembered, ever so briefly, an aroma of her baby's head. It smelled like the beginning of the living world. The pain she felt at that moment cut deep into her chest like a cold wind entering her lungs so that she struggled to breathe. A young woman was nearby picking up some Huggies. Her skin glowed with good health and the kind of tending that middle class girls get from their obstetricians. She pushed a cart with a little girl of about three. The child was the image of the mother.

She placed a warm tanned hand on Molly's skinny pale arm. Molly realized she must have been standing there for some time. Unable to move yet her face carried her message. She touched her face and it was wet.

"I'm fine." Molly searched for and found a crumpled tissue and wiped her eyes. It was all she could manage. No short sentence of I just lost my baby and it's still difficult. Not a remark about how pretty a baby she was. Nothing. One word more would have crippled her and a sentence would have caused her to scream out loud to a shocked young mother, do you know how very lucky you are, how precious and slippery it all is? She placed the bottle back on the shelf and left.

Later she rummaged in the medicine cabinet for the Valium the doctor gave her after the funeral, for her nerves she told Molly. She washed them down with some beer and by the time Javier arrived home she was not incoherent, she was unconscious. He must have thought she was asleep because he didn't even bother to wake her for supper, and she didn't wash her face or brush her teeth but slept until the morning.

Then it began, this spiraling down and she let it. It was so easy to not feel, to sleep when she didn't have to be awake. The next few days at school she faked it, the kids were given more written assignments and she gave fewer lectures. Their demeanor at first of welcoming her back changed to sullen soundless accusations that she, after all, was just as bad as the other teachers who punched the clock and didn't care.

Her stupor usually lasted till noon when she might rally for one lecture, and the lucky kids who got her at 2:00 pm got the benefit of her expensive graduate education. That ended too when her tolerance to Valium built up and the doctor wouldn't prescribe further. Without it she'd wake in the middle of the night, anxiety gripping her heart, making it beat faster.

She'd turn to Javier, nudging him with her arm, wanting him to wake and share her despair.

"Please," he'd mumble, "what time is it?"

"It's three o'clock. I can't sleep, I can't breathe" she would say.

"Querida, I have to get up at five. Please." And he'd roll over and dive deeper into his dreams.

Their schedules had always kept them apart but this grief was like a boulder in the path with mountains on all sides, no getting around it. There was nothing to share, not even the grief. She'd get up at five though she could sleep till six, and she dragged herself to make coffee while he showered. But Javier slipped out quickly, saying he'd grab coffee at the bodega, she needn't bother. And so she didn't. She'd come home to an empty house after school and sometimes make dinner which he barely ate, saying he'd eaten a big lunch. Yet she noticed he drank a six pack of Corona and so would she. Sometimes they shared a joint or two, and with all that beer, both of them stumbled into bed. Those nights she slept more soundly. He became haggard looking, his skin lost the healthy glow, so did hers. She hated looking at herself, the deep hollows under her eyes. Christ, she thought one day, I look like a camp victim.

She finally made an appointment to see Dr. West. It was the only way to get some kind of relief, and she told herself that pharmaceuticals were better than dope and beer.

The nurse called her name and she dutifully followed her into the examination room. The fair-haired, heavy breathing woman that Molly gauged was at least fifty pounds overweight took her pulse and blood pressure.

"How are you doing back at work?" She asked in a kindly voice. Molly spoke to her when Stella died, and it was her intercession with Dr. West that got Molly her Valium.

"It's difficult, you know?" Molly fretted with a ragged nail and looked at her dry and chapped hands. Maybe she'd stop for a manicure on the way home. The nurse left her, saying Dr. West would be in soon which was code for I hope you found a good magazine to read because you'll need it. The room was cold, always cold, and Molly rubbed her bare arms. She should have stayed in her own clothes. She grabbed her sweater and sat in the chair usually reserved for the doctor. She hated the exam table with its crinkling paper, where your legs dangled and where the only comfortable position was, sad to say, in stirrups. She leafed through the dog-eared New Yorker magazine, reading the timetables for off-Broadway shows. She always found it hard to picture New York in any but the winter season. She put the magazine down thinking she'd better begin to think what to say to Dr. West.

At that the door opened and a woman of fifty or so walked in. Her hair was reddish, curly, and therefore, Molly suspected, unruly hair, which was most likely why she wore it so short. Dr. West read some notes in the file and looked at Molly who moved to the exam table. She listened to Molly's heart and lungs, and asked her to lie down, and gently palpated the lower and mid abdomen.

"How are your periods? Regular?"

Molly nodded 'yes'. "I'm tired a lot, you know. Just really getting back to teaching again." She thought she sounded provisional, she hoped she did.

Dr. West put aside her stethoscope. She turned Molly's head left and right, and looked into her eyes. "You look tired."

Molly began to describe her symptoms, no need to lie now. It was an all too real nightmare. Molly's eyes shifted to the doctor whose face was without expression.

"I believe you have become dependent on the tranquilizer, Molly, and I really don't think that is the best option here."

The death knell sounded in Molly's ears. Death to any semblance of quiet and peace in her soul. No matter how drug-induced it was, she wanted it.

Dr. West spoke first, her face now full of true compassion. "I know how difficult it is right now. I'd like to give you some anti-anxiety medication and a recommendation to a therapist for counseling."

"Bereavement?" Molly asked. "Bereavement counseling? Is that what you mean?" Her composure slipped, some wild emotion took hold of her. "What will they teach me? How to live with my loss?" Her contempt was manifest as she tried to sit a little taller and hold it all in. "Fine, fine. I'll go to someone. Do I get to choose?"

After Dr. West left, she dressed, fumbling with her skirt zipper. Christ, I even shaved my fucking legs today for this. She picked up the prescription for the pills and the referral to the therapist.

* * *

The sun was high when Molly came out of Dr. West's office, prescription clutched in her hand. She fumbled for her sunglasses and car keys, her hands wet and sticky. Across the lot she saw some kids hanging around her beat-up old Nissan and was incredulous that they would bother to hot-wire it when the lot was full of late model American and Japanese cars. The clinic help couldn't afford the BMWs or Mercedes that were *de rigueur* among the medical staff, but even those guys were careful what they drove and parked in this neighborhood. As she advanced, the boys parted to let her get to the car.

"Hey, mama, you sho don't look like that ride." They snickered.

She didn't feel intimidated, not with ten years of teaching high school kids under her belt. "Bet your momma don't have a ride like this." She took her sunglasses off to let them see her eyes.

One boy, about nineteen, gently took hold of her arm, and said, "I can give you a ride." He was leaning into her face and she smiled up at him.

"Jimmy G. is that you? All done now with juvie hall?" She pulled away just as gently and unlocked the car door, slowly opening the windows to cool the car down because she wasn't sure whether her air conditioner was going to be obliging.

The boy dropped her arm as she said his name and

20

recognized her. He had once been in her tenth grade history, smart and quick, but his writing skills were poor to none from the years of elementary school shuffling he'd experienced. She might have felt sorry for him, but was too busy feeling sorry for herself.

"Hey, it's Ms M." He looked at two of the other boys who she remembered as her students at one time or another. "You know," he said, "Ms Morris". Hey, we wasn't going to steal your ride. You got that right," he sort of snickered. "We don't need no dump-me-on-the-freeway-when–I-most-need-help kind of a dog car." His delivery was not confrontational, maybe flirty but not disrespectful, at least not where he came from.

She extended her hand and he gave it a high-five, brother-to-brother slap. They smiled at one another now and she said, "I suppose I ought to feel complimented that you remember me. How are you?"

"Fine, doin' fine." He and the other boys began to wander off. The thrill of scandalizing a white woman gone now, and all they wanted was to leave her and the memory of Cabrillo High School in their rear view mirrors.

Molly shrugged. There was a time she cared, and now she couldn't muster concern for anyone but herself as she sat in her car, wiping the sweat from her face. Where to get her prescription filled? She knew from the nurse that this was only a week's supply of anti-anxiety pills. She wanted to get mellow, then get high, feel free of her life, not suspend anxiety. Fuck anxiety.

* * *

She stopped to fill the prescription, then drove home, the sun beginning to lower, the air getting cooler. The Camaro was parked out front and she silently cursed that Javier was already home as she dragged herself up the stairs and swung open the half-open screen door.

"Ola." He called out from the couch. He was already half lit, she thought, probably drank all the beer, as she checked to see there were two left. She opened both, swilled the first and then sipped the second. The pill kicked in, her heart wasn't beating as fast. Or maybe it was the beer. The smoke was profuse and dense in the living room. He had scored, so maybe there was some for her as well. She dropped down onto the floor near his feet and started to roll what was left on the coffee table. She wound the paper tightly to be sure none escaped.

"How was your day?" She purposely looked directly at him, and tried to take the edge from her voice because she wanted to say, "Is this it?" and he read that in her voice. He knew. It was the Indian part of him that read that shit in her remarks. Why does he bother with me? Why do I bother with him? Why is he here? Yeah, she thought, he reads that too.

He stretched his legs to better access the pocket on his tight-fitting jeans that were dirty with the day's grease under equally dirty and greasy cars. With some difficulty he pulled a neatly folded tissue paper packet out of the pocket and laid it out on the coffee table, carefully folding back the sides, being sure to contain the contents in the very middle. No one in this room wanted to lose anything but their souls, she thought.

"Gracias, mi amigo. ¿todos para mí?" She smirked as she looked up for his reaction. "Is this all for me?"

"Perra." His look was cold. "Always you laugh at me."

"Bitch? I'm the bitch? What do you call drinking all the beer and smoking all the dope? Don't tell me you saved this pittance for me. Oh, pittance? That's right, you wouldn't know what that means. "Pedacito minúsculo, minuscule." She gestured with her pinkie finger and he caught that her implication had more to do with his manhood than the size of the stash. She moved as quickly as his hand, but she felt the air brush past her face and knew it would've been quite a blow if he connected. She picked up her beer and moved away. Apparently he was smoking more tobacco than weed because he was definitely not mellow.

She lit the joint from across the room while she sat in a chair. She got up and, as a peace offering, handed it to him. He watched her with wary eyes, and took the joint, pulling the hot smoke into his throat. She saw him close his eyes as he sank back into the sofa pillows. His beautiful long eyelashes looked even more luxuriant than ever. She felt conciliatory toward him and slightly ashamed for provoking him.

"I went to see if the doctor could give me more Valium."

"Why do you need those? They don't help you feel better, just sleepy, all the time sleepy. Not good when you drive or work."

"They help me not remember. They make it mellow. That shit we smoke isn't as good as the Valium. I'd like to erase everything."

He leaned forward, his elbows on his knees and she saw how his biceps rippled and bulged. "But you must remember, Molly, or you will get sick." His voice was soft and reasoning, and it was clear that he had thought about this for some time.

"Yeah, Javier. It's not the same for you. You don't understand. I sometimes wake up at night and forget she's gone and then I remember all over again."

"Not the same?" He looked more closely at her, not angry, just perplexed. "I miss her. We were happy with her, with one another."

Molly had an overwhelming desire to be understood. "She was here, inside me for nine months and two days, listening to my heart, learning who I was. It's different. Now I am empty."

The pot was taking him somewhere because he said nothing further. She sat quietly next to him, and stroked his arm and he opened his eyes and pulled her closer to him resting her head on his expanding and contracting chest. She smelled the beer and the joint and the cigarettes and they smelled comforting and warm, as warm as he was. They didn't make love much anymore, sometimes if they forgot to not care. But now she felt a semblance of desire for him. As she looked up she saw that he was breathing more regularly and was asleep and recognized the other aroma she hadn't caught till now was whiskey, most likely tequila.

Weary, she pulled herself up off the sofa and deftly took the joint with her to the kitchen where she sat and smoked the remainder of the marijuana. Later she got up and scrounged through the cabinets for some food. When the munchie attack hit them both, they finally walked down to the stand for some carnitas and ice cream. This became their lives, they neither spoke to one another of anything of consequence. Had they ever, she wondered? That was all so long ago, she no longer remembered.

Midnight she awoke to his caresses and she knew that he was half asleep as she was. This became their impersonal sex, not lovemaking, just filling a physical need. He rolled off of her and she lay awake. The pills would run out and the pot wasn't doing it for her. She needed more. She knew a high was what she wanted.

Until The Darkness Goes

There was a party in L.A. that she had gone to with Helena. Molly had wandered off to a bedroom after too strong a drink and stumbled onto some of the guests doing lines. It was her first hit of cocaine and she loved it. The quick alertness, the feeling of superiority, yes, that was the part she liked the most, that she was the smartest person in the room. And, after another generous snort, the smartest in the world. From then on there was this nagging desire to consume more, much more of that wonderful drug. But it was too expensive for her pocketbook. She'd have to do some research, find a cheap substitute. Fuck it. I'm not going to some shrink just to get some anti-anxiety shit pills.

Drugs

It seemed odd to her that she would know what to do. Her innocent questions, eyes wide open about how things were in the 'hood began deliberately with her students. It was easy to turn the class discussion to drugs.

"Who can remember their civics class, the undermining of the Chinese? Which drugs were used for that?" Eager hands shot up. "Opium."

"Okay. How does that compare with now? And where?" She fed them and they gave back.

A hand shot up. Traverse Washington, a serious boy whose parents were both teachers responded. "Meth. Here, everywhere, and the color of the people it undermines the most is obvious." He looked from one classmate to the next, all rightfully smug in their considerable knowledge.

She challenged him, she needed to know. "Okay. Good. But it's not the same as having the government issuing and delivering the goods to the people the way they did in China." A whole room of hands was in the air. Discussion inevitably broke out, she heard snatches of what she needed. The name of a bodega near her apartment, most of all, the name of her local pusher, and as it turned out, her local savior.

Armed with this new information, Molly waited till it got dark and then headed to the bodega and roamed the tight dirty little aisles filled with cans of Goya products, mostly beans and refried beans, and she watched.

A young man with a do-rag on his head seemed to be in charge of things. He stood just inside the open door watching people pass by. There were always the little kids – ten and twelve years old – who ran about outside, and always they circled back to LaSheed. She knew he was watching her amble down one aisle after another. She picked up a loaf of bread because he stood nearest to it.

"Hey, mama. I seen you before. What you doin in this part of the 'hood?"

Molly pulled her wallet out, leafing through the twenties to find a five-dollar bill. "Same as you. I live here."

She handed the five to the grocer who studiously avoided eye contact with anyone standing near LaSheed. She held her wallet open to place the change in its proper place. "What you got?" she whispered close to his ear, as she placed the coins in her jeans.

He breathed close to her neck. "What you want?" He moved slightly away long enough to gauge her, check for the cop look, the undercover, slick chick, too fast to be real chick that would get him time inside again. He was so very smooth at what he did.

"Meth. I want meth." Her heart was beating extra fast in fear and excitement.

Javier had begun to drink more heavily ever since she dozed out on the Valium and beer, so now they could be out of it at the same time and high the rest of the time and from what she heard, cheaply.

Not one of her students could have believed she was looking to score. But not LaSheed. He got paid to know the target.

* * *

It wasn't long after Molly's first hit of crystal meth that Javier left. There was an inevitable sliding down in her relationship to everything surrounding Javier and Molly's tenuous coupling. Was Stella the lynchpin, no longer there to hold them together? It began that December when it rained the day after Christmas and for fourteen solid days after that. Living on the coast can be magical but there is a reality called fog and cold and damp days near an ocean.

On a Saturday night they began to drink heavily, as they had done on weekends that were now running into weeknights, and days. Molly knew the addiction to meth was deadly; so she used small doses and chipped on days when she was at school so that she could wake up after a boozed-out night. That weekend they switched from beer to tequila, and ran out of drugs and the money to buy more. Javier passed out on the couch, and Molly staggered into the bathroom to wash her face, remembering as she did that she stowed some money in a sock at the bottom of the hamper. She stuffed the money into her jeans and checked on Javier. He lay sprawled out on the couch. She stood right over him; he wasn't going to wake up.

She slipped out quietly to LaSheed, who on a Saturday night was holding court at the bodega, sipping a coke laced with rum and carefully watching the passing parade of young men and women. The rain stopped, so there was more activity than the last few wet days. Molly knew LaSheed positioned his ten-year-olds out there directing the 'traffic' to his door. Molly pushed past some chubby yet nubile fourteen-year-old girls in too-tight jeans that stretched across their ample bottoms, pumping provocatively to the rhythm of LL Cool J, Snoop Dog and Dr. Dre.

LaSheed, as though he was waiting all night, was ready for her.

"How's the weather?" she asked him as she approached.

"It's fine, all fine." LaSheed looked away and around as he spoke to her. "Times need something to make it good. You know what I'm saying?"

She handed off the money to one of the little boys who pocketed it and she left. Halfway down the block another ten-year-old walked by at a fast clip dropping the dope into her open palm. Molly ran it up the sleeve of her heavy sweater and walked slowly back home.

At 12:30 she was back at the apartment, but Javier was no longer asleep. He nodded as she walked by him. "I went out for some beers, we were running low." She dropped the six pack of Corona onto the coffee table and continued to the bathroom where she immediately cooked her dope, inhaling the fumes like a thirsty dog laps water.

Ten minutes later he kicked the door in. "You spend the damn money on shit? You give me nada."

Molly weaved, her legs entirely out of her control. She sat down on the toilet seat. "Javier, my compadre. So eloquent this evening. What could you possibly mean?"

27

"Fuck you, bitch. Where is it?"

"Ah, golden-tongued love of my life. Speak up, say more. You want something?" The slap across her face came with such force that she moved off the toilet to become a crumpled mess of limbs against the bathtub. She thought she heard the window casing rattle.

"Get up, bitch!" He was frothing and the spittle was sprayed on her face.

"It's gone. I used it all, it's gone," she repeated while he shook her, plunging his hands into her pockets, ripping at her bra, her pants, anywhere she might have hidden her stash. "Fuck you, shithead. I don't have anything. I already told you." The drug kicked in further as she became angry, braver. She tore at his bare arms, leaving red streaks on his flesh.

Javier was sufficiently sober to shriek with surprise more than pain. It was enough for her to get beyond him and out of the corner. She fled the room and the apartment and into the chest of a cop. The noise must have been too much even for her neighbors. Javier ran after her, and there was a second cop, bigger than the first, who had him in a choke hold, Javier's arms flailing, trying to reach her, trying for the powder that would make him as powerful and as all-knowing as she now felt.

* * *

Molly woke to find she was encased in a wool blanket smelling of beer and sweat, the blanket that must have been thrown over the shoulders of every victim of a freeway car mishap, attempted rape, and domestic incident.

A policewoman was saying something to her. "Molly? You're at St. Mary's. How's the arm?"

Molly looked dully at her left arm encased in a soft cast and held up in a sling. She was wary of the woman's badge, and the policewoman must have seen her stiffen. "I want to ask you again whether you want to press charges on Mr. Gutierrez."

Molly shook her aching head no. "I can't. He's her father." She was barely audible.

The woman was sitting on a chair across a quiet room in the emergency department, not the usual bay with curtains between people so that everyone could hear and smell and see life on any given Saturday night. She got up now and went to Molly's side, clipboard and pen still ready. "I didn't quite hear what you said. He's the father? Of who?"

"Whom. It's of whom." She suddenly was more aware and didn't wait to register the narrowing of eyes and the sting her correction made on the police officer. She was still very much in the control of the drug, and couldn't do any wrong. She looked at the woman, thick legs and arms, bursting out of her policeman's pants and shirt, wondering why they don't upgrade to a larger size after they've been on the force long enough to succumb to the bulge from too many donuts, KC and diet coke.

"You married to him?" She checked her papers, and said, "This Javier Gutierrez?"

Molly shook her head no. "He's my baby's father." She hurried on before the woman could ask. "Her name was Stella. She died at three months from SIDS." Her head began to hurt, the light in the room made her eyes feel as though she was looking directly into the sun. "Can I go home?"

"We have a few things left to do." The policewoman clicked and retracted the pen's ballpoint. She left the room and Molly lay back on the gurney. Her shoulder began to ache from where she connected with the bathtub. She very carefully opened and closed her stiff and swollen fingers, setting off a throbbing to the entire arm.

"That's not too good an idea." Dr. Suarez entered the room and checked her fingernails, his own fingers light and cool on her throbbing hand.

"What are you looking for?" she asked. "Doesn't it say I have a broken collar bone?"

He introduced himself. "I've been assigned to your case. I'm a therapist. But I did read your chart and yes, it is a broken collarbone. I was just checking to see whether the bandage was too tight."

"So why look at my fingers?" She tried to pull away from him and winced with pain.

"I'm sure you know I can't give you anything for the pain. Your blood work revealed some contents not normally found in humans. At least not in such large doses. I should say humans like you, because around here, the drugs are almost a constant. Just be glad we didn't have to do any surgery. The fracture was un-displaced." He made a note on her chart and she tried to read what he wrote. "Curious? He handed the chart to her. It's all about you and legally it belongs to you."

She grabbed the chart with her good hand and read the meticulous report about the fight that brought her here, testimony from her neighbor Carlos Nunez. She threw the chart on the gurney and sat up. "Addict? What do you know about it?"

"I know that you need some help. I'm not a trauma doc. That was someone else who fixed your arm. I'm a shrink and you have a choice. Therapy and N.A. meetings or they'll hound you till they catch you buying and using. I'm right here at the hospital and that's a quick bus ride from your home. I can see you next week." He looked up at her as he wrote something on a prescription pad. It was the time and date for an appointment that Wednesday. "I'll see you then. The clerk will get a cab when you're ready to go home. Javier is temporarily in jail. I understand you don't wish to press charges."

"It was an accident." She wiped the tears from her face and eyes. "It was all a big accident."

* * *

She slept part of the way home. She thought of Dr. Suarez, of all that happened tonight. How did he know I would need the bus? Someone must have told him that I cracked up my car last week and Javier hasn't gotten around to fixing it. She wondered if Javier would be there before her. She hoped not. She felt ashamed that they should come to this, that those very nice neighbors should see her as just some trashy white woman.

"You okay, Miss?" The cabbie, who must have seen her crying, was a thick-muscled white guy with a handlebar mustache. The kind that could just as easily work as a bounty hunter or a bouncer. As gentle as he was, he was also big. Bet he has many a woman ride home from St. Mary's E.R. in a similar bruised and broken way.

Life Changes

Six weeks and her arm almost healed, Molly was back at work. No one asked, but she heard the whispering and saw the averted eyes of the other teachers when she took a break between her junior and senior classes. Hard to know how to react to a teacher covered with bruises and an eye turning ugly yellow from the former black and blue. Things got quiet, then talk resumed in the teachers' lounge. The atmosphere became overly cheerful with a colleague, Tom Kelly's round face and belly laugh leading the conversation about football, usually USC against UCLA. Nancy Burrow, fiftyish and counting the years to an early retirement, nodded hello and lip-synced "How are you?" The rest ignored her with a fleeting smile before sipping tea or coffee, grading test papers or whatever else they were momentarily removed from before Molly showed up. She made short work of her half sandwich.

Tom gently touched her arm in its sling and asked if she needed Tylenol. She thanked him and crumpled up the wax paper, dropped it and the brown bag it came in, and faded from the room. She smiled to think of the calamity of voices that started up as soon as they were sure she was out of hearing.

She walked slowly down the hall to the front office bearing the short note she found earlier in her mailbox. It was signed by Robert Polesky, Vice Principal. She entered Polesky's office and sat down on the chair directly in front of his desk. Robert Polesky looked almost as nervous as Molly felt. He was wearing one of his signature K-Mart short sleeve plaid shirts and polyester tie. He was over six feet-seven inches tall, but too clumsy to have been any good on a basketball court. He picked up his coffee mug and thought better of the stale, semi-warm coffee that even a Starbucks brand latte could not make palatable.

"How's it going, Robert?" Molly straightened the long skirt so that it spread over her legs. She caught him watching, peering over the desk to catch a glimpse.

"How's the arm?" Without waiting for her to answer, he cleared his voice, and fidgeted with his tie, while glancing at some papers on his desk. "It's like this, Molly. It just isn't working out here. I know it comes at a bad time, but we're having all these substitutes and it's just not a good deal. Mrs. Parker and the board met..."

"Why not end it there?" Molly stopped him, leaning forward, bracing the arm still in its sling. Her voice was level, hiding the panic she began to feel. "It's okay. I need the break." She smiled at her own pun, and was thankful once again for the last of the Valium pills she found in the bottom of her purse, for taking some of the edge out of coming back here to be the object of everyone's curiosity.

Robert was nodding sympathetically, a simpering look playing on his lips. "That's right. A break. Good. It's really a leave of absence until you get healed." He sounded weak.

She wanted to slap the look off his face. Instead she stood up and left, her mind whirling around things like how much leave of absence meant in actual dollars, knowing it would not hold up her apartment, food, utilities.

Molly walked down the quiet hall, looking in each room as she passed, teachers engaged, chalk in hand, scribbling on blackboards, others pacing the room as students bent their heads to a surprise test while she felt like the outsider, the one out of sync with a world she had been part of until fifteen minutes ago. She alternated between a depression and an unexpected celebratory mood; elation for the freedom from this school, this vice principal, this ramrod curriculum she fought, trying to keep her class interested in a seriously irrelevant and whitewashed history she was forced to teach. Now that was going to be someone else's job, or not, if the kids weren't lucky. All the while she calculated the money she had against what she needed. Javier came to her thoughts. She threw that out. Her arm nagged with a small throb of pain. She hurried to catch the bus to her first therapy session.

* * *

Mired in thought she missed her stop by a block. She was ten minutes late and out of breath when she arrived at Dr. Suarez's office. He was standing at the door as she climbed the steps to the second floor. He wore khaki pants and a white dress shirt open at the collar. His dark hair was longish, and it receded to reveal a high and intelligent forehead. His right hand was casually in his pocket, and she wondered how many times he looked at his watch, thinking she'd forgotten or dismissed him.

"Got messed up with the bus connection?" He asked her this while he moved so that she might precede him into the room, and added, "Happens to everyone."

Catching her breath, she signaled a 'yes'. "Went two blocks past," she exaggerated. "Sorry."

They walked through the little anteroom into his office and he gestured her to a seating arrangement; she could take her pick between a chair directly across from him or the couch at a slight angle. She chose the couch. She was sweaty from the brisk walk, which added to a feeling of displacement, out of step with a greater world. She settled herself on the couch and looked up to find him already seated and looking at her, waiting. They were quiet now, but briefly, before he began.

"Here's a short schedule you will need for your N.A. meetings. I recommend you find those closest to work for weekdays and then near home for weekends. You know you must attend at least three times a week."

Molly looked at the address close to the high school. "Someone went to a lot of trouble to make sure I got there after school. But…" She didn't finish; instead, she laughed through her tears. "Lost my job today." She didn't wait for him to respond but went on, saying, "I'm thankful it's just a leave of absence but I won't be getting a full pay. So, I'll adjust my meeting to my new situation." She landed hard on the last word, her throat tight against this sudden torrent of emotion that wanted to pour out. All the time he was watching her, maybe weighing what she had to say.

"Let's go back to the beginning." He clicked the ballpoint pen. "Are you drug free right now? And, that means alcohol too."

She answered yes to the drugs. No meth but left room in her

mind for pot. She indicated yes, free of wine and whiskey, but discarded beer like the one bottle she drank last night because she sipped it with dinner. She wondered if he could see her reasoning it all out.

"I'm not going to say I don't want the relief. Christ. I just lost a major part of my income, and my car is dead. I feel like shit because I feel. All the time. I liked being numb from the Valium or high from the cocaine and meth. Wouldn't you if your life was falling down fast?"

He didn't speak and except for one or two notes, stopped writing, and again was looking directly at her, his eyes almost unblinking. She wondered how he managed that. Was it something you learned training to be a therapist?

"I don't even have a car." She repeated. "In fucking Southern California. Have you any idea what that means?" The words were meant to be confrontational but came out in a soft sigh.

"And Javier? Where are you with him?" She saw that, like a robot, he was going to stay on track, sounding, maybe a bit anal retentive, she couldn't say for sure.

She took a deep breath and brushed her hair back off her temples and let it drop. She was aware of its weight as it fell onto her back, and she liked the feeling. He watched impassively as she took strands of it through her fingers, so she stopped.

"He moved out before I was even released from the hospital." She thought of the days this past week, entering the empty apartment, a place that she pictured during the hours she taught at school, how the sun's rays slanted longer as the day progressed, the apartment still and quiet, the digital clock dropping numbers every minute. No one home, it seemed to say.

"I don't mind," she continued, "I like the quiet. The first few days I played the radio or turned on the TV. You know, just to fill the room back up with life." Her voice caught on the word. "But now, most nights I forget to even watch the news."

It grew quiet in the room. Dr. Suarez startled her out of a reverie that seemed almost too perfect. "Do you want to tell me about your baby?"

She continued to sit there for three or four minutes, her senses tingling with the risk she now felt at trying to discuss her loss. It wasn't the loss itself, she carried that in her head, Stella in all the aspects of her she remembered from the time she was born through the last moments of rocking the cold and lifeless infant before they took her away. So what was the hesitancy? Her slow response had more to do with the suddenness of the subject, no time to prepare or steel herself against the violence of her strongest feelings about losing her baby. Her baby, the only experience she'd ever had that approached nirvana.

"Stella?" She stalled for time. "You cut to the chase don't you?" She rubbed the back of her neck and it felt damp. She'd shower as soon as she got home; the image of yet another bus ride back home seemed daunting. "My baby. That was a question, wasn't it? Does that imply a choice, then, on my part?"

Her thoughts jumbled up. *Let me guess, from Psych 101, he wants to assess whether my recent drug interlude is symptomatic of addictive behavior, and/or a measure of the percent that can be directly attributed to the shock of the loss of Stella. Only she wasn't lost. Because I know where she is right now.* While she thought out her progressions, she saw him, that strangely impassive and expressionless look. Not someone she would figure for using so confrontational an approach. *Why push me? Do I look tough? Like I can handle this?*

"She's in a Catholic cemetery, in a white coffin. She's just not breathing anymore." Her face was awash again like the first days after Stella died. She wasn't crying but her eyes belied that and now she gave in and she cried very hard.

Dr. Suarez sat up a little straighter, uncrossed his legs and leaned forward toward her. She felt his humanity for the first time. Until now she thought of him as an unwilling player, court ordered, therapist for the low income-no income crowd. "How are you feeling right now?"

"Don't do that. Don't play those silly therapist games. Because I can do the same thing. I can say to you, how do you think I feel? And where would that get us?"

She looked for a reaction, a flash of anger, some impatience? Nothing. Well, maybe he was more engaged. She balled up her tissue and successfully lobbed it toward and into the waste basket that was placed not too far from where she sat, but enough to have made her effort a minor accomplishment. She saw him try to hide the beginnings of a smile at her childish toss of the tissue, and saw

35

him recover his professional demeanor.

"Molly, I am not trying to goad you into things you don't want to disclose or feelings you are uncomfortable with. I sense that you've never experienced therapy before and I am trying to help you get to some of the things that led to the crystal meth and the alcohol. So let's start again. Tell me what you would like to get out of these sessions for yourself." He held up his hand, a thick silver ID bracelet slid down his wrist. "And take your time."

Molly shook her head. "Isn't it amazing the see-saw of emotions in the last five minutes of my life? I chuck used tissues into your basket, cry because you mention my baby and now I'm wondering how the hell I'm going to keep my apartment because I am on temporary leave which may mean I lost my job. Maybe it's just life happening in a messy collage of things instead of neat and orderly." She stopped to think. "I want my baby back. And I know how that sounds. I don't care about anything else. So I'm trying to deal with that one thing." She stopped again. "And then there's the fact that I may not ever be able to get pregnant again. That doesn't stunt the loss of Stella. It accentuates my fears. Most of all, I want the fucking pain to stop."

She rested her head against the couch. Its softness felt rich yet it supported her head. "But then I think, I've always been something of a hedonist. I use to really dig the good leather of expensive shoes, and now I hunt for sandals off-season. Now that I have almost no money, I am so aware of this nice couch you have, and I compare it to the one in my apartment with cigarette burns." She paused, listening to what she just said. "I'm really very tired. My arm still hurts. Can we stop now?"

Suarez scribbled a note on his pad as he asked. "Were you fired?"

Molly explained the door was still open for her, that it was considered temporary leave.

"It could be good to take a break now, for the moment. From all I've noticed, I think you went back to teaching sooner than you should have." He stood and walked out with her. "Give the therapy, the N.A. meetings, all of it a try. Don't fight it."

She woke suddenly when the bus lurched to a stop. She must have slept the whole way because they were minutes from her stop. Her arm was stiff from having leaned into it and she tenderly touched the shoulder. God, I could use some pain killers, she thought as she carefully negotiated the steps down onto the sidewalk near the bodega. She checked her purse and stopped in to buy another pack of cigarettes. At least they were black market prices here in the barrio. Gotta have some benefits to living like this. She leaned into the freezer and looked for a Good Humor Banana Split ice cream bar. Sure they would have one, she was frustrated when she couldn't locate any.

"Jose." She called out to the storeowner. "Donde está el helado del plátano?"

Jose looked up from his copy of *La Opinion* and smiled at Molly. "No platano."

She was so sure she saw that flavor. She dug around and landed the last bar of Toasted Almond. The only reason she trusted it was almond was the fact that there were more almond trees in Southern California than anywhere else in the world. She didn't wait but tore off the paper and bit into the ice cream bar as she stood paying for it. She was short five cents, and Jose casually took pennies from a dish and dropped them into the register, smiling at her.

"Adios, Jose." She waved her hand, ice cream bar and all as she left the store.

Narcotics Anonymous

One more reason to have stayed home, and she was in that frame of mind when her neighbor Carlos saw her plodding along and offered her a ride.

"You got a ride back?" Carlos asked her as she opened the car door to jump onto the curb. He was a gentle guy with a family of three boys and one little five year old girl, an after- thought or midlife baby judging from Carlos's wife who looked late forties.

"It looks okay. I'll get a cab or grab a lift from someone here." She lied to him because she didn't know anyone and wouldn't accept a ride from a bunch of addicts. *Like me*, she thought. *Not just like me.* "The leader for our group said he'd find someone for me," she lied again. When she called Gary, the leader for the N.A. group, he had suggested there might be a bus back or she could get with one of the guys, but he couldn't commit because he never knew who would show. She understood. She watched as Carlos pulled away to circle wide into a U turn and drive back toward Redondo Beach Boulevard.

There was a flash rain earlier so it was muddy in the parking lot. She looked around for the building Gary had described, and picked it out, a low-lying one story attached to a Baptist Church that must have been the all-purpose rooms for children's Bible studies. It looked like so many built in the early sixties, weathered, losing its layer of cheap brown paint. She found it hard to believe that anyone worshiped in the church or that children filled the classrooms for stories of Joseph and his brothers on Sundays. The lights shone onto the dark parking lot, offering just enough for her to navigate the path of broken concrete sidewalk.

She swung open the door to find a woman in her late

twenties just inside, looking out, jittery, her hands shaking. Molly said hello and the young woman nodded and slipped outside for a cigarette, reminding Molly that they were in a public building and would be expected to refrain from smoking. She spun on her heel and joined the girl, lighting up as she spoke. "Do they start on time?"

Smoke from Molly's cigarette wafted in her direction. The girl rubbed her eye and Molly apologized, changing her direction. "Yeah, ten to eight. No worries, it's 7:45. She was looking furtively from the parking lot to the street lined with scraggly brush and unkempt hedges, and then back down the street Molly traveled to get there. The conversation ended as the girl's own agenda asserted itself. A car raced toward the side of the lot and stopped in one jerky squeal, and the girl rushed to the open window near the driver, who handed her something which she quickly pocketed, and just as quickly moved back to the curb, brushing past Molly into the building.

Molly blew out the smoke from a deep drag on her cigarette and noticed the car idling at the curb, waiting. Waiting for her, for another customer who might want, need, a soother to get them through an evening of self-recrimination, self-doubt, regret. Or just listening to the others as they played out the litany of their broken dreams, or more likely the broken promises they made as they scooped up the last bits of a paycheck to satisfy the monster habit. When she made no move toward the car, the man with the Fu Manchu mustache drove away.

* * *

Everyone settled into the circle of chairs surrounded by the half-light of weak light bulbs. There was John from Hermosa, a retired hippie who managed to live by selling beads to tourists because he occasionally flipped a house for a buddy who made good in the Hunt brothers' silver run-up in the sixties. Most of John's money went toward maintaining his habit. He introduced himself as they each took turns. Hi, I'm John, cocaine and pot." There were five others. The jittery girl was Suzanna that she pronounced with an "ah." She was stick thin and her little trip to the girls' room after her quick meeting with the driver of the squealing brakes rendered her mellow and slow speaking. The rest were guys between twenty and forty who were alcohol/pot; pills/meth and just plain meth/alcohol/pain pills. *Suzahnna* was coke/alcohol so, Molly decided, she must have been well heeled, as meth was the odds out favorite for this crowd.

Gary, the leader started the round robin. "Hi, I'm Gary,. They responded with a lazy, or very casual–sounding, "Hi Gary." "Hey, guys. I want you to meet a newcomer. Molly, why don't you tell us," he paused, "whatever makes you comfortable." The guys all seemed fairly attentive, most sat up straighter, and alert. No one else so flagrantly violated the rules of using the way Suzanna had.

Molly cleared her throat, "Molly, meth." She smiled a weak smile sent in no particular direction. "I'm court ordered, and I've never been to a meeting like this before." She paused and looked down, picking at her cuticles. "Because I never used before." She shrugged as if to signal Gary and the group of willing listeners that she was through for the night. Her immediate thought was no way am I wasting time with these losers.

There was a spattering of anemic applause made louder by the echo off the walls of the empty room.

"Okay," said Gary as he looked from one face to another. "Do we have testimony tonight?" He looked for a signal that someone was going to step forward. Molly knew enough about this process, bleed their hearts out in plaintive chords about how it all came to be. How they, the beloved son, or big brother or errant husband with a good construction job or telemarketing gig with a real future got fucked up and became what you see here tonight. A hand was raised, first tentatively then more resolutely. It was the twenty-year-old boy in the clean black tee shirt with the small tear at the neckline.

"Tony. Great, dude." Gary almost exclaimed in rapture. Otherwise, Molly sensed it would be Gary's ass nailed to the wall for the evening's entertainment if he couldn't bag a quarry and get someone, anyone, to bleed out.

Tony obliged as he told them he was "pot/meth" and how the one led to the other and all of a sudden he was out of school, kicked out and then the next three years were, wow, man, out of control, you know, living up there in San Francisco with some really great people who, he figured later, were not so great. He told his story with eagerness, with a deep desire to be understood, to be congratulated for being clean and sober, this time, for ten weeks, and finally to be forgiven. He wasn't disappointed because they all high-fived him, the guys anyway and Gary for sure.

"Good testimony, dude."

* * *

Molly hitched a ride with Tony, who graciously offered when he heard her ask if anyone knew where the bus stopped. He was reed thin with an innocence not tainted somehow by his drug addiction. She chalked it up to her maternal instinct because she could see the boy he was at sixteen. The sobering and cold fact was that arrested emotional development was what made him what he was now. He had a lot of growing up to do.

"Yeah, I got started early. My mom was drinking and doing pot while I was still in diapers." There was no hint of bitterness there. He could have been reciting the phone book. He piloted his car and them through the short cuts in the neighborhood where you appreciated locks on your doors, and stopped the car in front of her building and quickly turned to ask. "You coming tomorrow night? I mean, if you are, I could pick you up, no problem."

Molly smiled at his open and beautiful face, his wide dark-eyed stare that became nervous and self-conscious. "I didn't know there was a meeting tomorrow. I'll have to get back with you on that because I've got some stuff I need to do." She immediately thought of her finances and getting all that paperwork to SSI so that she could begin to collect, and watched as his look became disconsolate. "Can I call you?"

Her words were like a tonic as his face lightened. He gave her his phone number. "I'll call you around five then, to be sure, I mean, that you are coming. Or not," he fumbled.

As she left the car she felt a cold damp wind off the ocean and pulled her light jacket closer. She watched as Tony drove away, a bit distracted, almost not stopping at the Stop sign at the end of the street. Molly entered the dark apartment and felt for the light switch. The place had a rancid, closed-off smell to it as though no one lived there for a very long time. Though it was still cold, she bustled around to open windows to replace the stale air. She opened the fridge to find half of a dried up bologna sandwich and assorted plastic containers with old and, she suspected, moldy foods. She rummaged in the produce drawer and found an apple and bit into it provisionally. To her delight it was still sufficiently crisp. Further rummaging in the cabinets produced canned Wolfgang Puck lobster bisque and some crackers. As the soup warmed in a small pot its aroma filled the kitchen with something approximating the aroma you'd find in a place where someone lived.

Molly blew lightly on the soup in her spoon and swallowed. As she ladled another spoonful the phone rang. She looked at the clock Ten *p.m. Esther.* She punched the speaker device so she could continue concentrating on filling her stomach.

"Hi, Mom." She closed her eyes and felt the steam from the soup as she leaned closer to the bowl.

"I called twice earlier." Her mother did not remonstrate at her daughter's assumption that it could only be Esther calling. Instead, Molly knew, her remark implied that an explanation for her daughter's whereabouts in the last hours between the two earlier calls were owed, expected, overdue.

"Busy day, Mom. Shrink's meeting, Narcotics Anonymous meeting. Oh, and I lost my job." The pause was anticipated while Esther gathered all this new intelligence, the better to respond more fully, certainly in a meaningful way, the way a mother was expected to respond. And not just any mother, but one who cared. Above all, that.

"Nice. Those words. What a shame." Her breathing was close to the phone so Molly could hear it, quicker, deeper, as if she had just run up the four floors to her apartment.

"Which ones, Mom? Shrink? N.A.? Job?" Molly stood and stretched. She'd spent the day sitting in chairs, buses, couches and metal folding chairs. She roamed the kitchen opening cabinets, still hungry, and found an unopened box of ginger snaps. She tore at the damn wax paper that must have been sealed with enough pressure and heat to keep out G forces on earth reentry.

"What's that noise?"

Molly sat back down at the table, a sheet of paper and pen in place to begin a food list. She smiled as she sipped a cup of herbal tea, hibiscus, it said on the box. "Tomatoes." She said it out loud, forgetting for a moment that Esther was still waiting. "Sorry, Mom.

I'm writing up a grocery list for tomorrow."

"You'll have plenty of time to do that tomorrow, won't you?"

Molly scribbled around the border of the list and wrote down "Tuna," then followed with "mayonnaise, lettuce, bread." Funny, she thought, the natural progression of making a tuna sandwich will fill your cabinets and fridge.

"It's late, Mom. I'm going to ignore your reference to my current unemployment. I'll call the union tomorrow and find out about medical leave money." Her voice trailed off. It *was* late and these were not good late-night thoughts to be having. "Besides, Mom, it's late for you too." She refrained from asking why Esther was awake at 1:00 am New York City time because she already knew the answer and did not want to give Esther the opportunity for martyrdom at having to stay up so late to reach her wild and wayward daughter who foolishly lived on the West Coast.

"I'll be home in the morning. Why don't I call you?"

Esther deferred and said goodbye but not before she set a time to speak with Molly. Molly slid the ringer to off. Esther would call 9:00 am Eastern Time telling herself that 6:00 in the morning was late enough for Molly to sleep. As it was, Molly knew her mother tacitly understood why her daughter wouldn't answer her phone that early, but she'd try anyway. Otherwise there was no basis for her first carp of the day: "So, you slept in?"

Molly was surprised to find she was not quite ready to sleep. She flopped down on the couch and, not wanting to close the windows quite yet, pulled the throw over her injured shoulder. Her mind raced through the day, jumbled up with alternating things she said to Suarez, images of Javier, and finally a thought of her checkbook balance until the first check from SSI arrived.

Narcotics Anonymous II

It was almost ten o'clock before Molly raised her head off the pillow. She jumped as if an electrical prod hit her, ran to the shower, and was halfway through soaping up when she remembered there was no school bell calling her to teach history to juniors. Shuffling into the kitchen she started the coffee and dropped down at the desk to check email. A note from Symantec that her Norton super duper protection was about to lapse. The tone of the message possessed the gravity of a platoon sergeant listing the many ways a soldier could be sabotaged by the enemy. That could wait; she'd check whether the update was free, and if not, would   add this one more expense to her growing list of things she took for granted when there was a steady income stream. She trolled the remaining emails, lots of them, mostly from her friend Sarah. She opened the first to find a chatty note inviting her up to Santa Monica for a day on the Fourth Street Promenade. Sarah didn't know about the busted up Nissan and the enforced leave of absence. She wrote back in terse little remarks about her meeting at the school and its outcome. Sarah already knew of Javier's late night leave taking via police escort, and as a friend, was supportive through this time of loss. She'd call Sarah later today, much later, after she took time to settle her life in serious little rows of what she could and could not afford, and all the while knowing the 'could not' would far outpace the 'could'.

The smell of the coffee beckoned her to the table where she brought a pad and pencil to begin her list, preferring the more personal touch of a pencil over the clacking of the computer keys and the official looking print out. Her list included a bunch of "To Dos" for today, maybe for the rest of her life. "Call SSI" was placed at the top. She hesitated thinking she should call the Union first. A feeling of shame came over her at being dumped by the school, the vice-principal, Robert, and now that she thought about it, the board and superintendent. Had she really been an agenda item at their meeting after Javier's handiwork of bruises and sprained shoulder landed her at St. Mary's emergency room? Guilt took over, the kind that Esther was so good at meting out, guilt about the lifestyle that led to all this.

"Bullshit," she mumbled as she poured through the papers that Robert's secretary placed neatly in a large manila envelope, all pages stacked just so. In the back she found the Union phone number and sipped hot coffee while waiting for Kathy McDougall to pick up. A voice message greeted her.

"This is Kathy McDougall's office. Please leave your name and a phone number and I will call you back."

The burden of taking care of herself began to feel heavier. She stuttered through the message and hit the pound key to hear "options", and chose #3, to record a new message. This time she made it short and sweet. She tried for a light sound.

"Hi, Kathy. This is Molly Morris. I have some questions regarding medical leave pay. Please call me." She left her school's name and her phone number, and muttered a weak "Thanks."

* * *

Ten cigarettes and several cups of coffee later she located SSI on the Web and calculated her monthly allotments. It was going to be close, even living here in the 'hood was expensive and getting worse. Absentmindedly she pushed the phone ringer on and it rang immediately.

"Did you know it's after one o'clock?"

Molly rolled her eyes, "Yes, Mom. And it's 5 o'clock, too."

"Where?" Esther sounded impatient.

Molly looked distractedly around the room for something to eat. "Somewhere. Somewhere in the world it's time for a beer."

Esther didn't respond to the reference to alcohol.

"Look, Mom, I really have a lot to do. I've got to talk to the people at the Union about medical leave pay. I'm waiting for someone to call me back."

"Why are you on medical leave?"

Molly felt a slight jolt. Esther's remark signaled a real problem. She had no sense of the events that led her daughter to her life as it was right now. Sure, she knew Javier was *the father* of her daughter's baby. But the rest, Molly could tell, she half heard, or it was just so far from the life she envisioned for Molly. Last night's references to a Narcotics Anonymous meeting would not conjure the scene at the Baptist Church. Where to begin.

"Mom, it's been tough since Stella died." She lit yet another cigarette, her hands shaking. The silence stretched and she pictured Esther in her kitchen on the Grand Concourse, her lunch of homemade soup already cleaned up, a slight hint of an aroma remaining, evidence of a meal consumed. Molly looked around her own kitchen, the pot from last night's soup still on the stove, cracker crumbs on the table. She saw it all through Esther's eyes. How would Esther process someone like LaSheed, or her daughter taking a pipe of meth?

She began again, "I took some pills for a while after, to stop the nervousness." Her jaw clamped down on the words. "The pills helped but the doctor stopped them." She paused for an awful moment. There was no nice way to tell her mother. She thought of Suarez and what he might say about all of this.

The silence must have been even longer because Esther interrupted. "You took something, some other medication?"

"For a while. Look, it was not working out between me and Javier. He doesn't live here anymore. And I got some help because I was depressed so I'm seeing the therapist. And that's why I'm on leave." She knew the gaps between what was said and what had happened would fill the goddamned Grand Canyon but there would be a better time, not today, to tell her mother everything.

"I think I should come out there. I should have been there months ago but you wouldn't let me. You said, later, when the baby was older and now I didn't even get a chance to hold her."

Molly heard this from her mother all before. "I gotta go, Mom. I have work to do."

Esther must have realized she again crossed that barrier between them. This was their game, this rifle shot conversation that led nowhere, that entrenched them both even further into their separateness.

"Will you call me later? I want to know how you are." It was the closest Esther ever got to "I love you."

* * *

Molly slid on jeans and tee shirt, all the while ticking off rent, food, other basics that still left a five-hundred-dollar hole in her purse. Halfway down the block to the bodega, she knew in a sinking moment that she would ask Esther for the rest. Just till I find some part time gig. At the store she rummaged through the day-old bread for a dollar loaf and retraced her steps in the aisles for the few groceries on her list. Five dollars filled two plastic bags. She thanked God again for scaled-down prices in the 'hood set to the prevailing income.

Her beeper buzzed as she left the store; it was Sarah. Molly dialed her number at a phone just outside the store.

"Tried your home number. You're not at school. You feeling all right? She was glad it was Sarah, she could tell her anything and she did. She added to her list "search for a cheaper phone company."

Sarah breathed into the phone. Molly knew her friend was weighing what to offer, also knowing Molly wouldn't accept handouts. "Are you okay with the one arm in a sling?" Practical Sarah. Molly reassured her she was doing fine while she adjusted the bags over the shoulder of her good arm. "I've spent time thinking it through." She tried to sound upbeat. "Looks like I'll be asking Esther for some financial assistance."

"Will she make it impossible?" Sarah knew how Esther might treat her daughter's monetary dependency no matter how short lived. "Sweetie, you went back to work way too soon. Please do yourself a favor and use the time to heal."

"Not having Javier hanging around is a good thing," she lied, and knew it as soon as she said it. Remembering the sad look in his face when she convinced Suarez and the attending doc to let him in to see her before she left the hospital, he spoke softly in the voice he used when making love, or later, cooing gently to Stella. Yes, she missed him now that the drugs were out of her body, and she could feel. No time to think of that. At least for now. She said goodbye but not before Sarah offered Molly time in Santa Monica and a vacation from the 'hood. Molly thanked her for the offer and promised they'd get together soon when things got less complicated.

Her step picked up as she returned to the apartment, already framing the important words that would make her case. "It's just a loan," she said out loud. If only Esther was hooked up to the internet. Somehow a note out into cyberspace was less personal, less real, and quicker. Snail mail was five days coast to coast. After a quick peanut butter and jelly lunch, she spread out her budget to check her calculations once more with the concentration of a PhD candidate studying a new find in prime numbers. She finally dropped the pencil in disgust.

Without thinking, she dialed her mother's number. "Good, you're there."

"Where else would I be?"

"Look, I just finished going over my budget," she jumped in to it, "and with the car not running and needing an overhaul, I'm coming up short. I'm going to find a part time job, but I've got some bills and I'm not able to pay them."

Mercifully, Esther didn't wait, her response coming in nano seconds, "How much?"

There was a sound of movement on the phone. She pictured her mother's kitchen again, Esther's yellow wall phone that matched nothing else in the kitchen stretched so that she could sit at her table, a cup of tea and a Zwieback cookie on a platter, reading the New York Post.

"Maybe $500 a month?" Esther persisted.

Bingo! Esther was prescient. She must have calculated the short fall last night, knew with certainty that this call was coming.

"It's just a loan, I won't need it for long." She heard Esther moving about, the long cord not quite reaching whatever she wanted get hold of.

"I can go over to Webster Avenue. They have a Western Union."

"You could mail it. You don't have to go all the way over there."

"I need some brisket, I can get it at Gristedes."

She stared out the kitchen window a long time after the call ended, watched the curtain pushed by a warmer than usual breeze, then pulled back against the screen. She pondered the enigma that was Esther. Did her mother show this insight before or was this just the first time Molly sat still long enough to notice? She felt guilty, Esther trudging down the four flights, no way would she wait for the elevator. Always in Molly's mind Esther was slim, an inch taller than Molly, her hair darker in Molly's memory than it was in fact. The though that Esther might have aged, and was now gray was unpleasant to her, or, if her hair was still a deep red near brown, it have to be her hair dresser knowing for sure.

Molly snapped back to Southern California and to the numbing possibility that her mother's mission today had become one more point of contention between them. She opened the fridge and touched the bottle. A six-pack of Corona was chilled, so she sliced some lime and thought out loud, "But I need the money."

* * *

"Hey, uh, Molly. You said you might be going to N.A. tonight so I thought I could pick you up. Oh, I should tell you this is Tony, you know, from last night, I mean the N.A. meeting. I drove you home."

Molly sipped her second beer after chugging down the first, and listened to the young man struggle through his opening lines. "Of course I remember you." After her whirlwind twenty-four hours of negotiating with her mother, she'd forgotten the tentative plan to revisit the N.A. meeting, and wanted nothing more than to stay home and crunch on some blue corn tostados and of course drink the remaining Coronas. But she wasn't buzzed quite enough to slide into the oblivion.

"Sure, I was planning to be there, and my own car is busted so I'd appreciate the ride. What time?" She sucked on the lime and thought she should have bought tequila instead.

She felt Tony's hesitancy. "It's not that far, so maybe 7:30. I figure we can get there a little early just in case Gary needs help setting up."

It was an easy image to conjure, Tony pulling folded chairs from the stack and arranging them, making the coffee, putting the cookies onto a tray. "I'll be ready at 7:30, so see you then." She wanted to speed the process up and get off the phone so that she could eat something to absorb the beer, but she felt his crystal thin and fragile psyche out there on a line. She knew that anything, an abrupt word, impatience, could crack his sense of himself.

So she waited till he responded with, "Okay, then, so I'll see you at 7:30 then, Molly. Goodbye."

And she knew he'd be there at exactly 7:30; so she took another shower, put some ice in a towel and pressed it to her face to help clear her head, put on clean clothes, her newer jeans, and a blouse and tight little jacket and high sandals. Stuff she couldn't wear to school. She finished with some hoop earrings, feeling very much a muchacha from the barrio, only she still had the sling for her arm. And just as she knew he would be prompt, she knew he'd try to come around, be the gentleman and open the door for her, so she was at the curb and swept it open before he came to a complete stop. God, she didn't want the whole fucking neighborhood seeing more of this than was necessary.

"I got out of work late and then went home for some dinner. Just made it here on time." He registered a slight shock at the speed in which she had dropped down into the passenger seat. He spoke as he drove.

"Are you back now with your folks?" She resisted the temptation to refer to them as his parents, but she was sure his only other place of residence was with the druggies he had hung out with first in high school, then at community college, before ending up in an emergency room almost DOA. Just like me, only without the bruises.

"Yeah, uh with good ole Mom and stepdad. He's okay, I guess, but thinks I'm some heroin freak or something, and always looking at me if I wear a long sleeved shirt. Watches too many old movies." He looked over at her, and she was warmed by his genuine smile, beautiful and young, teeth young, face clear, hair dark but so very southern California.

"Do any surfing in high school?" She caught him looking at her for too long and wanted to change the tenor of where this was going for him.

"Yeah, some. Went out to Hawaii and surfed some really great tubes. Kinda like Kelly Slater, hell everybody wants to beat Slater, but I mean how can you?" He dropped down a notch from his enthusiasm, sensing it sounded sophomoric when all it did was

51

reinforce in Molly the picture of this boy who eagerly revealed his soul.

"Thought you might be a member of that club." She thought a moment, "but that's great, it's a way of life, and it's clean, can't be buzzed or high and surf. That's good." She watched him nod back emphatically and go back into his world again, and she was glad to derail him from making too much of a ride to NA with an older woman with a busted car.

* * *

Tony pulled up to the Baptist Church, found a spot near the front of the parking lot and stopped the car. The engine did a post ignition dance and settled down. Molly smiled inwardly thinking that Tony's car was headed to the same graveyard as her Nissan. She stood and felt a dizziness come over her, those beers she guzzled way too fast, and wished she'd eaten some crackers or something to tone down their effect. Tony was by her side asking, "Are you okay?" apparently alert to her condition though not it's cause.

"Just didn't eat much today. A little light headed." She straightened herself and took a deep breath.

Gary saw them as they entered the all-purpose room, an eyebrow raised in Molly's direction. *Guess he didn't expect me two nights in a row.* Gary was a spindly chain smoker with the voice and the loose rattling cough to prove it. This second encounter with him gave Molly a more thorough impression. She figured he made some spiritual twelve-step pledge and guessed at a cross below his bony collarbone where she spied a chain. He wore a sweater last night and again tonight, same sweater, different shirt. He was a guy who cared very little for clothes, or maybe he couldn't afford better. She knew from talk that he did school counseling via presentations to warn kids off drugs. His shirt was not garish, sort of a washed out blue striped thing with a collar on the way to being frayed. She guessed he bought it at a Swap Meet or Thrift Shop. She brought herself up from any further perusal, chiding herself for judging this guy. But left it at just that because she sensed him judging her now.

"Hey, Tony, Molly. Good to see you again." He stood close by and she could swear he knew she'd been drinking, even if it was only beer. "Hey, bro," he signaled to Tony, "Want to get some chairs out for me?" Tony obliged and left them while he unfolded some of the chairs he put away last night. She started toward Tony to help him.

"You think you should be doing that? I mean, with that arm still in a sling?" Molly looked straight at Gary and realized he'd been briefed about the state of her dislocated and sprained shoulder muscles. Great, no secrets here.

"I'm okay. Almost healed. Doctor says I'm out of this thing after tomorrow." She was glad her facial bruises had faded all the way down to a pale yellow which makeup was hiding rather well.

Gary slanted his head to the side, and lowered his voice. "I'm talking about the alcohol. Think it's fair to the others who come here?"

She lit a cigarette and they both walked out toward the doorway, the room being off- limits for tobacco.

"Oh. I'm really going to set a bad example for little Miss Paleface Suzahnna? Or the two bruisers who more than likely have tattoos on their tongues? They come here to meet Billy, you know, their connection?"

Gary blatantly ignored her remarks and studied her face. His was a noncommittal look, trying, she realized, to understand who she was. It made her uneasy, more scrutinized than Dr. Suarez with his active participation therapy that drove her nuts. "I was talking about Tony. He's making a real effort. No need to mess it up for him, is there?"

She blew out the last of the smoke and stamped on the butt, leaving it on the landing outside where they stood. Before she could reach for it, Gary picked it up and dropped it in the trash, but not before he checked for any vestige of sparks.

Molly excused herself to the restroom and entered the hall again as they were all networking. Feeling a twinge of guilt she snatched one of the stale Chips Ahoy at the table and crunched and swallowed it in two or three bites to staunch the flow of acid in her beer-sopped gut. The meeting began and she joined the others.

It turned out to be Suzanna's turn to speak, and Molly wondered how she could make such self-aggrandizing pronouncements with so much dope in her. The pale young woman was surprisingly calm, and began her tale as if she were reading from a menu. She scratched at her skin occasionally, and rubbed her nose every so often. She came from Beverly Hills, then moved away from her folks, gave up college. "But I'm getting it together now, and I'll be registering for the winter quarter at UCLA." She ended her story with that.

Gary threw a wary look at Molly. She arched her brow as if to say, "So?"

Bullets were being fired. That's what Molly remembered about the dream. She particularly felt the heavy crush of them as they pierced her back. In the dream she was running from someone or something and the more she ran, the closer the assailant got until the bullets hit her. The dream woke her, tearing the fragile veil of her unconscious self, forcing her to deal with the almost reality of it. The luminous clock glared 5:14. Too early. She turned the clock away, the glow of it was penetrating her eyelids, and tossed about, raveling the sheet and light blanket until she felt like a cocoon. The cold air off the ocean was not too pleasant against a sweaty body. She sat up and methodically straightened the bedding and lay on her back. The dream was still with her. Who shot at her? Esther was too easy an answer; besides it didn't feel like Esther; she would have known if it was. It was some nameless idea, something that followed her, some riddle she never solved. She dozed for what she thought was a little and woke to find it was 6:30. She decided to shower the dream off her body.

* * *

She knew she surprised Dr. Suarez. She arrived on time, and, she told herself, her head was on straight, no booze last night. But then she began to tell him about the dream. She hadn't meant to do that, it just became the only thing in her head when she started to talk.

"What do you make of it?" His question annoyed her because it was obvious. Why not offer something, why leave her out there trying to make sense of her life? She wanted to be angry, to flail at him with insults, and turn it all around.

Her words were tersely dealt. "I thought maybe you could help me with that one. Because I don't know. I mean it's obvious that it could be my money situation…or lack thereof. It could be dear old Mom. She's always the best guess, isn't she?"

Suarez didn't answer. He leaned forward. "The only thing that's obvious to me is that it troubled you a great deal. Let's explore it together. Maybe I can help you find your answer. Because, Molly, it is you and not anyone else that this whole thing is about."

"The whole thing is the meth, isn't it? That's what I'm getting from Gary, who by the way seems to know a lot more about me than what I've told him so far. So, was the paperwork shuttled to him? The part that says I'm to attend meetings or end up being prosecuted for using?" She chipped away at her nail polish and decided it was time to get a manicure/pedicure for twenty bucks in the little place run by the small-breasted, slim-hipped Vietnamese girls. Hell, Esther's money could spring her for just this one luxury. Suarez was waiting. "No, it's not Esther. Or if it is, then she's part of it, not the whole thing. She's coming out here, she says. I'm guessing in a month, at the latest. Meanwhile she's sending me some money to help and I feel cheapened by that. I don't want to accept because she'll make me pay."

"How?"

"Guilt. Guilt that I didn't use my Boston College degree to stay with the orthopedic surgeon. Guilt that I live like I do, where I do, teaching barrio kids, gang-banger kids." The room seemed to go round a bit for her, she wasn't eating well, she wasn't sleeping well, even being off the meth didn't bring her down enough, kept her racing. Her mind was a jumble, she wanted to feel good about something, anything.

"On Sundays, when I was a kid, my Dad and I played chess or we would read the Op Ed page in the Times and discuss what we read, or occasionally watch *Meet the Press* together. I remember my mom all those times, she sat near the window and looked out to where my brother Tory was down in the street and watched him play. She never talked with us, and I would feel…something." Molly stopped because she was crying, suddenly and very hard. "I felt her resentment, like I had no right to him."

"You had no right to spend time with your father? Did she ever say that to you?"

Molly shook her head no while she dabbed Kleenex at her

eyes and runny nose. "My Mom never said anything, especially if she felt that strongly. It wasn't often, but when my Dad and I did talk together it was great and yet fraught with this tension. He was okay, I don't think he ever noticed." She sighed and reflected on the picture that moved through her head, the sun coming in the window of the kitchen in the Bronx, lasting till one o'clock, and it was somehow always the darker days of fall and winter when they were together like that. Yes, she told herself, I remember. Because in summer he worked later and on Sundays if we didn't go to Jones Beach, he would go to the Baths.

She looked at her watch to see her time was up, but Suarez didn't seem in any hurry to have her end the session. "I don't know what the dream means," she repeated, blowing her nose and feeling drained.

Suarez stood when she did. "Maybe it's too soon, Molly." He touched her elbow. "Give it some time." He walked her to the door.

From the moment she left his office, Molly's mind whirred again over her money worries. Esther's $500 was bare bones. You can forget about the manicure; she chided herself for being so frivolous. She felt her face was tight from all the salt in her tears and trudged down the hall to the restroom. She looked at herself in the mirror and pulled out her makeup kit from the large woven bag she carried. No way am I getting on the bus looking like this. She applied some fresh foundation under her eyes where she'd wiped away the mascara from her crying jag, and smoothed out her clothes, pulled her hands through her hair to resettle its "just got out of bed" look. She stared for a moment longer at her reflection in the mirror, and silently thanked the engineers who designed the building for coming up with such complimentary lighting. She wondered how many years she had left to look younger than she was, and whether she'd ever not mind being the last woman in a room that a guy would look at. God. She shook her head to erase her feeble vanity and told herself she was a sicko.

* * *

Molly ran to the bus stop and just made it in time, queuing up impatiently behind several Latino women. The wind seemed to be changing, and she noticed some large drops of rain splash on the bus windshield, and she thought, great, no umbrella.

Two blocks from her stop a woman got on the bus. She was a big woman, tall and almost obese. Her hair was done in a soft Afro, and she tugged at two children to hurry on in. One looked just like her, while the other bore no resemblance in color or feature to her at all. He was a darker child, tall and very thin. The first child was dressed nicely, the tall boy was dressed almost in rags. Molly heard the woman speak to a friend she sat down next to and Molly surmised she must have been a neighbor. She found herself listening to their conversation.

With no thought to the boy or his feelings, the woman said to her friend, "Martha, that one is Dantell Jackson. He's the boy from Foster Care. Good thing they pay me to put up with his nonsense or he'd be out on his ass in no time."

Dantell sat directly across from Molly and looked straight ahead of him. Molly could see his jaw working to hold back tears of humiliation. He tried to be helpful with the younger child, talking to him, pointing things out along the way.

"Look there, Jesse. That's the school where I go." The smaller child, about five years old, stared out the window in wonder at the big building that must have looked impressive to him. He smiled at Dantell and scooted closer. Molly was glad to see someone offered love to the boy.

The woman was speaking softly now, but Molly heard her tell her friend the amount of her stipend from Foster Care. Far more, Molly thought, than the clothes or substantial food the boy was clearly wanting. Dantell caught her watching him and she spoke to him. "You are very kind to him." She gestured toward Jesse.

"Uh huh, he's a nice kid. Not like some." She gathered this was not the first Foster Home experience for Dantell.

"So you go to Webster? That's a big school. How do you like it?" Molly knew it was enormous, with 7th, 8th, and 9th graders, close to 400 kids.

The woman noticed Molly speaking to him. "He talking to you?" She turned to Dantell, "You being smart with the lady?" She leaned over brusquely and Molly thought as though to strike him. His reflex was to move back and away from her reach. Instead she straightened her son's collar, and fussed with his hair.

"He's good company for the little one." Molly quickly offered a distraction in case the woman was feeling particularly mean. Jesse's mother was sharp; her eyes narrowed as she picked up some sympathy for the boy, and Molly looked for a way to deflect her anger away from the boy. "I'm a teacher and might be looking at Webster for a job. Dantell says he attends there. Think it's a good school?"

Dantell's foster mother sat back against her seat. "Yes. He goes there. Takes the school bus, else he'd be walking for sure." She thought briefly and said, "Guess it's good, he got some good teachers there, one attends my church."

Molly forced a kindly expression at the woman and thanked her for the information and glanced at Dantell as she left the bus and smiled in his direction at both him and little Jesse. Dantell raised his hand ever so slightly fingers cupped, close to a wave, his lips were pursed, no visible smile, but his eyes told her thank you.

All the way down the block she thought about Foster Care. What did she know about it, nothing that the internet wouldn't tell her. She dropped her bag on the floor next to the computer desk and signed in to her account. Without pausing to check emails, she pulled up a bunch of places in Long Beach but thought better of it. Don't want that close a scrutiny, thank you very much.

She found some in Los Angeles, near Inglewood, close enough to get up there, not too close for them to get down here. What was she fretting for, she wondered, and decided it had something to do with her privacy. Would they poke through the rooms to be sure she kept the place clean before giving her a child? Right now that wouldn't be too good an idea. Without the high from meth, she was still experiencing listlessness and sometimes could barely get the few dinner dishes washed and put away.

The phone rang, and she answered to find Sarah. "I guess you didn't check your voice mail. I was hoping to get you to come up for the weekend."

"Your beau out of town?" She knew Sarah was dating a guy under contract to Universal for a pilot. Sarah was long legged and blonde and Beverly Hills above Sunset reared. The boyfriend was clearly the lucky one.

"No, sorry. Just got back from my visit with Dr. Suarez.

Forgot all about it being Friday. I can maybe make it for Saturday. Unless you're going to Temple." Molly liked to tease Sarah about her move over to Agape.

Sarah laughed. "Not lately, girlfriend. What time do you think you can get here tomorrow?"

"Let me tell you first though. I eavesdropped on this lady on the bus and she's got a foster kid. I was just looking it all up. Christ, it could save my ass. I might even have some discretionary income. Well, maybe not that good, but enough to buy a car down on Harbor Boulevard."

"That's good news, Sweetie. You know I'm good for some of that down payment." She waited for Molly to answer, then: "Don't say yes or no. Wait till tomorrow."

* * *

The first time she noticed Javier was when she left Theresa's Salon. True, Theresa was his cousin and he was particularly close to her, so it was natural for him to see her and maybe bump into Molly. Still Molly sensed she was followed on and off from the time she left the hospital. Hard to disguise a dark blue Camaro and it seemed that a blue something of that sort was rounding the corner out of sight every once in a while. For sure she saw it as she left the bodega just that morning and now she saw his handsome face peering between the slats of Theresa's as her hair was being styled. She looked directly into the mirror to assess Theresa's take on it and knew from the emotionless face staring back at her that Theresa hadn't missed a beat.

"I could just laugh out loud." Molly was chuckling.

"What do you mean? Laugh at what?" Theresa was extra fussy with the hair and Molly gently took her hand.

"It looks great, thanks." She looked over to the window, where Javier had been standing. No doubt he was at the restaurant next door. "You and Javier. I've been feeling his presence a lot lately. He's checking on me?" She smiled up at Theresa whose eyes were swimming in mirth, but whose lips remained straight as a ruler.

"Querida, he worries about you. Is she all right, he asks me. Is she taking care of herself? Is she eating, she looks too skinny."

59

"Why, is he planning on making me dinner? Besides," she added, "he likes my skinny ass. Isn't that true." She asked this in Spanish.

Theresa was laughing. "The way you talk. A gringa teacher from New York."

Then more seriously, she took her hand as Molly gave her the credit card. "You know you two," she said, shaking her head, "you both have so much love."

For just that moment Molly could remember her feeling for Javier. Theresa was telling her, something that seemed a long time ago, yet was only a few months ago. The two women hugged as family would, and Molly felt again that belonging she used to feel when she visited them all with Javier. That protection.

They had walked to the front of the Salon together, Theresa calling after her as Molly walked and waved back. And Theresa waved a quick good-bye then ran back to take care of Mrs. Medina who was dripping through her towel.

The strip mall shops were all crowded together. Molly took two quick steps and was inside Avila's restaurant. Her eyes adjusted for the subdued lighting, and finally made out Javier in a booth at the back. He, like Theresa, betrayed all with his eyes and nothing with his facial expression which had the same blank look. She walked toward him and slid into the booth across from him. He was eating a fish taco; the aroma was enticing. He placed one taco on a smaller plate and slid it across to her.

"Ummmm." She savored the fresh guacamole and dollop of sour cream and Avila's special sauce all over the tilapia. "Best fish tacos in Long Beach." She took a quick sip of his iced tea. "Good to know someone around here is sober," she quipped.

"And you?" he asked in Spanish. "What do you drink?"

He *was* glad to see her, she could tell, and all the old good feelings surfaced in her. How could they not? "I haven't been too bad. You know, occasionally have a beer, some Corona Light, that's all."

His silence was reproach enough.

She felt defensive. "Look, it's no big deal. I'm going to N.A. I'm getting there. No job, but I think I can get it back after a while."

"So, why are you here, then?" He was frowning now, and it

raised anger in her. She sipped some more of his tea and he reached over to lift her chin to see her eyes. "Hair appointment. Why are you at the bodega or when I visit Dr. Suarez?" He didn't respond. "No answer? Because there isn't one?"

He finally smiled at her. "I wanted to be sure you were well, not sick with drugs."

"Javier, I have a favor to ask. I want to apply for a foster child. If you have been following me then you know that I haven't been at the school for two weeks and I don't have any work. Maybe they will give me my job back. But not right away. I need money and the foster child could help me stay clean." And, she thought, a foster child will make it harder for you to come back to live with me.

Javier paid the waitress with cash, then stood as they both walked out together. They lingered just outside in the cool breeze and then walked down to the end of the strip mall where some kids were playing hoops. One kid was skinny but very fast, he looked half black, half latino.

"Lots of that around, but more so out in Westminster. It's good to see ethnic lines blending, maybe fewer people to fight with."

It must have been something in the way she said it that endeared her to him more, because he took her hands and held them in his big, warm one.

"Querida. I have not stopped loving you. So sorry." Tears in his eyes.

"Don't Javier. It was my fault. I feel like I've been running from myself all my life." She walked again and he with her. "That favor I need. Would you go with me to the Foster Care office?" She said it all quickly before she lost her courage. "They will give me a child if they think we are still together."

Foster Care with Javier

Javier wore a suit jacket that didn't quite match his pants, but his shirt was clean and he looked overall presentable. Molly chose to dress slightly down, sandals and a jean skirt. The two of them drove north on the 405 to one of a dozen L.A. county foster care offices. She had spent a day researching the internet, and speed reading every one of the independently owned agencies to find one that was near, but not too near. She defended her decision not to be scrutinized. She told herself it would interfere in any bonding that could occur between her and the little stranger. Always in her mind, it was some Mexican kid or some biracial mix. Always the child had to be a boy, and never a baby. Besides, she reasoned, she couldn't have a job and a baby and live alone. Javier was glancing at her as she adjusted the vent to blow some cool air her way.

"Please watch the road. I hope you haven't been drinking today." She turned as he quickly looked back to the road.

"Nada." His lips were tight as he squeezed out the word. "I do this for *you*, Querida. Not for me." His hands tightened on the steering wheel. "Have you had something to drink?" He had layered the sarcasm as he would have spread butter on bread.

"It will give me some money." She ignored his remark about drinking, and left off her temptation to say she needed the money because he'd jump at the chance to wiggle himself back into the apartment. She figured he was staying with his brother and didn't want her to know.

Molly began to read through the information she had downloaded from the website, fumbling with the papers while she searched for her birth certificate. She found the battered piece of paper and clipped it to the forms along with the copy of the lease on the apartment, their names enshrined, and worried that someone might challenge that she had a different last name. She was almost sure that none of the women at such an agency would have a difficult time understanding her desire to keep her maiden name. With Javier's job, and she, the stay at home mom, she reasoned they were in a good place. Nonetheless, her hands shook. Thank God she didn't have to wear the sling and the swelling under her eye was all but gone. She had to apply a few dabs of concealer here and there. Somehow she didn't hold it against him; maybe it was because she couldn't remember much about that night, just the inherent aftermath in the form of breaks and bruises.

"God, I need this twelve hundred." She whispered her unholy prayer.

Javier had not spoken since his remonstrance at her rude questioning of his sobriety. Now he spoke, still sullenly, "You get the baby today?" He looked more fully at her as the traffic in L.A. slowed to the inevitable crawl. She saw all over again what had drawn her to him, the fierce animal fire in his eyes. Christ, she thought, I'm beginning to sound like a goddamned romance novel. He was biting his lip nervously.

Molly placed a placating hand on his arm, which he pulled away from as though it were a lighted torch. He was still clearly harboring anger or hurt feelings or both from the last time they were alone together. She knew he didn't remember too much about that night either, and that was okay with her.

"It may not be a baby." She left out the fact that she had already pointedly told the agency she did not want to take care of a baby. Javier would consider her not wanting a baby a reproof against what they had together with Stella, and curiously she felt the opposite.

"They give you what they have and babies are very popular." His knitted brow signaled that he did not understand her. "Everyone wants a baby. They need homes for older children."

That seemed to mollify his machismo, which was not characteristic of him. Javier was handsome, and intelligent. She knew he had left school in Mexico with good grades, but language was a barrier as he had come to L.A. and to school late. It was almost a badge of honor among the family of men, his own and his barrio's, to keep with the old ways, staying close to Latino friends.

She knew he did not personally know one white person, or for that matter, one black person either. What if they gave her a black kid? What would he do? For that matter, she hadn't thought about white, black, Hispanic. What about Esther who was threatening to show up anytime now?

They were exiting the freeway. The trees on this side of the road were scraggly, with evidence of the desert that is L.A. surrounding them in scrub brush, stunted trees and lack of the red flowers of bougainvillea. They parked the Camaro under a fichus tree thick with leaves. It would stay cooler. Javier entered the tall, white building ahead of her. She admired the Art-Deco- tinted-blue-windows look to it. Molly remembered seeing this building in a 1930s movie. They were always shooting in certain neighborhoods; she couldn't count how many times she saw the cameras and trucks in San Pedro for a movie meant to look like the 1930s. Inside there was a tiny elevator that held two uncomfortably, so they took the stairs to the third floor. Javier climbed two at a time only to wait on the landing each time for Molly to join him. Now that they were here, he seemed eager, which bewildered Molly.

They walked into the agency together, holding hands. Suddenly she had become nervous and Javier was offering her his support by lightly cupping his hand under her elbow. The intake person was a woman in her fifties, gray showing at the temples through her blonde bob hairdo. She was California-tanned, and a set of deep creases and wrinkles were stretched into a smile as she spoke to them. Molly had prepared the paperwork in advance and had faxed it to Mrs. Terry Wilson.

"I'll copy these and give you back the originals," Terry said as she held up the birth certificates, the lease on the apartment under their names jointly, and their driver's licenses. Molly was right; Terry Wilson showed no concern over Molly's use of her own last name. Terry, dressed in a white skirt and navy blue and white striped tight little tee shirt, was back in a flash. She sat down across the table from them.

"Now, it won't take too long. In fact, we'll have someone for you right away, as soon as we have our agent visit your home." She smiled her bright smile again. "Any questions?"

Molly had heard all sorts of stories. Her friend Sarah had mentioned babies born with fetal alcohol syndrome, and that the children may only begin to exhibit symptoms as they neared puberty. "Is there a chance of a child older, no younger than pre-school?"

Terry's face went back to its resting stage, no furrowing of the brow, the eyes bright and shiny. "The age groups come and go. I couldn't begin to tell you what age child we have now. Although we try to place these children as quickly as they come to us." She filed through some papers, her French-manicured nails clicking on the computer for a few moments, then turned back to Molly and Javier, this time looking at him while she addressed them both.

"Mrs. Robertson will be the visiting agent. She'll call tomorrow for a time to meet with you." She smiled again. This time Molly saw fatigue and a sadness, perhaps for the eager foster parents who didn't have a clue what they were about to encounter, or maybe it was for the children who, with luck, might reap a cornucopia of warmth, food, love, or the whirlwind of a monster posing as a real parent.

* * *

Molly's beeper buzzed as she stepped off the bus. It was Sarah. There was a public phone on the corner where she dialed Sarah.

"I'm headed in to see the therapist. What's up?"

Sarah's voice always had a soothing effect on Molly. Even in her rush to get to her appointment she felt just a shade more relaxed to hear her friend's voice. "Just a reality check. How did it go at Foster Care?"

"It was cool." She answered Sarah's question. "Good thing my medical leave is non-specific."

Sarah responded. "Hell, they'd pretty much say yes. How many middle-class types do you think they get?" She kidded, "Bet they said, 'You're Caucasian, so you must have a good reason to be on leave with a decent roof over your head, a spare bed.'"

Molly laughed. "Yup, just like that. If only they knew about this white girl."

Sarah listened to all the reasons her friend might soon have a child in her home.

"How about Javier? What's his take on things?"

"He thought they were giving me a baby right then. He's

ready to move back in, but I made a quick end to that. A kid is enough for right now. "Listen, going to Suarez. Call you later from home when I get to safer ground."

Molly crossed to the shady side of Redondo Beach Boulevard at a fast pace, the light on the opposite side already threatening to turn yellow, leaving Molly waiting on the median and fair game for cars whizzing by at 75 miles an hour toward her liver, spleen, and other vital organs.

As usual she ran up the stairs at Suarez's building, not wanting to wait for the pokey elevator. It gave her a few minutes to stop in the restroom to do something with her disheveled hair and swipe some gloss on her parched lips. Dr. Suarez' greeting her at the door had become a part of their routine. Or maybe all his patients were as unreliable and late. She was aware of his cologne, something very subtle and clean smelling without the danger of bordering on medicinal. She looked at him appraisingly, would she date him? She decided not, having shared too much of her soul. He already knew her too well.

She sat on the couch again but this time slipped off her wedged sandals and flexed her toes. If he noticed she couldn't say. He maintained that sphinxlike gaze that she swore he and all other therapists learn as part of their PhDs and their training.

She said as much to him. "It's amazing how I never know what you think of me." She waited but he said nothing, almost as though he hadn't heard her. "I mean, it's not the most important thing to me. I know how my friend, Sarah, feels; she loves me. I know about Esther. But not how you feel."

Dr. Suarez remained quietly alert. "Does it matter to you to know how others feel about you?"

"Yes, people close to me. My mother."

"How about Javier?"

The question mentally unseated her. She had not expected it. She thought awhile about Javier whom she knew she took for granted, his good nature, the way he still loved her.

"I feel guilty that I don't love him as much as he loves me." When it appeared that Suarez was waiting, she continued. "I can't help that. In any relationship, one person always loves more than the other, is more dependent on the other's love. My dad loved my mom more." She stopped, remembering Esther as a young woman, her hair that reddish brown, her father darker, opposites in everything, even their coloring. How patient and happier than her mother he'd been, his good mood helping to erase Esther's moods, all dark and colorless. "My dad used to say mom is in one of her February moods."

"Do you know what he meant?"

"Oh, everyone knew, I guess you don't have that kind of weather here. February on the east coast is the worst. Days are still short, the snow has melted, everything is brown and muddy, the ground way too hard to grow anything, and the sun rarely comes out for any plant to sprout a leaf. It's a long way from spring. And Mom was always a long way from spring, too." For a moment she felt a curious strength of her visceral connection to her mother, flesh of her flesh, and a sorrow that she could not make her mother happy. She remained quiet in her thoughts, her vision inward, almost forgetting him. When she came out of her inner looking, and saw him again, he was waiting.

He uncrossed then crossed his legs again before he spoke, the action Molly thought, gave him time to think about what she had said. "Molly, I think it will be more helpful if we establish a pattern to your visits here. You are a very closed person."

"How? Closed? Because I don't rattle on?" she was defensive, stung by what she perceived as an insult.

"Wait. You're way too intelligent and were schooled in child psychology at some point in your education, so you must know that when I say you are closed, I mean that like some patients, you're less inclined to share your feelings than others. You just happen to be among those that are less so. It's your work here to make yourself more accessible. I am suggesting that we develop a give and take dynamic when we meet. I will respond to things you say to gain a better understanding. Just now you said your mother had moods. Do you have any idea why she may have been withdrawn?"

Molly inhaled as though dragging on one of her cigarettes and wishing for one right now. "It's just that she is so very hard to understand. I don't know why she's so unhappy. We weren't rich but we had an untroubled household, no violence, not outbursts of shouting. Life was quiet. But there was this hole, almost like an abyss and it was there when my mother would get quiet and inside herself." What did he want from her? What more could she say?

68

Suarez settled into his chair and she swore he was committing all of this to memory because he seldom wrote anything down. Finally he spoke.

"How are the N.A. meetings coming along?"

The smile that had begun to play on her lips faded as she thought of her run-in with Gary about the beer she'd swilled that night. Had he called Suarez? "It's getting better. A few interesting characters, for sure, but hell, I bet they say the same about me." She quickly moved on, not wanting to dwell on N.A. and the occasional beer she'd entitled herself to. "Foster Care looks like they'll be checking me out for a kid."

"Do you feel ready for the responsibility of a child?"

She hunched over to place her arms on her knees much like a guy position. "What I need right now is money to keep my apartment, and at the same time give a kid some food, clothes— just enough."

"Enough?"

"Enough so I can maybe send Esther back her checks if I don't like the way things are going."

Suarez raised an inquiring brow and Molly answered as if he'd already asked. "If she becomes too intrusive, I can just drop her and her hand-outs." She fidgeted on the couch, and an entire roll of film unleashed in her brain and with it a dialog in her ear of Esther and her relentless digging into her life, settling her values on top of Molly's actions like so much fine dust, like so much judgment.

"What about the child and why did you say him? Did Foster Care indicate a boy?"

"Obvious isn't it? I gave a preference. Don't need a little girl to remind me." She felt compelled to say more. "It's easier that way. And I want easy, Doctor. I want relief from this emotional speeding train I've been on for so goddamned long." She looked at him, the sun framing his dark hair, and marveled at the light pouring in from the windows high above them, like a clearstory. So clever, she thought, they engineered it so the sun could cast its light without the unforgiving rays hitting us in the eye.

"And the child?"

"You mean will I be a good foster parent? From the time I thought of fostering at all, I've thought about that. I wasn't physically abused as a child, so he'll have a safe haven from that."

She ticked off her list of arguments he or anyone might use against her fitness as a parent, foster or otherwise. "Until recently I was a teacher whose classroom of kids was entrusted to me by the Unified School District of Long Beach. He'll even have someone to help him with his homework. More than that I can't tell you right now because right now he doesn't have a name or a psyche or even a damn batting average at Little League."

"Do you think you can be something to this foster child right now? I know you've given this some thought, but what about affection for him?"

"We can just wait and see." She was damned if he was going to talk her out of it.

"Do you think you could talk about Stella a little now?" Molly felt him lying in wait to jump out and pounce on the unresolved Stella.

"You caught me a little off guard. I mean, I wasn't expecting." She fumbled for words. "Yes, I could tell you a little about Stella, and that I think about her a lot. I wake up in fact with her in my mind. She's always just this side of floating away, like she's just this side of alive. You see, then I get to lose her all over again when I am fully awake. Makes me want to find something to occupy my time with, like coke, too expensive, so meth. That stuff will kill you, and besides have you seen how people lose their looks?" She said it all in a joke, she thought.

* * *

It was just as Terry Wilson said, Foster Care was back to Molly in less than a week. Only thing was they hadn't alerted her that a social worker would call and then show up at the apartment in the same day, and with a foster child in tow.

Mrs. Robertson was an imposing figure of a woman, very tall; Molly estimated she was near six feet, with linebacker broad shoulders. She wore a stylish electric blue dress with matching sweater, and her linen shoes were chosen for the closely matched shades of blue threads interwoven through and closely matched the dress ensemble. She wore her abundant hair straightened, but it was already very silky. Her face was broad with sharp features, and she was very dark-skinned so the vibrant colors played beautifully off her equally beautiful skin. She wasn't a health club enthusiast, which made the trek up the backstairs of the apartment house a workout. Molly saw that her skin glistened. The boy was very thin and jittery. His large dark eyes did not meet Molly's, though she tried to engage him because the conversation was openly about him much like the conversation had been about poor Dantel, the boy on the bus.

"Say hello to Miz Morris." Mrs. Robertson let go of the boy's hand as she spoke.

Molly offered her some lemonade, which she hastily prepared when she received the call along with a whirlwind lick-and-a promise cleanup to the apartment. Everything was in place, he would sleep in the small extra bedroom, planned as a nursery for Stella. There was a twin bed with a nondescript blue and yellow comforter that could not be classified for boy or girl.

"Would you like a cookie?" Molly took hold of the boy's slim hand and gently shook it, telling him her name, dropping the Miz Morris and telling him to call her Molly.

"He just came in from intake yesterday. The boy was staying with a neighbor of his father's at Pendleton down there in Oceanside. The father passed on and the mom, well, she's been gone for some time. They think she's down in Mexico with some boyfriend or whatever."

Molly watched the boy. Surprisingly, his curious eyes were roaming the kitchen and into the living room. He seemed not to care, or at least didn't register emotion, at the woman's remarks.

She considered that he didn't know he should be bothered or ashamed, and Molly took him to be naturally quiet and shy. Although he was slight, she figured his height at the top of the percentile for his age. His father must have been tall. The boy had Anglo features and medium- dark skin.

He was wearing jeans that fit, not the baggy pants she could tell he'd prefer. His Lakers cap was in his hand but she noticed he wore it backwards. His sneakers were untied, the dirty laces trailing alongside, the shoe opened wide so that he made a clomping sound, the heels of his feet awkwardly coming out of the shoes as he walked. Nugent would fit right in with the boys in this barrio, though they all called it the hood.

"Boy, answer Miz Morris when she speaks to you." Mrs.

Robertson snapped at the boy, who stood straighter. She looked to see Molly's expression which must have registered a frown and disapproval, and so softened her own to match.

"Tell me your name." Molly handed the boy a cookie.

"My name is Nugent Alvarez." He took the cookie but did not immediately bite into it although Molly was sure it was tempting; it was a big Amos's Famous Chocolate Chip. Molly poured a smaller glass of lemonade and ushered Nugent into the living room, put the glass on the coffee table with a napkin serving as a coaster, and showed him the sofa to sit. She turned the television to the Disney channel.

"Mrs. Robertson and I are going to talk in the kitchen. If you want anything just come in." She had not left the room when she heard the remote expertly clicked to a sports channel where a rerun of a Lakers game was playing. "So, do you think Shaq is the best?" She called over her shoulder.

"Him and Kobe. They a real team." His words tumbled out as his head snapped to look at her. He almost smiled.

Mrs. Robertson was waiting at the kitchen table sipping her lemonade and brushing some cookie crumbs off her paperwork. Molly had the impression that she devoured the cookies quickly feeling it unseemly for a professional to eat in the client's presence.

"Some general information for you about the boy." Mrs. Robertson handed Molly the intake form, a blur of names of others the boy was assigned to after he was picked up, including a street not too far from her own. As she read, Mrs. Robertson handed her the next sheet, and the next, slowly, the only sound came from her heavy costume jewelry bracelet.

"Like I said, the authorities think his mother is in Mexico with her boyfriend." She looked through her papers. "A Mr. Rayford Chandler. He's wanted in Nevada for a meth lab he started there that blew up, killing ten cookers and three children." She was frowning as she read. "This boy here is sure lucky to be away from her and her friends." She must have sensed that Molly wanted to know more about the boy and his family. "His mother's name is Ana Alverez, she had Nugent when she was eighteen. The father was a Marine at Camp Pendleton, lots of violence between those two. He was African American, died in a fight, they think with another dealer, from gunshot wounds. They never married. The boy has his mother's last name."

"How long has he been in Foster Care?" Molly sat down and refrained from lighting a cigarette, accurately sensing that Mrs. Robertson was not a smoker or a drinker, but someone who attended church regularly and who, with her husband, was raising two boys who attended a private school.

Mrs. Robertson gently lifted one of the papers she gave Molly and turned it over, placing her well-polished nail on the line for her to read. "Nugent Alverez, age six, fostered through kinship program for one year, however unsuccessfully. The Alverez family voiced opposition to his biracial status and returned him to the county for Foster Care."

"He's been in Foster Care for three years?" Molly was surprised. "He seems to be pretty normal." She knew as soon as she said it, it might have been the wrong thing to say. "I mean, that's a long time for a kid to be with strangers."

"I know what you're trying to say." Mrs. Robertson placed the paper neatly on the stack in front of Molly. Molly wished the house were cleaner, this woman was way too tidy. "I've known Nugent for the three years after kinship didn't work out. He was lucky. The family he lived with had two children, one a boy near Nugent's age. They were ready to leave for assignment in Germany. They knew Nugent's father before he got hooked on drugs. They couldn't take the boy out of the country and couldn't afford to adopt him." He's been back with us only two weeks. Not long enough for it to take hold if you know what I mean." She reached into her briefcase for a large manila envelope, and opened it, leafing through its contents. "His birth certificate, his food stamps. You'll get the stipend by mail tomorrow. Go online to have direct deposit if you want. That usually takes two weeks, sometimes more." She handed the envelope and its remaining contents to Molly.

"I don't understand." Molly stuttered the words out. "You mean that's all?" She stood also and walked quickly to the door before the woman, who was fairly sprinting to leave, got out. "Wait, I mean, is that all?"

"Ms. Morris, there isn't any more to say. You seem like a decent woman, you have a place for him to stay. You were a teacher? If you could see the places he isn't going to be sleeping tonight." She smiled in earnest and patted the hand she had been shaking. "It's going to be fine. Any questions, you can call Terry Wilson." She handed Molly a card with Terry's office number, and a neatly printed home phone number underneath. As she opened the door, she leaned out to heft two plastic garbage bags, Nugent's worldly goods, and placed them inside the door.

Getting to Know You

Nugent sniffed at the green beans, eyeing them suspiciously. With his fork poised in one hand, he bent over the food. Molly could see he wasn't exactly diving into his plate. He spoke softly like he really didn't want to be heard. "What's this?" He sniffed at the beans.

"You don't know green beans?" She was genuinely surprised but could tell he was wary of her response to his skepticism. "What kinds of foods did your foster mother cook? I mean, that you really liked."

His eyes got bigger, rounder as he jumped back to his most recent home-style cooking. "Maryann made stuff like Krafts with applesauce on the side. And it was good too," he added, just in case Molly didn't realize that it was something he liked. Or maybe it was a hint for her to cook in a similar way.

"Krafts. Is that some new type of food or recipe?" She was confused and was searching her students' acumen of food crazes; she couldn't find anything that came close.

Nugent finally speared a tomato from the salad she made. Molly guessed he recognized it as something he'd eaten before. He munched on it from all sides of his fork then popped the remaining morsel into his mouth and chewed some more.

"You know, Krafts. Comes in a blue box and has the cheese right in there too, so it's convenient." He sounded like a commercial. He licked his lips where the vinaigrette dressing began to dribble. "You don't cook Krafts?" His voice was quieter, afraid, she thought, that he might have given offense. "I like the hamburger though."

She heard the concession he made for the hamburger, which

she took to mean that salad wasn't a part of his regular diet either. He took another bite of his burger. "I never had a burger like this. I always order Big Mac, and once I asked them for a fish sandwich and it was good but only with that special sauce it comes with."

Molly was getting the picture, and wondered what the kid's blood cholesterol looked like as he regaled her with a litany of fast food restaurants his foster family ate at in a week. Once in a while a home cooked meal came in a Kentucky Fried Chicken bucket. There was a serious dearth to anything fibrous, fresh, unfried. He remembered once he tried a banana. "Only it was brown on the outside and sour tasting on the inside, like rotten, my friend Julio said."

Molly made a mental note of the foods he liked and thought she might be able to approximate those without the deep-fried. She noticed how he looked about the room as he ate, and talked.

"I can tell you one thing that's really different here." He had propped his elbows on the table and rested his head between his hands. "We always got to see TV when we was eating at Maryann's. She just didn't like little kids at the table, all talking at once and she said it gave her a headache. Sos, we got these little tables? And we put the food on them? And that's how we did. I didn't mind none cuz I don't like all that smoke they do while theyz eating."

Molly noticed his green beans were all that remained on his plate. She took one onto her fork from her plate and chewed and swallowed. He watched, wrinkling his nose.

"You like them beans?"

As she chewed she nodded yes. He absentmindedly put his own forked bean into his mouth and chewed. There must have been enough butter and salt and a hint of garlic powder to flavor it because he didn't spit it out, which she half expected. Instead, he cut another bean and ate it as well.

With the dinner ritual over, Molly suggested that he help her clear the table. He placed his dish, eating utensils and glass on the counter and watched as Molly cleaned up, the only sound now was the tap water and the splashing of soapsuds in pots and pans. She glanced over to see Nugent sitting at the table watching her intently. The silence became broader as neither broke it.

Molly wondered whether he was deep into his own thoughts,

or was like most kids she'd known, all vibration of nervous energy and life, passing time slowly, watching ants building mountains of sandy mounds. She hadn't thought this way for such a long time, for as long as she'd lived in Long Beach.

"I'll take you to school tomorrow because it's your first day. Then the bus will bring you back home." Home. So that's what this was. Creating this space into a safe haven for him.

"I didn't know I was going to be on some bus." A look of dark concern shadowed his face, and she realized he was afraid not just about how he'd get back after school but, she knew, of who and what she was or would be to him.

Molly dried her hands and sat down at the table to light a cigarette, hesitating when she thought of Maryann and the other adults smoking, filling the children's lungs with secondary poison. She got up to open the kitchen window so the cool air pulled the smoke out of the room and away from him.

"It's not so bad. The bus will bring you and all the other kids from the neighborhood home together." He became suspicious, fearful. The new school, new kids, all of it seemed overwhelming, and each time she tried to resolve the fear she only added new reasons to worry. It suddenly depressed her how out of her league she felt, so out of control, certainly not someone who should or could be responsible for a child.

"Look. The bus driver knows where to stop, and you can see the house because he stops right in front. And I'll be here."

The shadow seemed to pass. She wanted to believe he was calmed by knowing she'd be here to greet him upon his return. She reached out for his hand and he followed her out to the front steps of the building. It was a three-story yellow and white wash owned by the brother of her neighbor, Carlos Nunez. The street was quiet; most families were having their dinner. Carlos was outside standing near the curb, and he nodded to Molly as he absorbed Nugent's biracial mix. He stepped toward them, speaking to the boy in rapid fire Spanish. The boy responded in kind. Molly caught phrases here and there. Nugent deftly answered with his age, his mother's full name and "nada" to a question about his mother's family.

Carlos turned to a friend he was speaking with and bid him farewell, and retreated from the curb to speak more to the boy. She saw Nugent's shoulders relax as the man spoke to him, and watched the boy's interest increase as Carlos called Ramon to join them. The two boys spoke first in Spanish then a mix with English until they had abandoned the Spanish entirely and sounded almost white-bread L.A. to her.

" I gotta skateboard too, but I left it with some friends in Oceanside," Nugent was saying. Ramon quickly offered his spare board and the two boys walked away to try their moves together. Molly smiled and silently thanked Carlos for the language, for Ramon.

Out in the cool evening air, she lit another cigarette and sent the thick stream of smoke upward where it was caught by the air and pushed away from the ocean.

* * *

The days with Nugent were a stop-and-start affair. She was learning about him at every turn, and Nugent just absorbed whatever came his way. That first night was followed by similar nights when she often fried two hamburgers and somehow came up with a concession to Big Whoppers, using Thousand Island dressing, lettuce when she had it, and some sliced tomatoes. She watched as Nugent opened the burger to check on the fillings. She substituted milk for soda from the first night and he didn't seem to mind or notice the difference, or care. And she thought that he got milk at school and whatever Head Start program he'd gone to as a preschooler.

The first night he dropped into the bed and slept until she woke him the next day. Molly was equally tired and chalked it up to emotional exhaustion on both their parts because the next day was not Friday, but Saturday, so no new school and plenty of time for Nugent to get the feel of the neighborhood. She thought Terry Wilson must have set it up that way.

Molly planned his breakfast ahead, with cereal and less ripened and unspotted bananas. He pried himself away from the television and the usual Saturday array of cartoon shows to find her piling his clothes onto the bed and folding them. She opened the drawers and did the traditional socks and underwear in top drawers and jeans and tee shirts in the bottom ones. She saw his attention riveted. Later she went back into his room to straighten the bed. He didn't see her as he slowly opened the top drawer and touched each neat pile of folded underwear, and each rolled up pair of socks, then moved to the lower drawers and looked at the tee shirts, long sleeves in one pile, short sleeves in the next. She decided the bed could wait.

* * *

Saturday night Molly sat in the chair where she could train the reading lamp on the manila envelope that came with the boy. Nugent dropped onto the couch and handed her the remote. "You want to choose?"

"I got some stuff to read." She opened the envelope and knew without looking that he wasn't missing a single one of her movements. He slid to the floor and sat cross-legged and clicked onto the Disney channel where a sentimental stream of music signaled an equally saccharine movie about a coach and his hapless misfit pre-teen baseball team. She half-watched the side of Nugent's face for signs of emotion, wondering why he'd choose such a show. While she leafed through the paper to find his school information, she wondered less about his choice of evening amusement. The coach in the movie was all about tough love, believing in the kids, even the one outcast who wants to come back and help win the big game. Nugent was in awe, his mouth slightly open, relaxed, his eyes big. He must have sensed her watching because he turned. She saw a small boy full of wonderment and hope, and she supposed he saw yet another woman, not his mother, whose strange ways, food and apartment were now his home. And she knew he wondered for how long.

* * *

Molly's dread of Tuesdays was coupled with her dread of down time. Time she wasn't busy reading the want ads or surfing the internet to look for a job that would get her home in time for Nugent. Tuesdays were the longest day for Molly. It was Tuesdays that Nugent was late at little kid basketball practice that kept him at school until 4:00 o'clock. The bus took even longer to get him home because the traffic began flowing down from L.A. at that time of day.

This Tuesday was hot and terribly dry. The slight breeze

rustled the fronds of the palms out front, setting Molly's nerves on edge. She reached for her cigarettes and then pushed them away. Even with black market prices her habit was too expensive. She walked through the apartment straightening up the magazines on the coffee table in the living room, rinsing the stale coffee out of the pot in the kitchen, smoothing the sheets on Nugent's bed.

As she plumped the pillows in the sham she noticed a piece of cloth between the bed and the wall. She tugged at it to find it was a pink infant's bootie sent from Esther only days after Stella was born. Her idle mind filled with a dozen scenes playing out. Stella's perfect little mouth, her fair skin and dark hair, the baby milk smell of her when Molly kissed her warm forehead. She saw it once again, like a movie playing on a screen in front of her eyes. The big feast her neighbors gave after Stella and she came home from the hospital. So many people, maybe too much noise. Was that it? Was there something there that weakened her baby? She would have moved home, back east, she might have endured Esther's interference, her carping, anything to hold her living, breathing daughter again and know she would live beyond the three months of her short life. And on Tuesdays, she'd chip away at her feelings with a beer or two

Part Two

The Clinic

This bus's shocks must be fucked, Molly thought. They were jostling along and hitting every bump. Nugent was too busy sucking in the air from the open window to hear Molly, so she gave up trying to tell him to pull his head in. Molly checked her purse for her house keys, never certain she didn't forget them, though she checked for them every five minutes since she left the apartment.

She needed the anti-anxiety pills that Doctors Suarez and West were monitoring, and the drugstore was right next to K-Mart where she'd get them. She pushed a letter for Esther out of the way to find the heavy bulk of keys. Each time she saw the letter she wrote to her mother, she dreaded sending it. Esther twisted her words, she knew. Esther would call her then and rehash every phrase, every thought. She wanted Esther to read that the boy, Nugent, a foster child, was staying with her daughter, and so, wrote to tell her mother. Molly finally decided the letter could prevent the phone call sure to come afterwards. The bus came to a stop, a broad woman, very pregnant, waddled down the aisle toward the door. The driver watched her as she descended the stairs.

"Buenos Dias," he said to the woman.

"Gracias," she replied.

Molly watched her closely. Must be in her tenth month, she thought, like me with Stella. She remembered hating the bus ride down to the clinic toward the end of the pregnancy when her car broke down yet again. Testament to the great teacher's pay. Stella moving around inside, little thing that she was. Maybe that's what it was, she started out so small. Even when she got off the cigarettes in the second trimester, it might not have been enough. Her eyes misted over for her daughter, for the sweet milk smell of her, for the nights she nursed her and never once found it a burden. How much love she felt, she hoped, prayed that Stella knew, could feel it. They followed the pregnant woman off the bus and walked to the clinic.

* * *

Once inside, Nugent was shuffling the heels of the new sneakers to make them squeak against the highly polished clinic linoleum. "Hey guy, you want to stop that?" There was no edge to Molly's remonstrance, just a slight impatience that said her medication was wearing off. Or maybe it was the hot day, a carryover from the buzz she felt last night from the beers. Good thing a piss test wasn't going to show much this late in the day. She was busy picking white lint off the cheap black sweater that found its way into the wrong wash load when she heard her named called.

It was a loud bellow, "Morris!" that rankled her. She felt stripped of her privacy, on stage, in front of all these people. The others were mostly a mix of colors and cultures who long ago divested themselves from the personal aspect of the calling out of names, knowing the nurses and everyone else didn't give a damn who was being summoned. But it mattered to Molly even as she looked around and saw no one looked up, in fact no one cared.

"Stay here," she said to Nugent. "You all right if I leave you alone for a little while?"

Nugent nodded in a distracted way, playing with the computer game an uncle from his mother's family gave him. Good thing someone in that family half cared about him, though none of them, his mother's family, would take him. She was afraid he hadn't really heard her and would get bent out of shape if he looked up and found her gone.

"Nugent, look at me." Eye contact usually assured her he heard her.

"Yeah, I hear, I hear. Molly, hey look at this guy. He moves in and 'crash,' he explodes the two bad guys."

"Will he be okay out here?" A tall and heavy black woman who processed most of Molly's requests for her antidepressant refills and knew enough of the story told her it was okay.

Inside the treatment area Molly followed the dark blue line to the weigh-in station, the blood pressure and temperature station, and the urine and blood testing station. Each time she was greeted by a different woman, but they all seemed variations on the same theme, African American, Latina. The last one, Anita, handed her a plastic cup with a screw-on top for her urine sample. Molly hoped again that the lateness of the day and the fair amount of coffee and water consumption this morning had cleared her of any trace of the Coronas she guzzled.

"Put the cup here when you're done and go to room five."

* * *

An hour passed and Molly sat on the exam table, stripped to her panties in a white paper exam gown, reading a paperback. She applauded herself for bringing something to read because she usually got caught staring at a dumb white wall for over an hour waiting for the nurse to remember that someone was behind door five.

"Emma Morris." It was a statement in a flat, disinterested tone. Nurse Practitioner Sheila Lawler continued to peruse the chart, never looking up. It was a wonder she didn't fall on her face and good if she did.

"Molly. I don't use Emma."

"You were here four weeks ago."

Molly muttered a yes in a voice stale from not speaking for over an hour, and the nurse finally looked up, because she hadn't heard her. She stared blankly at Molly for the space of a minute and Molly finally responded again.

"Four weeks ago, and I don't use Emma. It's Molly." She was Molly's least favorite substitute for a doctor, a sour woman usually capable of making Molly feel trodden on and victimized.

"How are the moods?"

"Fine." Molly rustled in her paper gown on the paper-covered table.

"Any relapses? Sleeplessness? Suicidal thoughts?"

"Nope. Just fine." As if she would admit to any of the above. Molly looked around the room and at a picture of mauve and pink flowers in a white frame. All attempts at making the room less institutionalized were squelched with the white frame.

"Molly." Lawler must have caught Molly's daydreaming. Whether she meant it or not, it came out sharp, the way she might address an errant child.

"No feelings of suicide. No problem sleeping. Seeing Dr. Suarez once a week." She looked down at her hands as she spoke distinctly, the words pulled out of her. Each bit of information, each tiny drop of Molly's life spilling out in the room, one less drop of self-pride she got to keep for herself.

"Are you still at 844 Magnolia?"

"Nothing's changed. Same phone too." She never divulged more than she had to, no email address, and least of all, no list of academic credentials because she sensed this woman resented her, felt challenged by her.

Lawler read the chart for a few minutes more, then rested it on the instrument table and adjusted her stethoscope to her ears. She listened to Molly's chest through the flimsy material of her gown. Molly wondered what ever happened to the blue flowered cotton gowns they used in hospitals that some marketing maven sold to every hospital in the country. She smirked at the thought of some guy in the Caymans, his bottomless bank account keeping him in tequila shots and island babes. Lawler moved the stethoscope and asked Molly to breathe several different times, then pocketed the instrument in her white lab coat.

"How many packs a day?"

"Pack, maybe pack and a half," she said, then added, "low tar, though." And immediately felt foolish. *This bitch doesn't give a rat's ass whether I smoke or die.*

"Well, I guess it helps for all of you to do that." The nurse's heavy brows shot up. She spied Molly's book and picked it up. It was an old copy of *To the Lighthouse*. The pages were browned from twenty years of moving from one brick and wood bookcase to another, from one side of the country to the other.

"Oh, I see you are reading poetry?"

"No."

"You're reading this?" Lawler persisted almost in response to Molly's recalcitrance.

"I'm reading it, but it's not poetry."

"I see." The nurse put the book down and for the first time Molly felt her looking closely at her, her steely blue eyes narrowing in their deep-set pouches of flesh. She read over her notes again, and asked again when Molly would see her therapist, noting the date on the chart. "You can pick up your prescription out front. I'm making it for the rest of the month because you should be re-evaluated."

"Re-evaluated? Why?"

"It's routine to reconsider whether this drug or a new one is preferred." Her lips tightened against any remonstrance that might come from Molly.

"I've only been on this medication three months. How can you tell so soon? I mean, I'm feeling good on this one." She broke the cardinal rule of never seeming needy or dependent on anything that could be deemed addictive. The anti-anxiety pill was why she slept at all, was the reason she was not tearing this woman's blonde hair out by its dark brown roots, was how she could be trusted to care for a foster child. She knew it all came out sounding like pleading, weak and mewling, and she hated herself and blamed Lawler for making her so weak.

"I am sure that it is, but you should be seen by the psychiatrist appointed to your case." Lawler handed her the form that carried the magical word naming the drug, how often to take it and with a "no refill" box checked and an amount of pills that would last Molly till she saw Suarez, but not enough until she could see the psychiatrist. She felt the danger in the timing between seeing the two doctors, the danger of having her blood levels down without the pills and what that might do to her.

"Be sure to make a return appointment with Betty up front."

"Fine." Molly snagged the piece of paper from Lawler and slipped it into the book like a page marker.

Lapsing

For Molly it was a hard and bitter pill to swallow, so she took a swig of Corona Light and began to write the weekly letter to Esther so that her mother would continue to send her that extra money. The magical foster care check was not enough. Her words flowed better too with the beer, and two more bottles sealed the deal, as she tapped onto her laptop, filling the screen and marveling at how easy it was after all.

"Just so you know, I have Nugent, the foster care kid still living with me." She wrote this and then highlighted and cut it off the screen, weighing whether Esther would find it a sign of responsible adulthood that the boy lived with her, or whether her mother's repugnance for his half-Mexican, half-black heritage outweighed the fact that the State of California bore proof to Molly's ability to care for a ten year old.

In the final analysis, she pasted the sentence back in its original spot and tapped on. The first beer was guzzled before she knew it, so she took a cigarette break and opened another, this bottle colder than the last because she placed them in the freezer to speed up the process. Molly cut a thin wedge of lime and squeezed the juice as best she could into the bottle before plunking the lime through the narrow neck. She blew a stream of smoke, and the cold breeze at the window pulled the smoke out of the room and into the night air to be mingled with the smells of Magnolia Boulevard, which had its share of Mexican salsas and roasted Island jerked chicken.

Molly didn't think too often about it, but tonight as she paused to consider what to say to Esther to appease her so she'd send the small stipend that kept her daughter's roof over her head, she herself wondered what a white Jewish girl was doing in the 'hood. Magnolia was only a few blocks from the coast, and from Ocean Avenue where any night of the week and all day Saturday and Sunday there was the constant parade of the upscale, well-dressed seated in outside cafes, only blocks from a darker and more dangerous part of town. That Molly lived in the latter and seldom had anything to do with the former would be a constant surprise to most of the teacher friends she drifted away from, so that all that remained was Sarah.

Esther was threatening to come out to see things for herself. She gave a short and bitter laugh. To say they didn't get along was to say that the Gibraltar was a large stone. Molly sometimes could feel the relief in her mother's voice that her daughter was three thousand miles away. Yes, a source of immense and constant embarrassment that her daughter was not only that far away, but single, lately the lover of a Mexican by the name of Javier and the foster parent of Nugent Alvarez, so-named for his mother's family because no one knew much about his father's family. There was so little history. He was a marine, got mixed up with Nugent's mother, Ana and she pulled him toward her addiction until he went up in smoke in a home grown meth lab.

Molly continued to write stream of consciousness, filling up the computer screen. Hell, I'll edit later, she thought.

"I'm still looking for some kind of job," she wrote her mother, reinforcing the prospect of an end to the monthly dole her mother sent her, which she came to rely on. Foster Care money turned out to be largely insufficient. The landlord raised the rent when the boy arrived, she thought for fear his precious semi-slum would be wrecked by a skinny ten-year-old kid.

"I think something will come up now that it's fall and school has started." She slumped in her chair and lit yet another cigarette. She thought of the futility of trying to quit nicotine when she still toked an occasional joint, something her psychologist and her Narcotics Anonymous sponsor would freak about if they only knew. *At least I get a momentary kick out of nicotine, and the prospect of an early death followed with a marijuana mellow.*

She didn't pause to think too closely on her remark, made out loud. Now she regretted it because Nugent might have heard her. He was still a very light sleeper, some nights waking in a sweat and bumping along the hall looking for her, making sure she was still here, still someone he could depend on not to beat him, starve him, leave him abandoned. He never said, and Foster Care never confirmed it, but she guessed that if they saved him from a meth lab, there was rampant neglect throughout his earliest years. *How could they?* Her own short acquaintance with meth told her very well how they could, though she reminded herself often that it was only after her baby died that she turned to the cheap fix, something that would blur the edges of her pain and make her feel on top of it all.

She turned off the overhead light which cast a glare on the screen and opted instead for a cheap little gooseneck table lamp she found on one of her runs to the Swap Meet. It was a Southern California phenomenon onto congregate on Saturdays in Tustin or Santa Ana where ninety-five percent of the population was Asian or Hispanic, and rummage through other people's junk which fast became your own little treasure. So, for fifty cents you became the proud owner of a lamp that held a 60-watt bulb and whose gooseneck could be trained on your computer screen — something you bought while you were still gainfully and most respectfully employed. She preferred the more subtle light so she wouldn't be reminded that the kitchen needed a paint job better than the one she got before Stella was born, and where the curtains could use some washing and spray starch. Still, the place was clean, Esther would be glad to know.

"You taught me well, Mom." She raised her beer bottle up in tribute to the Mrs. Clean of The Grand Concourse, the Bronx, New York. "I'll finish this tomorrow." Her voice was just a tad slurred, time for a deep and dreamless sleep. "Besides," she reasoned. The editing needs the bright and sober day." She needed to get the letter out first thing tomorrow, or risk the dreaded phone call, or worse, the threat of Esther on her way to the west coast to check out things for herself. That would never do.

It was her turn to bump along the dark and dusty hallway to the room across from Nugent's. It held a queen-sized bed with a mattress meant to last her at least another five years. Javier bought it when she became pregnant with Stella. He was so delighted, so proud in that Latino way, of his machismo. He made a baby. She reminded him that it took two. She fell across the bed and pitched and rolled until she could find enough pillows to bolster her, hold her in one position so that she might not wake herself, so that she might not dream, so that she could find some peace and push away all that she did not want to visit again.

Esther would come out, letter or no letter. It was just a matter of time. And then the nightmare would all begin, and she'd be forced to live it again. Her loss was the constant topic in her therapy sessions and her countless N.A. meetings. "Molly, crystal meth addict. I'm here tonight because my baby died and I couldn't face the pain." Or, hi, I'm Molly, meth addict. I just got my first chip, 30 days, clean and sober." *Am I?* She pushed the question away for some other night when soul searching came up on the menu again.

She fell asleep and dreamed in spite of her efforts otherwise. She dreamed in Technicolor, and it was beautiful and Stella was there of course. This time she was a toddler, running through the grass in a park in Long Beach. She wore a yellow pinafore, and matching bonnet, and she looked back at her mother, smiling a secret smile to her mother, and running some more. And Molly couldn't get her. She called out to her daughter, thinking how beautiful she was, how sturdy on her little legs, how fast she ran. "Careful. The street." She yelled out and Stella stopped in time and Molly picked her up, swooped her overhead and the baby laughed that full-belly giggle that only a baby can. And Molly held her and held her. She woke when the cold air off the ocean hit her uncovered shoulders. Her face was wet with tears and she looked at the digital clock to see it was 2:00 a.m. She thought of her dream, it was so real. Her mind raced through the dimming memory of it. Stella as a two year old. Did she look like me? Did she have any of Javier in her? She recalled the bonnet and the hair under it was dark, dark, so yes, she was Javier's child in the dream, not some wished-for resemblance to a child, but someone who could have been theirs. She turned over on her back and forced herself to deep breathe, forced herself to relax first her feet, then felt her legs sink into the mattress, then her thighs and so on until she was concentrating on her neck and was gone, mercifully gone into the dreamless sleep she prayed for and which now had finally come. And she slept in a tangle of bed clothes and pajamas, the light blanket draped over her bare shoulders while Nugent slept on in the room across, their breathing both deep and rhythmic and forming a unified bond in sleep as they were forming one in life.

Tomorrow would be soon enough for both of them to take up that other rhythm of being in the world, the one they were forced to live in, next to the one each was forging for themselves in order to survive. Molly would wake first, at five and remember half her dream but not that she actually awakened. Nugent would sleep on as a child does, and he would dream a different dream, of competing on the basketball court with the bigger boys and he'd be triumphant like the father he was told he'd had.

References

The job didn't come from an ad. It was one of those neighborhood things, one person telling another and so on. Javier's cousin Theresa heard there was a teacher's aide job open at the day care. "And, Querida, they pay day to day because the people come and go." That was a relief to Molly, nothing to declare on top of the Foster Care and the SSI, and of course, Esther's checks. She purposely let them slide and did not ask Esther if a check was late or didn't arrive, waiting instead until Esther mentioned them when she called. It was their little game, who would be the first to speak, who would say, "Oh, I forgot the check, I'll get it out tomorrow." Or, "Hi, Mom, things are a bit tight until the Foster Care check arrives." She did that only once and then decided it wasn't worth the indignity of having to ask. So a teaching job might be the answer for now, even if it was an aide's position.

She was almost thinking out loud when she told Sarah, "But I know they're going to want references."

Sarah was dubious. "Why will they? You said it was under-the-table kind of pay."

Molly thought some more. "Kids, it's because they're kids. Even if the job is supervised, they'll catch hell from the State if something happened to a kid caused by a temp worker. Which means, I'll have to talk to Robert." The thought of having to see Robert made her stomach turn.

"Write him a note, can't you?" Sarah understood how distasteful it was to have to bend a knee in supplication to that asshole.

"Wish. I'll just go in for a quick visit, nothing too formal, and just ask him." She saw the event unfold as she spoke, and knew that she'd better do it today, before she changed her mind. But first she called the Brewster Day Care and got an appointment to meet with the principal.

* * *

She chose the clothes carefully. The navy blue cloth skirt and the peasant blouse with her tan sandals. She tried on the blue and turquoise feathered native earrings and opted instead for the plain silver hoops. It had been so long since she dressed for an occasion, and one that might mean more income at that. Nugent waltzed into her room as she laid the clothes on the bed, alternately choosing to include pantyhose or not.

"You go to the school today, Molly?" He backed up when she swished the skirt in front of her to check it for heavy wrinkles.

"Back to the high school first to see my old boss. I see the day care principal tomorrow. She touched his wet hair, and pulled the towel from him to rub the hair dry. "It's cold out this morning." She went through the litany of things to remember for school, he finished his breakfast, don't forget the math homework sitting on the table from last night. "You better hurry." The boy piled everything into his backpack, chosen to resemble the type Ramon carried; no Batman logo that was way too childish. It came as no surprise Nugent wanted a Lakers logo with signatures of his heroes.

She heard him leave when the door banged closed. She hurried into her clothes, brushing her hair, and at the last minute deciding against the pantyhose and risked a run by pulling them off so quickly. She thought through the short description of the day care, "Just to help out," was how she phrased it when she spoke to Robert late yesterday. He was unresponsive and so she kept it light. "You might get a call because I've been interviewing a bit."

His heavy breathing on the phone sounded like a horse in heat, and he was eating something while he spoke. It was too distasteful. "Sure, Moll, I can see you tomorrow...." His chair creaked as he reached for his calendar. "Ten okay with you? The superintendent wants me to drive down to his office for lunch, so I'm outa here after I see you."

* * *

He looked that pasty-pale, sweaty type that he was, his skin

96

glistening, which to Molly always suggested greasy. She sat down but not before the requisite handshake that confirmed the greasy part.

"You got some job coming up?" He looked like he'd attempted to wet down and comb his thin blondish hair, and she was surprised to realize he was ill at ease in her presence.

"It's not much of a job, just to get me over this economic hump right now." She sat a little straighter, reminding herself to be careful and not give too much away.

Robert shuffled some papers in front of him, pretending, she thought, to read them. He was thinking. "So, uh, does it pay good? I mean you must be finding it hard to keep ends up. It cost a lot when you had that habit."

At first she found it troublesome in understanding Robert. "Habit?" she couldn't believe she was hearing this from him.

"Yeah. That heroin or cocaine? Must cost some real money." He smiled weakly. "Did they make you do time?"

She leaned close to the edge of the large desk that separated him from her and that separated him from the wrath of her fingernails that she would have gladly racked across his silly face.

"Robert, don't you remember anything? How many years did I work here?" She stopped and regrouped. "After my baby died, I became dependent on the Valium they gave me. I didn't steal it, it was prescribed." She left out the meth, that wouldn't do for someone as brainless as he was. "But that's all over now." She added this quickly to reassure him.

"So, what do you do for the little extra money you need now? I know that SSI is not doing it for you. Not with the price of apartments."

She knew he had no idea where she lived, and thanked a silent, most likely absent god for that. "Guess that's why I'm here. A part time gig will help."

"I was thinking we could get together, you know, kick back with a few brews at RJ's pub down the block. And we could see where that might go."

She dug her nails into her palm to avoid the violence she might otherwise do to him, and tried for a smile. "Maybe. Sure. You got a meeting today? You said soon."

"Huh? Oh, yeah with the super." He looked toward the door

then back at her. "Maybe you could do me here. You know as kind of a get-to-know-you thing?" His pale blue, almost colorless eyes blinked behind his thick glasses, his K-Mart tie looked too tight for his thick-with-too-many-Burger King lunches' neck.

Molly stood up. She walked slowly toward the door. "Robert, the law is clear on what you can or cannot divulge about my employment. Hell, I'm on medical leave, so I am technically 'employed' here. You wouldn't be harassing me sexually or otherwise, now would you? I mean, I could be carrying a tape recorder. Just in case you started suggesting sexual favors. There were those little mishaps. What? A year ago? With that girls' basketball team you coached?" She let it all linger like so much fetid air, from the cesspool she thought he belonged in. She smiled, "Let's talk again sometime. Okay?"

The Interview

Molly took two more drags in quick succession and blew out the cumulative smoke in one long billowing cloud. Now or never she reasoned, as she ground the butt into the sidewalk. She crossed the street to the large and sprawling white one-story building. "Brewster Day Care and Nursery" was emblazoned in blue on a white sign in front of a gate. Molly pressed the buzzer and waited for what felt like an eternity.

"Yes?" A blurred sounding-voice came back over the speaker.

"Molly Morris. I have an appointment with Mrs. Dickenson."

The buzzer sounded and Molly pushed against the gate, which opened easily, and climbed up two steps and into the school. Directly in front of her was a short hall with doors leading either left or right into great rooms. The lights were out, the window shades were pulled down against the blazing sun of mid-afternoon. When her eyes adjusted to the dark, she saw children lying on mats in various levels of sleep or wakefulness. Some tossed about against the restrictive motion the mats imposed. Others were lying in fetal position on their sides with or without thumbs in mouths.

"I'm here, Ms. Morris." The voice came from immediately to her left, and spoke in a half whisper. Molly picked her way past a floor filled with four- and near five-year-old sleepers, and one very alert little girl whose head pivoted to watch her. Molly reached out in response to the director's hand.

"I'm Mrs. Dickenson. Thanks for coming today." Mrs. Dickenson was a thin woman of average height. She wore a dark blue dress in a conservative cut, and her hair was in a neat bun at the nape of her neck. Molly could see in the dim light that she was a light-skinned black woman in her mid-fifties.

Mrs. Dickenson gestured to a seat next to her, a child's chair near an equally low work table. She looked directly at Molly.

"Did you bring a resume?" she said, then fumbled through a stack of papers. Molly's heart began to sink. Were all those papers other resumes? "Here it is." She waved the one-page rendering of Molly's professional career in front of both of them, and then read through briefly. "I was wondering. Why would you be interested in this position? I see you have some very good credentials. High School. History and Social Studies and Junior and Senior levels." She looked up.

"I have a child who gets home early from school."

"Couldn't you make arrangements for your child and teach at a local high school?" Molly knew this was the direction the interview would take. Mrs. Dickenson continued to rummage through her papers. A child stood up at the far end of the room. Mrs. Dickenson stood so the child could see her. He pointed to the hall and most likely the restroom. Mrs. Dickenson nodded assent in his direction and he scurried out in his socks.

"I am having a hard time believing you will find this work rewarding."

Thankfully she hadn't given Molly a chance to answer the first question. "I took some time off from high school. They are all farther away, and I would have to take two buses to get there. I don't have a car." There was a quiet moment. "And since I was planning on a new beginning, I thought I'd go back to working with children who are really at the beginning of their lives. Nursery school would be their first experience in a structured environment." Molly wondered as she spoke, where she came up with these things. *Hope I don't sound too flighty.*

Mrs. Dickenson pushed her glasses back up her nose to focus on the resume, and then squinted at Molly. "You live very nearby on Magnolia." She looked closer at Molly. Molly wondered, was she looking at her white skin, her light brown hair with blonde highlights?

"Why don't you tell me a little about yourself?"

"Well, I do live nearby, which makes it easier for me to be here early in case you needed someone to open or if any one of the other teachers were delayed because of freeway traffic." Molly's head began to whirl, thinking of Robert, thinking of who she could possibly get for references? What about Robert? That was a closed case, for sure. She'd get someone to call the school and check for a reference with Robert. That way he'd be on the alert that someone might be testing him; if he said anything negative, he could be sued. As she talked about her work experience she ran down a list of teachers she knew at the school where toward the end, she turned up only occasionally and only when she was not high, so not all that often.

By that time, the substitute knew her class better than she did. She thought about the therapy she was forced into and N.A. meetings and the sad cases she shared her life with on a weekly basis. Couldn't use any of them for references, but if she could, they might impress this woman.

She could ask Marion Stein, a friend from her old life, the one where English as a second language was not the norm. Marion stayed in touch; she remembered Molly when she loved her work, the Molly whose students started out dark and sullenly wary of her because she was a white woman, but who were won over and thinking of history as a door to a real job in the real world. Some of them maybe even thinking of teaching careers instead of pie-in-the-sky dreams of making it as a gangsta rapper or basketball star. She could call Marion.

"It *would* be nice to have someone who lives nearby." Mrs. Dickenson's eyes softened. Her smile encouraged Molly to continue.

"And my son, actually my foster child, his bus route takes him back to the apartment at 3:00. He's one of the first to be dropped." Molly immediately cursed herself for having given up that much. Why say foster child? She nervously added, "Nugent's mother may be dead, no one can find her. His father is known to be dead but they can't find any family for him. They think he might be from back east somewhere. His mother's family is scattered, mostly here, some in Mexico." She chided herself for non-stop blathering.

Mrs. Dickenson returned to the resume, then removed her glasses and again looked at Molly more closely, smiling at the corners of her mouth. It was a knowing but kind smile. "Our demographics must be obvious to you since you live here." Then, in a quieter tone: "These children, a lot them, are from homes like the one Nugent had." She hesitated. "You realize you'll begin as a teacher's assistant. The pay isn't all that good."

"I'm just getting back to work. I wasn't well for a while. My baby died." Molly's voice faded, the breath forced out like a bellows with holes in it. "She didn't live very long. They say it was SIDS." Molly was relieved that she got it all out, a rote little statement that helped her stay an emotional distance. The words no longer meant anything to her as long as she didn't stop to think what or who they referred to. No longer did they actually mean Stella at eleven pounds and looking healthy whose heart stopped when her breathing did, and her mother didn't even get to say good-bye or hold her while she was still warm. Nor did they allude to the shabby little coffin she bargained for with the funeral home, and that Javier's brother paid for, or the absence of any of Molly's family or the Catholic burial for a half-Jewish infant, or the long ride to the cemetery deep into Long Beach's 'hood on Pacific Coast Highway. They did read the psalms of David at least.

One of the children, a girl, stirred near Molly's feet, and she instinctively reached out to her and stroked her head. The child turned on her side and slept on. Mrs. Dickenson reached out and pressed her cool hand into Molly's hot one.

"I'm very sorry for your loss." The director's eyes conveyed her genuine feeling.

"You'll begin then as a teacher's aide. And I am truly sorry that is what is open right now. Are you all right with that? And the pay is just above minimum wage."

"I really want to get back to work." She shifted in the little chair, her knees aching from being so low for so long.

Mrs. Dickenson stood and Molly followed. "When can you begin?"

* * *

Molly burst out of the doors, her lungs feeling like she hadn't taken a deep breath in hours. The traffic was getting heavy on the boulevard. It was near time for the bus. She walked, then found herself jogging until she arrived, panting, at her corner. Five minutes. It only took five minutes if she ran all the way in case there was an emergency and the school called to say that Nugent was sick or something. This could work. Her thoughts turned again to Marion, and the pain of dealing with creditors for late credit cards or the guy who threatened to shut off the electricity. She'd have to call Marion and ask. But not right away. Molly planned to take care of that with a call to her. And Robert? Well, she was pretty sure he wasn't going to interfere. He stopped thinking of her the moment she was gone from his office.

A smile played on her lips. She felt almost like a citizen again. She remembered telling her kids in class how money was the rule for American hierarchy. Being without it was the best and saddest lesson.

A Job and Toya

The distance between Magnolia Street and the school was alternately short or long depending on the time of day and Toya. In the morning Molly rushed there because she was always a little late in getting Nugent out the door for his bus, or late getting her hair dried, or just late. In contemplation of Toya, she dragged her feet and then hurried when she noticed by her watch there were only minutes before the poor and often hungry pre-schoolers descended on the school. If Toya called in sick or didn't show up the day before for one lame reason or another, Molly would be glum because odds were she'd be back today. If she had been there the day before, Molly would have plenty of slights, real and slightly real to chew until they festered into something that needed a strong antibiotic. Toya was that bad, or good, depending on how you calculated her barbs, insults and snide, just-out-of-hearing remarks about Molly.

It was a hot day and the air conditioning unit was a full-scale disaster. The windows were open on the ocean air and the breeze was mercifully blowing cool into the room. Molly began to pick up the paper plates filled with French toast and slathered butter, and poured syrup onto each serving. No sooner had she placed the plates at the table settings than four year olds appeared as if from nowhere. The first were LaShya Thomas, pretty with very large eyes, and Marlinda McBride, whose clothes and manner bespoke professional parents and upscale living conditions, probably somewhere on Cherry Street. The other children, mostly boys, filled the table for twenty, including Markum Standard. He was wiry thin with a nervous energy. He could not talk without almost screaming, and he was unintelligible. His language skills were below his age, and his physical motions, often imitating men in pursuit of women were mature beyond a teenager's, unless you lived in the 'hood.

"Here's your breakfast, Markum. This is French toast. Can you say that for me?" The boy stuffed large pieces of the bread into his mouth, his cheeks puffed out. Molly saw him eat this way yesterday and every day she worked at this table. She knelt close to his seat with her hand on the back of the chair. "Chew, Mark, chew it all before you choke." Predictably, Markum shot up and out of the seat and Molly grabbed him with one hand.

"Let go, fool." He spat the words and a good deal of food and pushed at Molly.

Molly saw Toya and the cook watching her. "Mark. You have to chew before you can swallow. There's plenty more if you want it."

Markum began to chew the food and then gagged. Molly placed a napkin to his mouth. "Spit it out. I'll get you some more. Go ahead." The boy spit into the napkin.

Molly moved a plate in front of him, but he continued to stand. She cut the toast into small pieces and skewered a portion onto a plastic fork, and handed it to the boy, as she steered him back into his seat. He accepted the fork and the food and chewed it but immediately stood and ran to the other side of the room. Molly heard the cook and Toya laughing as she brought him back to his place. "Sit here and don't get up" she said it sternly. The boy did as he was told as he watched her monitoring him.

Toya and the cook were smirking and making very little effort at hiding their enjoyment of this scene. The cook shouted, "Markum, you know the name of that food, boy?" Markum looked confused and tried to speak with his mouth still full. The cook and Toya laughed again and Toya growled in Molly's direction. "What you think you're doing with him?" Toya began to move closer to where Molly stood.

She feared this encounter, but now that it was here, Molly was too angry to care. "Helping him learn to eat like a human being. While you laugh at him."

"You don't think he's human? That what you're saying to me?"

" I know he's human. I just don't think he knows."

Toya's voice was thick with rage. "You say he's an

animal?"

Molly put a plate back on the table and met Toya as she walked toward her. "I know where you're going with this. Whether you like it or not, that boy can't eat without bolting. He's like a dog that hasn't seen food in a while."

"You making fun of him? Think you're better?"

"If you were so concerned about him, why haven't you helped him?" She glanced over at the cook and said, "And why haven't you shown him how to hold a fork instead of grabbing his food off his plate? He's been coming here, how long now?"

Molly noticed the noise in the room was not lessened, yet their conversation was distinctly easier to hear, both for them and the several teachers and aides who now made a great effort at not looking like they were listening. Toya stopped where she was.

"Let me guess, Toya. I'm discriminating against him?"

"That's how I see it."

"How do your boys eat their dinner? With both hands? Doubt it." She took a deep and ragged breath, her body shaking with anger. "Markum needs help with his food. I suggest you lodge a written complaint about this incident. In fact, I desperately pray you do, so that I, in turn can bring attention to this situation. Toya, this is something has been going on way to long."

Toya was a tall and heavy woman whose movements were hard to miss. Now Molly was almost shocked to see her back away and turn around. The cook lowered her gaze and retreated from her window where she began to place paper plates on the window sill while teachers and aides walked by, picking up and serving the breakfast to the other children. Everyone was eating in silence.

* * *

Molly went back to helping the children. The shiny eyes of Malcolm told her he might have a fever. She placed her hand on his forehead and he was warm. "You feel okay, Malcolm?" She looked up to see Toya's back as she bent to address a child at the next table. Her eyes came back to Molly and they stared at one another until another child asked for help at Toya's table.

* * *

The children were at recess when Mrs. Dickenson stopped Molly in the hall. "Could we have a few minutes?" Molly tried to guess her reasons. Toya reported her? The cook? She felt anger, and some fear, hating to think that there was some retaliation for preventing the boy from choking and needing the Heimlich maneuver. Molly followed the director into the soundproof closet she called an office. She smiled at Molly and put a hand on her arm which Molly wanted to find comforting.

"How are things going?"

Molly thought a moment, then a moment longer. "Pretty good."

"You seem to be settling in okay?" Molly felt this was the lead in to the bigger questions that now would come.

"The kids are great and the staff seems to show a genuine interest."

"Molly, I know what happens in there." She gestured with her head toward the main room. "You seem to fit well into the curriculum and with the teachers."

"But?" Molly wanted to pick up the word as quickly as she flung it out.

"No buts." Mrs. Dickenson settled further into her chair. "You're a teacher's aide but we all know your education and background. I'd like to think that you set an example for the other teacher's aides."

Molly wanted to say that Toya and most of the aides couldn't stand her. That she heard them mumbling about her having attitude. Instead she sat there.

Mrs. Dickenson stood and so did she. "Keep doing what you're doing" she said.

* * *

The back of the school was a fortress of nine feet of cinder blocks. Two teacher's aides, Darren Cooper and an older woman, stood just outside the door, cigarettes in hand. Darren felt in his shirt pocket and handed a cigarette over to Molly without her asking.

"She's quitting." He motioned to the woman. "She quit smoking her own." He lisped in a pronounced way. His shirt was a riot of colors and fabrics. He pieced together pants were torn on the legs of the inseam. Molly could see white thread that did not match the gray pants.

"Darren, what happened to your pants?"

"Where?" He looked down self-consciously to the white thread. "I was trying to peg them, give them a 50s look. Ran out of gray thread, wouldn't you know."

"My name is Beryl. I just started here," the woman said to Molly. She had thick gray hair that was unkempt, strands went everywhere, and looked like it could use some shampoo.

"You seem to know one another." Molly took a light off of Darren's cigarette.

"Oh, Darren and me. We play leapfrog. Every few months one of us finds a job and gets the other one in." Beryl leaned up against the building, with no regard for her clothes. She was dressed in slacks and a tank top that showed gaunt arms bereft of any muscle tone. Her face was lined and her fingers were yellow with nicotine. When she coughed, which was often, her chest sounded full. Molly felt the woman's lease on life had dwindled. She contemplated a one-room efficiency over in Westminster, the half-eaten sub-way sandwiches and two cans of coke with some cheap rum thrown in that she consumed before falling asleep on a sofa bed that never got rolled out. "How them witches treating you in there?" Her voice was conspiratorial.

"Be more specific." Molly stubbed the cigarette out in distaste. She had a pang that hit her deep. Is this where I am headed? She asked herself. Engaging in this discussion? She thought about Ms. Dickenson and what she said earlier. Was she setting an example for others by legitimizing the worth of this encounter? Or was she now just being a snob? She chided herself; for someone living on Magnolia in the 'hood', there wasn't much to contemplate from that street address.

"All of 'em." Beryl winked at Darren and then back at Molly.

"Some, yes." Molly liked the teachers, and could not speak ill of them. Then: "The kids are great, though. Do you like working with children? You and Darren work in this type of place before?"

"Nah. First time. Most often we do the telemarketing gigs. Lots of them, mortgage companies especially. Right now those guys are having a heyday. Orange County's full of them too."

"Why telemarketing?"

"Because the money's a little better and because Beryl and me can speak English."

"And read. Don't forget, Darren. Read those goddamned scripts they put up on them computer screens. Now I got computer skill too."

"Beryl, you're full of shit. You got bupkis for computer skills." Darren laughed out loud then quieted down when Chondra appeared in the doorway and motioned to Beryl to come back in. Molly sensed a change in Darren, and looked up to find tears standing in his eyes. "I know what I look like to you. I'm not all black, you know. My father was mostly Mexican and my mother was part Pacific Islander."

"You're a whole cornucopia, aren't you?" Molly could see the slight slant to Darren's eyes. Could be Pacific or could be Vietnamese or Chinese, more likely. She'd been up to Costa Mesa to experience the melding of cultures and colors. "I'm getting enough money to start designing clothes. Have a friend who does Indie films. He said they looked at some of my stuff."

Molly studied Darren's tattered shirt more closely. It was colorful; he'd shown a flair in the choice of fabric, and she supposed, if he owned a decent sewing machine or mannequin to sew with, he might be half good. In the space of five minutes Darren continued to share his life with Molly. He spoke of his particular hell, growing up in the barrio, Latino and gay in a family of boys and men. Though he spoke mostly through damp eyes of hurtful reproaches both on the playground and at home, Molly admired his resolve to remain connected to the neighborhood and what was left of his extended family. His parents were dead, his mother from overwork and a bad heart, and his father from a needless industrial accident.

"I sit with my girl cousins at family fiestas. Give them tips on what colors work or don't depending on their particular shade of coffee."

"What do you mean?" Molly paid closer attention to what he was saying with this expression. A flicker of recognition came to her. "You mean color of skin, don't you?"

Darren nodded. "Gloria is café au lait, Dolores is black, and

Lourdes is a splash of cream."

Molly smiled at him. "And Nugent is a mix of Dolores and Lourdes."

Darren stepped on his cigarette. "Nugent. Your stepson or something? Chondra said. 'Cause lookin' at you I can tell there's nothing mixed, 'cept something European. So he ain't your blood."

"He's my foster child. I had a little girl, but she died as an infant. She was more like Gloria."

She saw how Darren appraised her knowing her child would've been half non-white. It was the same when people in her apartment saw her living with Javier and then her big belly. They surrounded her, protected her as though she were carrying the link from their world to hers. And in many ways, that was the way of it for women who blurred the lines. But she was sure that was not how Toya would see it.

Toya came to the door just as they were leaving. Darren hung back long enough for Molly to enter the building and for Toya to come out.

"Darren. Miz Dickenson's looking for you."

Molly turned to see Darren make a face at Toya's back and shake an exaggerated limp wrist.

The Cut

Molly ran up the stairs to catch the phone on the fourth ring.

"This is Betty Miles at Nugent Alverez's school? His teacher, Mrs. Guzman? Asked me to call you to make an appointment to see her?" All of Betty's pronouncements ended in a question mark even where there was no question, as if she were asking permission to actually be Betty Miles and the secretary at the school.

"Did Mrs. Guzman say why she wants to meet?" It was Molly's turn to ask a question, only hers was meant to elicit an answer. Betty was quiet a long time at the other end of the phone, which made Molly nervous. She felt that *she* was somehow being judged by this little secretary and it pissed her off.

"She said to just tell you there was an incident at school today." Her words were clipped and signaled that there was an end to the discussion. If Molly wanted to know more, she'd have to meet Ms. Guzman.

She wanted to say that getting off from work in the middle of the day, and from a new job, might cost her that job. She wanted to tell Betty that she was tired, even mid-way through the day, tired because she stayed up too late and drank way too many beers, something her Narc and Alcohol Anon session mates disapproved of, but that was how she got through her nights.

* * *

"I have to make arrangements at work. I'll call you."

When Molly asked for the number, Betty seemed somewhat surprised. Molly guessed she was used to some welfare chick. Or some type who made side money giving blow jobs to the locals, and not a real live gringa with a job. One who might just have to check with her boss before she ran over to meet Ms. Guzman.

She told herself to relax, settle in to the end of the day. The boy would be home and he needed her to be calm, even if he was beginning to act out in school. Her mind seized on Nugent becoming a pre-teen gangbanger, and she wanted to lecture herself about making way too much of this. Yet she knew there was that possibility, if not now, then certainly a year or more down the road. And how would she be able to piece her life back together if that were to happen? She pulled a beer from the fridge and took a long hard swig from the bottle. She had not been to an N.A. meeting in a week. She toyed with the label, ruminating on the thought of her many transgressions. Yes, beer was alcohol, and therefore outside the regimen, easier to fall all the way back to using if she was getting a buzz from booze. She didn't want to think about that now. Her eyes hurt; the kitchen looked bright to her with the sunrays bouncing off the clean floor. How easy it would be to lose what she gained if her desire for something stronger than beer took hold. She opened a kitchen drawer full of odd pieces of things, straws, toothpicks, a can opener, a broken figurine of a small angel and on top of all of it the photo she was looking for. Stella's christening. Javier's family insisted, and she didn't care. She thought of the joke on her mother, and what she would say if she knew her Jewish granddaughter was baptized, and a Catholic.

There was a close-up of Javier holding Stella. Stella's round baby face was beatific, the first curl of a smile where her father kissed her cheek. "Stella." She whispered her name and stroked the picture, and the loss of Stella became a keen and sharp pain. She took another long pull on the bottle and swallowed, the fizzy taste, the lime, all tasted good.

Molly thought she heard Nugent coming up the stairs, but it was too early for his bus to have dropped him off. And the footsteps were too heavy for a skinny ten year old. Instead Javier was standing in front of her with just a screen door between them. He reached to push the screen at the same time that Molly tugged and opened the door.

"Perfect end to my day." She glared at him and the smile that momentarily played on his lips faded to a thin and bitter line. He looked tired, yet sober, in control anyway.

"Yes, Querida, I know how glad you are to see me." She instinctively moved back although he had not moved forward.

"Nugent will be here soon." It sounded like a lame excuse even to her. She knew that if Javier wanted to, Nugent coming home wouldn't stop him from violence any more than it would stop him from making love to her, which was its own kind of violence. Molly told herself she was overreacting. He had a right to feel hurt. She used him to get a foster child. While he conjured images of the both of them together raising this boy, she pulled the rug out.

"I don't see you too much anymore." He must be reading her mind.

She felt tired and shaky from too much coffee and too much Toya. She opened the fridge for another Corona, cut the right size piece of lime and wiped the lime juice around the rim of the bottle before she expertly dunked it in. She kicked off her sandals, and stretched her legs out onto the chair in front of her, using it like a foot stool, and lit yet another cigarette. She knew he watched her drink, watched her stretch her legs.

"Nugent? That's the foster kid? Funny name for a kid. I never got to meet him."

This was a calmer Javier. He initiated the conversation with something benign, almost polite. She couldn't decide if it was the beer that was marring her judgment or something new in him. She had to give it to him, he was something to look at. Dark, dark hair that flopped over his brow, taller than most other Mexican men she knew, maybe like a conquistador ancestor she liked to tell herself, and smooth skinned like the Mexican Indian blood that claimed most of him. He looked healthy, something the drugs never really made a dent in. His tee shirt was worn not too tight, just enough to push against the toned biceps, and tight abdomen. He'd probably look this good when he was sixty.

"You got the place looking nice." Javier looked around the room at the fresh paint, the clean curtains in the windows. It wasn't hard to notice the difference from the hovel they both made it in their drugged glory days when sweaty sheets stayed on the bed for weeks until she came out of her haze or the sun was slanting into the rooms in a way that she couldn't ignore the dust, the grime, the mess she lived in.

She offered him a beer but he shook his head, no. Odd. The

Javier she knew started his day with a shot of tequila and a joint.

"What, you just said something?" She was having trouble staying focused. Javier stood, leaning against the refrigerator and she felt overly scrutinized. He lit a cigarette and dropped the match into her ashtray, then moved away from her as if to say he was giving her space.

"I said Nugent is a funny name for a Latino. But he's half black, no? So I guess that is where it comes from."

Molly smirked. In the past, she thought, he exhibited a much more overt racism. "They could have just as well named him Jesus." She pronounced the name in the Spanish, to sound like Heysuse. "His mother was Latina." Her slur was not lost on Javier. His eyes narrowed, a sign in the past, anyway, that like a panther, he'd strike. But whatever storm lurked behind them seemed momentarily quelled.

"He going to be here very long? You like this kid?"

She could see how hard he was working to keep this even keel. Okay, she thought. I'll be nice. "I don't know how long. He's the product of a messed up mother they can't find. She took off with her boyfriend, to Mexico somewhere. The father is dead." Her bottle was empty and she wanted another. She became impatient. "So what are you doing here?"

"Can't I stop to say hi? My brother just moved on the street, so I was seeing him." Javier opened the fridge and took out a bottle of water for himself.

"Making yourself at home? Give me another will you?" She held up her empty bottle. "Have to replenish."

There was a puzzled look on his face, and she knew why. His English was very good for a first generation Angelino, but certain idioms and turns of phrase eluded him. It touched a nerve if he thought he was showing this deficiency, and now that nerve summoned a dark look, as dark as his hair because he most likely never heard the word replenish.

She was more than slightly buzzed having guzzled three beers, and to prove her own point she didn't wait for him to give her a beer, but stood to take one from the fridge while he still held the door open. It was the wrong move, because her position placed her directly in front of him, all the ammunition he required to gently but firmly pull her to him. Javier stood so that their bodies were in alignment, and Molly felt herself come alive in a way she hadn't felt since before Stella. The memory of his body, the memory of them both, carried her along. One side of her watched and stood back while the other gave in to what was comfortable and familiar. Yes, she told herself, he could be wonderful, he could be gentle in his lovemaking. And then, just as suddenly as she succumbed, she forced herself away from him.

"You drinking a lot?" He released her almost as if he read her conflict.

"What the fuck?" She became incensed with his remark. "Who are you, my mother?" She twisted the cap off the bottle and cut her palm as she did it. Javier tried to take her hand to look at it, but she pulled away and moved to the other side of the room.

"You go to the meetings, si?"

"Oh, I get it, you're reformed. How many months, Javier? How many?" Her laugh was so full of irony that it might have choked her. "What? Let me guess. Six. Six goddamned months off of meth? Off of weed? Who the hell are you to tell me? Look at you, you're this close to drinking a beer. You're already breaking a cardinal rule being near someone who does." She ran water on her bloody palm and wrapped it in a paper napkin and pressed it tight. But the paper filled up and was red immediately.

"Querida. You're hurt." He took her hand, which she let him, and removed the napkin, and stretched the palm. She winced. "Just let me see." They both saw a pulsing of bright red blood in the center of her palm.

"It's an arteriole." Molly put pressure on it again with a kitchen towel. "I've cut a small artery. It needs to be stitched." She pushed past him to the back porch. "I gotta get someone to watch for Nugent when he gets home. Carlos should be home."

They left the apartment together, Javier gently clutching her elbow to steady her. She was glad for the buzz, although unsteady on her feet. Carlos was at the landing of the third floor as they descended. "Can you wait for Nugent? He should be home soon?"

Carlos nodded recognition toward Javier. "Sure Molly." It was the nod of one man to another, of one compadre to another that all was well or would be, that all was in control. He did not ask her how she hurt herself, so she was quick to tell him that she cut it on the beer bottle cap. Only after she told him did she realize that she didn't want him to think it was Javier. She remonstrated to herself that maybe that was the first time she was kind to Javier in well over six months.

As she walked to the curb, she felt watched. The neighborhood was home. Everyone congregated at their front doors or on the back porches of the semi-slum they lived in. There were calls from the men to Javier in rapid fire Mexican Spanish that she couldn't always follow. It was small talk. How are you? What's new? Hey, I see you have a new car. Buena. The subterranean message was more like, She's your woman again? Because to all of them, a woman of her age alone was against nature. She slid onto the highly polished leather seat of his vintage Camaro and thought how he must have massaged the oil into it until it was no longer thirsty, until it was as luminous as he could make it.

"Do you know where to go?" She flipped the mirror down to view her hair and she saw him smile at her vanity.

"Santa Maria, no?" The car's engine purred, telling her that it was as well cared for inside as out.

"Yes, just drive to the Emergency Room. You don't have to wait."

"Fuck, Molly." He whispered the words. Then, "Buena." With a nod to his head.

The heat of the late afternoon blended with the beer and the motion of the car to lull her into a semi-sleep. She dreamt vividly in ultra-Technicolor, a hot sun, a man with very white teeth smiling at her, caressing her face, and woke startled as she felt Javier's hand on her face.

"Molly. We are at the hospital." Javier parked the car at the lot next to the entrance and escorted her inside where a wave of cool air hit her. Someone brought a wheelchair and she heard Javier saying her name slowly for the intake nurse. "Morris." She told them her address. She heard Javier say, "Her husband." The nurse didn't seem to find the last name he gave for Molly juxtaposed against his surname as noteworthy. She probably thought Molly was just one more very independent woman, making her stand, holding onto her identity.

She must have fallen asleep again and woke to find herself on a gurney, hooked to an IV and Javier sitting next to her, gently touching her fingers. The hand was bandaged.

"It was as you said, arteriole. You lost much blood." If anyone wondered how worried he was, his expression answered the question.

"Nugent." Molly tried to sit up. Nugent would worry not to find her home, and while Carlos wouldn't burden the boy, someone in the neighborhood might get the story all wrong. Besides there was blood in the kitchen, she remembered seeing it in the sink and it dripped on the floor before Javier pressed the dish cloth onto the wound. What a mess that kitchen must be.

Javier steadied her and the nurse wound the bed up so she could sit. "I talked to the boy. He is okay."

St. Mary's

"Hang in there! Here's something to read to pass the time. We love you."

It was signed by Helena Schmidt and Sarah Fein. Molly recognized the handwriting and the Santa Monica postmark. She picked up the card again, Winnie the Pooh on the front, a flower close to his nose. Nothing could be more innocent. She took the "we" to mean the small group of women who found one another in the first weeks of their Master's program. Molly had a momentary feeling of unease that Helena or Sarah had spoken to all of them. What would she have said? She remembered calling Sarah the day after the accident, and Sarah told Helena. What was the harm that they knew? It was the way it happened. A stupid beer bottle. They should have discharged her a day ago, but when her blood work came back, the ER doc was concerned at her low hemoglobin, said something about anemia, and suggested a blood transfusion.

The room was close to the nurse's station and to the alternating noisy day chatter or the subdued tones of the evening and night shift. A board kept Molly's arm straight so the needle wouldn't move, and prevented her from turning to her side. She napped fitfully for most of the two days in the hospital room which made her nights unbearably stark and wakeful.

The haze from the beer was cut in two and all that was left was her sense of how far down she'd slid. She vacillated between wonder that went from sobriety to chipping with beer and an occasional joint to the consequent sick recognition that she had no control of any of it. And now it was visiting hours Friday night. The halls were full of human traffic stopping occasionally at her door.

A plump woman with a bouquet of flowers wearing a pink fleece sweat suit emblazoned with shiny little rhinestones stopped in looking for her sister Grace. Molly rang the bell and the nurse came to escort Mrs. McMahon to the room across the hall.

That first day, a tentative knock on the half-opened door was accompanied by Nugent, his big eyes seeming larger. Javier held the boy's hand, and Nugent glanced nervously at Molly's bandage, fearing, she thought, the sight of blood. She beckoned him to her, and he let go of Javier's hand and Nugent quickly surrounded her awkwardly with his skinny arms. She pushed his dark hair away from his flushed face to see traces of a Popsicle red on his lips.

"Has he eaten today? Since lunch? What did you have for dinner?"

Javier dropped some mail on the bedside table and poured a glass of water for the boy, who drank it down in one gulp. "He ate burritos and frijoles and some chicken mole at my mother's. Now he is thirsty."

"I ate it all. It was good. And then Javier stopped by the house to pick up the mail before we came. Just junk mail, no bills." He smiled and handed her the mail which she laid on the blanket near her.

Javier found a chair. He too seemed excited, almost festive. She guessed he was just glad she hadn't thrown something at him.

"He's been staying with you." More a statement than a question, and she reasoned Javier would not want to stay in her apartment without her. There were too many memories to brush back all alone.

"When are you coming home, Molly?" The boy leaned his body against her arm, and Javier cautioned him because of the IV. She had never experienced Nugent this physically close to her, and she reached out to graze his cheek with her free hand. It was so natural that he should lie against her left side, the most natural place for a child to seek or a mother to give.

She struggled to keep her voice even. "Maybe tomorrow. The doctor will be here early, so I can ask him." She turned to Javier to say, "I've been bugging them all day today, so maybe they'll get tired of me."

A nurse's aide opened the door. She propped a thermometer in Molly's mouth.

"Time for your vitals," she said and brushed past Javier to take her pulse, watching her chest rise and fall to check respirations, then moved both Javier and the boy away from her right arm while she took Molly's blood pressure. She did this by inserting her physical self between Javier and the bed. He tried to smile at her but the aide ignored him, looked a moment curiously, then appraisingly at the boy and asked, "You go to the Caesar Chavez Elementary? You in Mrs. Guzman's class? You know Monty Ferris?" Nugent nodded yes to the bombardment of questions. "He goes to that school too," she continued. "He's my neighbor's child, I pick him up, and I seen you there one day." She read the thermometer, noted the temperature on a piece of paper and began to stroll out, but stopped to speak again, this time addressing Javier, "She need her rest. You best leave now."

They stayed for a few minutes more, taking turns sharing neighborhood updates. Ramon got a new skateboard and gave Nugent his best old one. "And Molly, it's an Almost Banana, really cool."

Molly must have furrowed her brow because Nugent quickly added, "That's the name for the board, *Almost*. You know, they have one called Almost Hot Dog." He rattled on about the banana painted on the board, and she remembered seeing him on the skateboard website checking out prices.

Javier edged himself closer, held and absent-mindedly stroked her right hand. Occasionally he would look closely at her, holding her gaze until they both looked away. She had a sense of this scene, *we're almost happy again*, and then laughed at the 'Almost' skateboards.

"It's late, muchacho, let's go."

Javier bent over to Molly, brushed her lips with his, saying softly, "Querida."

Nugent's eyes were all over the two of them. His face was mobile with a rash of expressions she could not fully decipher but she thought were a mix of relaxation to see her well enough to talk, jealous or at the very least covetous of her when Javier's moves signaled an intimacy, and yet some relief from the inevitable Oedipal thing that he didn't have to be the man. She pulled the boy to her one more time and squeezed him. "I'm fine. I'll be home, this weekend for sure."

* * *

Molly woke Saturday feeling trapped, pasted to the bed, the IV still pumping fluids into her and now she had to pee. She pushed the call button but knew she could wet the damn bed before the nurse would arrive, so she slid out and pushed the IV pole on its little wheels to the bathroom. A nurse poked her head inside the door as Molly sat down.

"You shouldn't be out of bed without assistance." Perky little Lisa Kelly from the Emergency Room followed her patient from admission through nursing care. To most it was the new and improved way to ensure continuity of care, but to Molly it was a source of daily agony to have this saccharine sprite hovering over her every move.

"Don't you ever go home?" Molly groaned. "I think I can do this by myself."

Lisa pulled her head out of the bathroom like a turtle trying to hide, and waited till Molly came back out to the room. She guided the pole and Molly walked, a bit unsteadily. She couldn't have been more than a year out of training, eager, energetic. She got on Molly's nerves with her perfectly cut, short blonde hair and bright blue eyes. Molly felt seasoned next to her.

"I worked a double, last night and today until three."

"Christ, when do you sleep?" Her peppiness rankled Molly. It made her feel foolish for her drug and booze transgressions, as though she were an errant almost senior citizen.

"Who do you have to blow around here to get a cigarette?" She twitched uncomfortably as Lisa helped her settle into a chair, with much pillow plumping and more fussing. Molly had the impression that Lisa tuned out when language went in a colorful direction. When she asked whether Molly needed anything else, she withered at the hostile spark in Molly's eyes and hurried, finally from the room.

As soon as she left, Molly steadied herself and quietly rolled her IV pole down the hall to the side entrance of the hospital where all manner of patient riff raff stood, pulling nicotine deeply into their lungs. It was the last bastion of hope, the one concession that St. Mary's Hospital still allowed for people whose addiction was profound, though in a few weeks hospital policy makers would change the standards, and smoking for nicotine addicts would be gone for good.

Molly surveyed the assembled crew for a kind compatriot who would lend her a butt. A man, about fifty, was staring at her in her hospital gowns, one opened at the back and the other, worn in lieu of a robe, opened at the front. His dark blonde hair was perfectly coiffed, with silver at the sides that she swore he must have tinted. There were deep creases on the sides of his face from squinting into the sun, she guessed, on his yacht. She stared back, but he was not deterred. He'd already caressed her long thick hair as much with his eyes.

"Michael Dunn." He held the cigarette in one hand and extended the other.

She thought it was an unusual thing to do. Like they were at a cocktail party in the Valley or something.

"Molly." She shook his hand.

"Yes, Molly, what?" He stubbed out his cigarette.

"Morris." Something made her not want to say. Until now she had been anonymous among the crowd of those who smoke, poorer, barely able to pay black market prices, but who long ago gave up good nutrition for tobacco. She noticed the cut of his robe, hand-made and tailored just for him. His nails were manicured.

"I just thought that if I told you my name, you'd tell me yours." He smiled a soft smile and she could tell Michael Dunn won most of life's daily wars with a smile and with an absolute minimum of expended energy.

"Morris. My name is Molly Morris," she repeated.

She felt rewarded for having deferred to him, because he held out his warm hands and held hers in both of his. It was only a second, but a second longer than casual.

"Almost sounds like the rap star."

"My real name is Emma," she stammered. Maybe, she reasoned, he came from more money, more position, more everything tangible, and therefore he might be more in the world that measured human worth, and she felt measured.

"And you're from New York." He brushed an imaginary speck from his robe, and she wondered, did anyone really wear robes anymore? Maybe only rich, white Angelinos.

"And you're from L.A., some hot-shot director." She felt

obliged to follow suit and cast him as a type.

"Something like that. Did you hurt your hand?" He pointed to the heavy bandage.

"Something like that." No more excursions, the day trip was over into who and what she was.

Dunn must have sensed this. "I am an attorney at SONY."

"Not too surprising." She pursed her lips into something close to a smirky smile which she thought he was quick to notice. She scraped the cigarette butt out against a low wall and flipped it into the bushes, then thanked him again, and he held the door open for her as she negotiated the IV pole inside and back down the hall toward her room and toward Dr. Suarez who came out of nowhere to walk with her, taking control of the IV and gently guiding the pole.

A patient chart with her name on it was closed and fitted snugly to his side under his armpit. "Mind if I look?" She stopped and removed the chart, flipping it to the back to see the admissions form. She'd learned enough about the system to know that her case would be presented in the fewest and most meaningful words on this intake form. Name, age, address; her eyes skimmed down to diagnosis. In neat handwriting, a nurse for sure, an intern maybe, a doctor no way. "Patient presented with torn arteriole." She grimaced at the word 'torn.' She read on, "Loss of blood, confused, crying, incapable of answering basic questions. Appears intoxicated, rule out drugs."

Suarez watched her. "What were you looking to find, Molly? Not pretty is it?"

She closed the metal cover with a slap and handed it back to him. *I'm not a pretty picture, am I?* Her face was hot with shame.

"It's really all up to you. Not your mother, Javier, Nugent, Toya, that difficult woman you work with. It's you." His voice was no longer conciliatory. "You're going home today, which is Saturday."

"You don't have to orient me to time and place. I know what day it is," she shot back at him.

Dr. Suarez stopped and held her arm to steady her, and to turn her in such a way that she could not avoid his face or his expression of fatigue and dismay and certain anger.

"Do you? Know what time it is? Look, girl. Your being a gringa doesn't carry much currency anymore. The cops are watching you. One trip to the bodega for bread and to LaSheed for whatever he carries, and it's over. Is that what you want? What happens to the boy, then? Are you that stupid or selfish?" Her humiliation tripled in the wake of this stern side of him. "I'll see you Monday. Figure out a way to be there, tell the school principal whatever you have to." He stopped to turn down another hall away from the direction of her room, leaving her and her IV pole. "Oh. And call your sponsor, Greg, for an N.A. Monday night."

She wanted her anger to take over, she wanted to be indignant. Instead her heartbeat thumped against her chest as though she'd had ten cups of espresso or ran ten flights of stairs. The threat of losing Nugent was a most palpable fear. Would he be better off without her? Pathetic as they were, they were together in their makeshift little life, their shared dinners, weekend breakfasts. She bought him sneakers and worried about improving his math skills. What life would he have if they sent him somewhere else? Worse. Because it could be lots worse and she knew it. She walked more slowly.

"It's time for your medication." Lisa Kelly was waiting for her when she returned to her room. The young nurse sounded disappointed that Molly broke a rule by going outside for a smoke. Molly was hoping just once for angry. She could deal with angry, but disappointed would summon guilt, and Molly could not deal with any more guilt on a sober stomach. Even less so from someone like Lisa Kelly who may have seen a lot in her young nursing career that would sour most people into a cynicism. All it did for Lisa was strengthen her resolve to make it better for the poor, homeless, or derelict that crowded St. Mary's Medical Center Emergency Room.

"I told you I needed a cigarette." She popped the pill, iron supplement she assumed, and swallowed with the little paper cup of water. "When do I get out of here? The doctor said today. It's almost 2:00, and he hasn't even been here to see me."

"He wrote up your discharge five minutes ago." Lisa helped Molly sit on the edge of the bed as she deftly removed the IV needle, sponged off the area and applied a dry bandage.

"God, I am out of here." Molly tugged the hospital gown off and began to rummage in the closet for her clothes. Lisa actually turned away in the face of Molly's nakedness because implicit with it was Molly's wantonness and an animal sexuality Molly thought she'd hidden so well. A sun-dress was neatly pressed on a hanger, and her sandals were on the floor. Javier must have brought them.

Before stepping into her own clothes, she washed her face and brushed her tangled hair. Her mind raced to the little to do list of things left at home to get done, she packed up the remaining personal stuff, makeup, toothpaste, and turned to leave the room to see Esther standing in the doorway.

* * *

"So you cut yourself. Nice. Blood everywhere." Esther Morris settled her shoulders so that her back was ramrod stiff. Molly noticed it as her mother's signature move, ready to do battle, and always it was with Molly. The freshly ironed sundress and the sandals in the closet were explained.

"You went to the apartment? Who took you there?" Molly backed into the room, the rush to leave now mollified by her mother's presence. Certainly made more sense than her first thought of Javier ironing or even having his mother or his cousin Theresa doing the woman's work of preparing Molly's clothes. She cringed to think her mother saw the apartment before she had a chance to straighten it because she knew for damn sure Javier would not have done much to clean up.

"What a question. There were those shuttles but I took a cab. You never know about those other people in the van. If they drop you off first, some man knows your address." Esther surveyed her daughter's face, dusted an imaginary fleck of starch off the sundress. "You're skinny. No food?"

Molly hated to admit feeling weak and reasoned it was the trip out to the curb for a cigarette that pushed her endurance. Not wanting to get into 'it' with her mother, she glossed-over Esther's remarks. She picked up the hospital phone and called Javier at her apartment. He answered on the first ring, his voice eager. "I'm ready to go home." Javier said he and the boy would be there in fifteen minutes. "If there's enough room, my mother is here."

"I cleaned up that boy's clothes too. His jeans, a mess." Esther was prattling on. Molly pictured her mother, a regular whirling dervish with her bottle of Mr. Clean scrubbing all washable surfaces and chasing the dust down from under her bed with a broom. Her mother would have found and used one of the oldest

128

towels and some safety pins, and pinned it to the broom which she'd have found by rummaging through Molly's junk drawer, and use the cloth as a makeshift mop. She knew this as well as she knew the first thing Esther would do when they got back was either walk to the bodega to buy a proper mop, or commandeer Javier or Nugent for that particular job. Her mind steered back to her mother's remark, and she cupped the phone so that Javier would not hear.

"What do you mean *that* boy? He has a name. Don't start your shit with me about Nugent."

Her mother was impervious to Molly's remarks; in fact they gave Esther license to add to her own martyrdom at the hands of her wayward, gypsy of a daughter. Molly could hear her mother as she complained of Molly to her sister Minna, always when Molly was just slightly out of eyesight but surely within earshot.

Molly had almost forgotten Javier was still waiting.

"Querida, no worries. Nugent is too skinny to worry." Javier's voice was unmistakably buoyant.

Molly tried to ignore the sweet soap and water- clean smell emanating from the sundress, uncorrupted by smoke, beer, days of not bathing. It smelled like her life before she began to ignore herself, and worst of all, what was best for Nugent. Yet, right now she was wishing for a beer or a joint or both to get her through whatever Esther came up with in bad behavior, bad feelings, alienating the entire neighborhood.

The need for fresh air was so severe that Molly directed her mother and herself out of the room, ignored Lisa Kelly's plea to wait for a wheelchair and took the elevator to the first floor lobby. The whoosh of the revolving door sucked them out onto the curb where Molly sat down on a bench and searched for and found a short stub of a cigarette at the bottom of her purse. Mercifully there was a break in their conversation but Molly lighting up put a neat end to that. She almost winced with the pain of regret as soon as she realized this.

"These things will be the death of you." Esther all the while pointing a rigid finger. But it was an entrée to other chat. "I saw that man there, at your apartment."

"Javier." Molly blew out the thickest stream of smoke she could manage. "He, too, comes with a name." Molly looked out on the sunny day from the shaded building. The air held the clear and quiet beauty of a Saturday afternoon with all the promise that stretched before her, freedom from the IV pole, from little miss perky Lisa Kelly, and the prospect of getting home to be with Nugent, even Javier. She almost forgot her mother was standing there.

Esther's lips were a thin line across her face, her eyes were hard. Most likely her thoughts were with the name Javier and all that conjured for her of an illegal Mexican and any number of Hollywood stereotypes.

"Don't start." The admonition from Molly came with the last of the inhaled cigarette, and the cough that erupted from trying to talk and inhale at the same time.

"I'm just going to say one thing. Just one." Esther fidgeted, igniting with anger at what she perceived was her daughter's downfall, the depths she had come to. And it was Javier. For Esther it was wrapped up in the sleek, dark-skinned Mexican in the tight-fitting white tee shirt. "I thought that was over."

"That is not saying *one thing*, Mom. That's meant to start something, but guess what? We're not going there." Her hands were shaking and her legs a little, too, when she stood up to move away from her mother. She turned to see the man in the robe and silk pajamas in the revolving doors walking toward her.

"You left this outside." He placed a small lighter in her hand. He smiled at Molly and then at Esther. The lighter was silver and monogrammed.

"It's not mine." She handed it back to him, wondering if this was some ploy. "Try one of the nurses, they all smoke except for Lisa."

He looked disappointed. "I doubt it belongs to any of them. Won't you keep it?" She remembered his name, Michael Dunn. The lawyer from Culver City. She saw Esther's eyes smiling on her and then him, surmising a liaison, with an older man, a provider, a term Esther used for any man who owned a business, had at least one college degree and the promise of a pension, a 401K package or the golden parachute Goldman Sachs rewarded its favored sons. And he wasn't even Jewish. She knew Esther had all but given up on her daughter ever attracting a man from their tribe.

The Testimonial

"What time do you think this meeting will end?" Esther didn't look up, fussing with clearing the dinner table.

Molly was ready to forget the N.A. meeting but she knew Gary would be on the phone to Suarez if she didn't show. She looked over at Nugent who carefully placed his folded paper napkin next to the dish. *Where did he learn that?* Molly wondered again whether leaving Nugent with her mother, even if it was just an hour or so, was such a good idea. "Nuge, have some dessert." She handed the boy an ice cream sandwich and added, "You can eat it while you watch your show." She gave him the napkin for spills.

She turned to Esther as soon as he was out of sight and range of her voice.

"Look," she whispered, "I have no choice about this meeting. It is required." Not a total lie because Suarez was vigilant about 'helping' her stay on the straight and narrow.

She continued, "I am leaving the boy to have his dessert and to brush his teeth and get into his pajamas. He knows the drill, so there's no need for much interaction between the two of you." She stopped and locked eyes with her mother. "I'm saying this very slowly so there's no misunderstanding. Do not, *do not,* in any way make that boy uncomfortable."

Esther straightened up as if preparing to set her own rules in place. "I don't even know what you mean. What am I supposed to do?"

"I really don't care, Mom. Go lock yourself in the bathroom, go read *War and Peace*, it's on the bookshelf. But leave him alone." Molly ran some water on her dish and placed it in the dishwasher. "You have the church hall number if you need me. I'll keep an ear out for it, just in case."

A light knock on the screen door announced Javier. As always he took her breath away with his strong, healthy looks. She thought all that beer and weed dulled her to her own libidinous emotion and halfheartedly admitted, for now, it was okay to be clean and sober after all.

She was quiet as they drove to the church and Javier suddenly filled the car with talk. So unlike him, she thought, and here he was, asking about Esther. Was she well? Had she rested enough from her plane ride? She noticed he'd been exceedingly solicitous, deferring to her, asking her how she was feeling. Esther, for her part, was actually nice enough to answer politely.

"What time should I return for you?" He rounded the corner and pulled into the parking lot.

"Don't worry. Carlos is supposed to pick me up. I'll call to let you know for sure just before we end the session. I never know how long. Depends on how many show up."

* * *

She knew as soon as she entered the building that this was her night and that she'd be expected to give something more than the token few words she managed in the past, to forestall her own active participation. While not mandatory, her absence and a relapse made it clear she had not been following any of the rules. They all seemed to know it too; they were all there and they were waiting for the ice princess – their name for her – to deliver. She was less than friendly with them, had not bought into the team spirit and even took pleasure in staying away from the close-in kind of talk, the telling of your most intimate life to a stranger on a plane kind of stuff. Even the guys and some of the women who still used but who came to this dumpy church all-purpose room for some salvation gave more of their hearts to the assembled than she did. And so tonight it was a reckoning for her.

She was nervous. Her voice shook a little; then the teacher giving a lecture kicked in. "For a long time I tried not to remember anything." Molly stretched in her chair sticking her skinny legs in her skinny jeans out in front of her. The words were tough coming out, and she felt that she wasn't saying it the way she actually felt at the time, the way it became a path to her drug addiction.

No one spoke and, except for a few throat clearings, the room remained silent. Molly suddenly wished she wasn't there. She might even brave Esther's company to avoid this.

"Molly, could you be more specific?" Gary sat two chairs down from her, in the semi-circle of that same make-believe maple wood kitchenette shit they got from The Salvation Army.

She continued on in a litany to justify her life, and for taking up space on this overpopulated earth. "I just put everything out of my mind and went back to work."

"Can you describe this for us, Molly." Though gentle, Gary sounded irritated with her.

"Okay. I didn't think about Stella. I pushed her memory out of my head. As long as I was working, it was easy. It got harder after." She stopped. Gary riveted her with his no-nonsense look. "After work, and all night." She knew what he wanted.

She sighed. "How did it make me feel? Numb and detached. Like I wasn't a part of anything or anyone. I began to sleep more, and when it got harder to do that, I'd relax with some weed."

She thought about what she was saying and began to see the picture of it all. First the marijuana to relax, which propelled her into further depression and then the uppers and then the cheapest of the cheapest of any high, crystal meth.

"Then I didn't think at all except one constant thought to score drugs, use them, find money to score some more. And if I stopped, the pain was worse as it all wore off, like losing Stella had just all happened again." Her voice broke so she stopped. "See, meth kept in control of it all. *I was the one*, I was the top of the heap. I know that anyone who has done coke or meth knows that feeling. And I needed to be in control."

"At the worst moments, I was not doing my job and the kids I taught saw it, and pretended not to notice.." She controlled a sob that was welling up. "I looked a mess. One day, I woke up and the bed was wet from sweating, so I thought. But I knocked myself out with something so strong that I didn't even know I needed to pee." The thought repulsed her when she remembered it, saw it all over again. "One day…." Tears flowed now, genuinely. "One day, I found a photo someone had taken of Stella just as she began to smile." She looked around the circle of light they all sat in and continued. "No surprise that I called in sick to work that day and went on a week of meth to get high, went to movies late at night, went to places I'd never go to before or since." She stopped, reviewing a snapshot, frame by sickening frame of her life then and before Nugent.

"Where are you now with things?" He whispered the obvious question and now Gary looked around the room at the others.

"Things?" Well the meth stopped but not everything did. She thought how Nugent had changed her nights of roaming and but she was wary, saying nothing about him.

Her senses were fine-tuned. She pushed her hair away from her face and she felt it fall heavy down her back as it had done what seemed like an eternity ago. "I smoke." They all laughed. "Not weed," She lied; well, not lately. "Occasional beer." She half lied. *Oh fuck them. So they all guessed I was doing both.*

Gary must have read her mind. "Wanna share with us? How many? How often?"

"Maybe with dinner." She leaned back and picked at the bandaged hand. "Not since this accident. She gestured to the hand. "I am clean right now and boy, I could use anything to soothe it all away." Molly's eyes wandered around the room and then back at Gary.

"Look, my mother is visiting me and I don't know when she'll actually be leaving. And I'm doing this recently clean and recently sober. I can't say I don't miss it. It took the edge off." There were a few titters of recognition which meant to her that she wasn't alone in having interfering relatives. She couldn't decide to what degree Esther cared more what she might have to tell her friends if her daughter ended up OD in an emergency room.

"But now I see the meth meant I was out of control. And the beer and the weed were a substitute for the high, so I am really just at the beginning. I've got a long way to go, maybe a lifetime."

Gary stood up, perhaps to stretch or just to emphasize his point. "It took some strength to be honest about the beer. Molly could have lied. How would we know? And, if you all don't think that we know about the lies that go on in this place, you're wrong, stupid or dead. It's more important for all of us to look at the positive side of this and build on that part. So Molly drank a beer or two and told us about it. Now when I say that the beer is going to get in the way of her recovery, she may think twice about the next beer she takes. Maybe you all will."

Someone entered the room, and as he emerged from the shadows into the circle of light she saw first very highly polished shoes followed by sharply creased slacks. She knew it could only be Michael Dunn because absolutely no one in this neighborhood dressed like this and then came to this N.A. meeting. After much shuffling of chairs on the streaked linoleum floor, everyone settled in again. Those few who were nodding off from the weed they shared before the meeting came to attention. It wasn't often that this neighborhood experienced a white guy of this caliber. Some others, not dozing and feeling the hard edge of drug withdrawal, became stone-faced with hard eyes and a 'what the fuck?' quizzical look on their faces. They were, after all, from the 'hood: Black, Mexican, some biracial, one other white guy, but he lived in a homeless shelter during the rainy season, so he didn't count.

Gary was cool, no trace of whatever he was thinking got by him. He spoke to the newcomer. "We've been at it a while."

Michael responded in a soft, but not mumbling voice. "Sorry for being late. I thought I'd stop here on my way down to Orange County." That produced some guffaws and a few snorts that sounded more like jeers. "I saw your meeting on the list at my church last week."

He looked over at Molly in an unapologetic for-crashing-her-crib attitude. She saw that and decided he didn't get to SONY by being polite. "I'm Michael, alcohol and cocaine, and I've been clean for five months." Despite their deep mistrust of him, they applauded. He was a fellow traveler after all, on a road they all knew, and the wisdom born of their collective experience in addicts' hell made him a card-carrying member regardless of his Bruno Magli shoes.

Gary asked him if he'd like to speak, but Michael demurred, saying it wasn't fair to take up their time if the meeting was ending soon.

"No, man, we did some testimonials this evening." A slow-talking thin black man who bore a remarkable resemblance to Samuel Jackson spoke.

Michael looked again at Molly, but she chose to look beyond him as though he was not there. She sank further in her chair waiting for him to reveal himself to this group.

"I work in L.A."

"No shit." Came from the same black man. It was an unimpressed no shit, not an exclamatory no shit, and it said tell us something we want to hear. Gary sat up a bit straighter and the others quieted down.

Michael sat more relaxed into the chair. Molly could see how his manicured nails, his expensive haircut, his trendy tie were a slap in the face to these guys because he was something out of a movie. The only real thing about him was his addiction, his risking his life on big, lethal drugs.

Michael nervously twisted his watch on his wrist. "Surprise. There were no wild Beverly Hills parties. I didn't use because of the demands of the job, deciding whether we're going to call Dustin or Kevin or Cruise to tell them the box office wasn't as good this time so we all lost a bundle. No, it was an accident at home that no one could say how it happened. How did we forget to lock the gate? Just one of those stupid things that happen every day, only I wasn't lucky and neither was Gabby. That was my little girl, three years old. She wandered to the neighbors' and she fell in their pool." He paused for a moment and all his sleek look faded away as his well-muscled shoulders slumped into his shirt. "But it wouldn't have happened if I wasn't drinking the night before and just kept on to that day."

He sat forward, leaning toward them all. His voice came very harsh like a bad cold with laryngitis and his head was slightly bowed. "It was all over so fast. Everything was all over so very fast. Drink wasn't helping anymore. I did some drugs right after the funeral, the kind your doctor prescribes, harmless. It was too easy and then taking them with a drink and then looking for something stronger."

Molly saw Gary stir. You could count on him to get through to even a guy like Dunn. Michael's eyes finally locked with Molly's and he looked down again.

"The truth is I was drinking and taking the pills before she died, not just after. It's the lifestyle, but that's no excuse for what happened. That day I was drinking more than usual and, combined

136

with the pills, I dozed off." He stopped and it was clear he wasn't going to say much more.

He looked again at Molly, whose eyes had not left his face. She saw the tiny lines accentuated in the light, tired and driven lines like their owner. "So now I work and when I'm not working, I'm working. I consider myself lucky to have that. I come to meetings and I go to church. It's something I can say I live for and has most to do with my being sober this long."

"Thank you, man." Gary applauded, and the others followed suit. Molly looked around at them and saw shiny eyes wide open to hold back the tears they didn't dare show.

Molly and the rest began to push the chairs back to the wall. Some of the guys were gone but others lingered around the coffee pot, one of the women brought a coffee cake, and those who stayed were busy with that, the homeless guy, Marty especially. Gary snagged Michael immediately and she heard morsels of conversation having to do with SONY and the story that Gary himself had to tell about Hollywood. She poured herself a cup of coffee and laced it with artificial sweetener. She didn't look in Dunn's direction, yet she could hear the tension in his voice that said he wanted to get away from Gary. He was polite and finally ended it with, "Yeah, we should get together next time so I can hear more. Right now, though, I want to say hello to a friend."

And he was there, filling a cup from the decaf pot. "I can't do the high-test stuff this late, I'd never get to sleep."

She said nothing, vacillating between anger for his intrusion into her world and a foolish form of flattery that he took the time to find out where she lived. Mostly she was glad he wasn't there when she had spoken. It was easier to share with these strangers, yet she didn't want him to know about her life.

He answered her silence. "I sneaked a peek at your hospital chart and got your address. I wanted to see you again. I can't say that I like you, I don't know you, yet. But I like the fact that you strolled out of that hospital with an IV pole to snag a cigarette. I spend a lot of time with people who are afraid of their own shadow. You living here and that IV pole tells me you aren't one of them."

"Yeah, very strong. So strong I can't stay away from weed and booze. Real, real strong." She leaned on one foot, then the other, tired of standing and ready to leave.

He must have caught the body language because he spoke quickly. "I can drive you home, if you're ready to leave." They sipped their weak decaf coffee until she threw her cup in the trash.

She began to walk toward the door and he followed. She sped up her pace to the wall phone and dialed Javier's brother's phone. Thankfully Javier answered.

"Carlos will drive me home." He was fine with that, the sounds in the background told her he was with his family. She hung up and peeked out to see Carlos's car.

She turned again to Dunn. "My neighbor is here to pick me up. Thanks." She waved at Carlos, his motor idling in the fire lane, the N.A. attendees cutting a wide girth around his car to avoid the somewhat smoky emissions. "Ola, Carlos." He nodded his head and, she knew, was watching the tall well-dressed, out-of-place stranger talking to her. She hoped he'd keep this one to himself and not be too eager to share with Javier. Maybe if he thought there was nothing to report..., so she tried to affect a casual stance as she continued to walk.

"I'll see you next week, then." His words were clear. He would be back.

"Oh, sure. See you." She was off and didn't turn.

* * *

Molly was munching on a Granny Smith apple while Esther cleared the table when she mused, "There was this old proverb, or maybe it was some philosopher's remark. I learned it in an undergrad course." She saw Esther look up as she spoke. "It was something about staring at death too closely because, like the sun, it will blind you." Esther turned the water on full force as she continued to scrape the dinner dishes into the sink's disposal. Molly continued to chomp through the apple. "It means maybe we shouldn't try to figure things out too much, certainly death, because it invades our lives altogether, hurts us."

"How can it hurt us to look at death? I lost your father, it wasn't easy, but I faced it. Sometimes you talk nonsense." She pointed an accusatory finger at her daughter, a gesture Molly hated. "You need to face things, that's what's wrong with you. You think all this therapy mumbo jumbo is going to make it easier? Life is hard."

Molly lobbed the apple core into the sink from where she stood. "That was different. How can you lump everyone's experience, my experience, in with yours or anyone else's? That's just like you, taking some simplistic approach." She watched her mother furiously wiping the counter beyond the need for it. She realized that Esther could never understand therapy and N.A. meetings. "You know Mom, I named Stella for Dad."

Esther stopped the cleaning and nodded. "I figured as much."

Molly thought her father would be pleased to have a granddaughter, and that eventually he might have come around about her Mexican Christian lover. She smiled, picturing her father seeking a common ground in conversation with Javier.

Her phone rang and she picked it up to hear Michael Dunn's voice. She wasn't surprised, knew this would come; after all, he read her chart.

"I'm having trouble hearing you." She raised her voice. There was a lot of interference on the call.

"Sorry, wait. the window was open. You mentioned something back at the hospital about Agape and I thought you might get up to the meetings in Santa Monica." There was an eagerness, almost boy-like.

Molly laughed to herself. "Not been there lately, no wheels. I went to a few meetings with a friend." She didn't ask him why he mentioned it to her because she knew if she waited a beat, he'd tell her. Nugent sauntered into the kitchen, and she automatically reached into the cupboard for three Chips Ahoy chocolate chips. Esther began to hover, waiting to hear enough to tell her who Molly was speaking to. She'd been there for five days and she could expertly tell it wasn't Javier because the language construct of Molly's conversation was more complex. Molly walked away and down the hall, glad for the remote phone. Her mother's snooping pissed her off.

"I was very interested in their more casual way they worship. What do you think of the minister?" Dunn pursued the subject.

Molly thought of the thin man with a small build, light complexion like a café latte. "I think he's a guy who has come a long way from where he started. He's certainly made a place for himself." She wandered back toward the kitchen where she could hear Michael clearly, even over Esther's return to her scrubbing an already gleaming stovetop.

"I thought you might like to go to a meeting with me Friday night." Dunn brought it back to the beginning.

She admired how cool he was about it. There was more energy in his dialing her number than asking her out. It wasn't a lack of energy, just a lack of excessive energy. Unlike guys recently divorced whose last social contact was college, Dunn was a man who never stopped looking for new women. She wondered about the ex-wife. Well, if he hung around long enough, she'd ask.

Her energy however was flagging. It just took too much out of her to be with anyone other than Nugent right now. Even her mother was easier; she didn't have to begin again, explain again, live it all again. Molly wanted nothing more than to end the conversation with Michael Dunn. His remarks about Agape though prompted a response, however unwittingly. "I wouldn't have figured you for Agape."

"Thought I'd try something new, you know, experiment a bit." There was a slight pause. "Are you going to N.A. tomorrow night? I thought we might have some coffee after. You know, something simple."

Esther finally stopped running the water in the sink and Molly felt her mother might hear Dunn in the stillness. She knew Esther's choice to favor someone, anyone, even a California Catholic over Javier. "I'm not sure if I will be there tomorrow."

Esther was now gesticulating wildly at her with the dishtowel. "Say yes," she mouthed, "say yes." So, she could hear him after all.

Molly cupped the phone and turned away. "My boy has homework and tomorrow is my first day back at work."

"You have a son?" He sounded profoundly disappointed but quickly recovered. "How old is he?"

Molly walked into the hall determined to finish this conversation without a cheerleader. She whispered so Nugent wouldn't hear. "He's my foster child. He's ten."

The expected "oh" was left unsaid. "How about I call you after school? You should have your schedule in place, and we can plan accordingly." He was almost business-like except for the slight lilt in his voice. It was the lilt that kept her on the phone talking to him. This left her confused. Why should she defer to someone so far from the world she inhabited? Yet he'd spent the last several days trying to drag her into his and she was giving in to it because it was new and therefore unexplored and it was nice to be desired.

"You can call me after 3:30. I should be home by then." She thought of the walk from the school to her apartment, and that she'd have to move fast to get home in time first from Redondo Blvd, then to her street. Why, she wondered, was everything such a chore for her? The edginess, she knew, was from her withdrawal from the nightly beers. You wouldn't think a few Coronas could be so potent. She was drifting away from his words.

"I didn't hear what you just said." It wasn't just her mind drift. Nugent was bouncing his rubber ball against the wall, the thud punctuating Michael's words and interfering with her ability to hear him. "Excuse me, I have to take care of something. Can you hold for a moment?" She covered the phone with her hand and opened the door to Nugent's room to yell. "Cut that out."

The boy must have been deep in thought and mechanically throwing the ball from across the room where he lay on his bed. He sat up like he'd been shocked with a cattle prod. She smiled to lessen the intensity of her sharp request.

Dunn repeated himself. "You never said whether you were going to N.A. tomorrow night. I could pick you up."

The thought of Dunn coming into her neighborhood sent a stab to her gut, followed with a similar stab by the thought of Javier just dropping by as she graced Dunn's Mercedes convertible with her presence.

"That wouldn't work. I mean, I've got to get Nugent situated after dinner with homework and stuff. Why don't I just see you there?" As he talked, she moved up and down the hall, staying far away from the kitchen and Esther.

He was quiet a moment, and she imagined the quiet inside his car. No large swooshing noises emanating from his vehicle. She smiled at the difference of his car and Javier's semi-souped up 'pimp my ride' Camaro.

He spoke again but she drifted again. She thought he said something like, that will have to do. Dunn cleared his throat. "I just said good, I'll see you then."

Esther was within an inch of her nose when she turned on her heel and entered Nugent's room. "Sorry, Nuge. I was trying to hear. And you know? That nice paint job that Carlos' brother did will be all messed up with that dirty ball." She picked it up. It was a pinky, and tossed it back to him. "Did I ever tell you how I use to play stick ball with these where I grew up?" Nugent, looking solemn, nodded no. She hugged him loosely through his thin tee shirt and he hugged her back. It felt good.

Then she felt Esther's breath on her neck. "God damn, Mom. Can you give me a little more than an inch?"

"I wanted to see where all that racket was coming from." She zeroed in on the boy with one of her withering looks.

"I've got it covered, Mom. He's cool, aren't you bro?"

Dating

That Friday night she rushed to be ready for her "date" with Michael Dunn. She felt like a teenager, her mother hovering, making suggestions, what she should wear. She couldn't believe her ears.

"Mom. I think I know what's in my closet."

"I was just saying that you never wear dresses."

"I'm not going to some goddamned senior prom. I don't need a dress." She was busy consulting her wardrobe for something that appeased Esther and yet would leave her with some sense that she and not Esther made the decision. She sifted through the skirts and found the flouncy one that looked like a peasant skirt. The short-sleeved little white sweater stretched across her breasts and was the best bet with the multi-colored Mexican skirt.

"Don't you have something a little more comfortable?" Esther was eyeing Molly's snug sweater.

Molly finished brushing her hair, finished with the lipstick and eye makeup and shot a look at Esther. "Mom. It is what it is."

Esther sat down heavily on the bed and appraised her daughter. "I guess that's the way, so informal."

"I'm going up to L.A. for chrissakes, to a cavern of a place for some quasi-Christian singing and prayer. It will be dark and no one will give a damn."

"Nice talk." Esther must have had a delayed reaction to her daughter's words because she answered now, "Christian?"

"Nothing to worry about. No one tries to recruit, least of all me." She dragged her fingers through her hair one more time, and it was shiny and all golden highlights and it felt good. She looked at her watch. "It's late. He'll be here."

They heard Nugent talking as they entered the kitchen to see Michael Dunn in deep conversation with the boy who was leaning against the doorjamb, bouncing his pinkie up and down, up and down. Dunn just finished saying something. He straightened when he saw Esther and right behind her, Molly.

"I was just telling Nugent about the ball we play squash with. Same size but very dense." He turned to the boy, "Hey buddy, I'll bring one with me next time."

Nugent was provisional, "Okay, man, cool." His loyalties lay elsewhere, but he'd still like to get his hands on the "dense" ball, and Molly knew he'd be invading her computer to look up the game of squash before she got off of Magnolia Avenue.

Michael took Esther's hand and shook it gently saying, "Good to see you again. We met briefly outside St. Mary's." For her part, Esther was all quiet smiles and short sentences. "Good to meet you again." Calling him Michael at his insistence. Molly and Dunn said their goodnights and left.

Molly couldn't wait to get out of the barrio, fearful that Javier would see them. If he wasn't spying, he might have someone else doing it for him. Either way she preferred not to run into him. The neighborhood was quieter than usual, dusk falling heavily on the cool night had mercifully cleared the streets. Still, his silver Mercedes was like a beacon shining under the street lamp.

They drove, not saying much, as he navigated onto Bellflower Avenue and then the 405 freeway to Culver City. She refrained from suggesting taking the 710 Freeway because she wasn't sure about traffic. "So, Agape is close to work," she said as she realized that he could go there often.

"Yes. You'd think that I'd go there more often." He read her mind. He eased into the late afternoon traffic, lighter because most were headed for the weekend to the beach cities. He touched her arm softly, not in a possessive way but as someone reminding her what he thought about being with her.

It was a long time since someone courted her. He was different from Javier, softer in some ways, yet more deliberate and, she suspected, with a stronger resolve underneath it all. "Thanks, Michael. There is such energy in L.A. that you tend to lose sight of it down closer to the old O.C."

Michael looked at her as they slowed down to the LAX

crawl. "Thanks for what?"

"For a nice night out. For a good reason to dress up, though according to my mother, this is not being dressed up." She noticed his short-sleeved collared knit shirt and thought Nordstrom and thought very expensive, even when it was on sale twice a year.

He smiled and she knew he could conjure a history between them.

"How do you come by being so wise a man?" She had to know. "You seemed to have figured out who I am, where I am. I am guessing, better than I know myself."

The question was left in the air between them as he moved beyond LAX and onto the exit for Culver City. When they stopped at the light, he looked more closely at her. "Who knows why these things happen?" He shrugged. Ultimately, it's just being alive longer than you. Experience." He touched her arm again, and she liked it more this time than the last.

* * *

Molly remembered the Agape building and parking lot from her trip here with Sarah. The place was a cavern of dark shadows and sudden bright lights playing on the dais and then swooping around to a chorus of men, women and children singing with all the vigor of those who are saved. And they were. They were people who found hope in a simple message of the practice of love to help them come to terms with a world gone greedier, crazier, sadder. But Molly saw little evidence of any sadness, just a lot of very uplifted souls. She watched Michael whom she knew to be from an Irish Catholic breeding.

Michael Dunn sang wholeheartedly, she thought she heard a tenor. He sang unabashedly in the spirit of all the others. He was genuine, no mover and shaker, just a man trying to make peace with his losses. The sermon and singing ended and he took her hand as they walked out to the front lobby. He waved or nodded at people, lots of them women, and occasionally said a few words above the crowd's chattering.

As they left the temple and the ceremony and the last word of hope and love to send them all on their way, she asked him, "How is it for you coming from such a disciplined institution like the Catholic Church?"

He took her hand again and softly held it as they walked out into the parking lot, stopped near his car and took her other hand. "I think this sort of rounds it out for me. I can add this like so much cream to the top of my religious sundae. Agape sets me free from a lot of unnecessary rules." She saw they were sheltered by a tree with low hanging branches just in front of his car. He brought her closer to him and embraced her and she responded as easily, feeling protected and appreciated. His face and lips were in her hair and then on her face near her temple. "Can we be together tonight? I'd like to take you to my beach house. Would you come with me?"

And she said yes.

* * *

Michael Dunn's beach house was on the sand facing the ocean. She lay in his beautiful big bed with a headboard made, especially for him, of bleached and winged pieces of driftwood. The colors of the room were built around the colors of the headboard, some grays, lots of shades of light blues, so cooling that the glare of the sun could not change. They skipped the light dinner for the ride down to Orange County. Though they never rushed, she found they were both out of their clothes in very short order. He explored her arms, her legs, and cupped her breasts and her crotch. Though none of it was orchestrated, it felt perfect, and it was.

She found herself watching him give in with equal abandon to the feeling of her skin, of her mouth as it moved over his body. He was a man most comfortable about himself, and she told him so. As they lay in bed at near midnight, he wanted to know more about what she meant. "It's just that you seem so well organized. No, I don't mean that." She watched him grimace at the words. "I'm saying this all wrong. So fuck it, forget it. What do you want from me? That's what I can't fathom."

He turned over toward her, leaning on his arm and placing his hand palm down on her naked abdomen. "I knew you were intelligent. The eyes, see, they tell you everything. That you were distinctly *not Hollywood*, and *not Beverly Hills*, that was the attraction." His voice grew quieter. "I knew there was suffering. Silly perhaps, but I knew we shared a loss."

It became difficult for her to lie there with him with the

thought of Stella surrounding them. She asked herself whether she considered anyone but Javier appropriate to make love to and then to think or talk of Stella. "I don't want to talk about it." Her words came out harsher sounding than she wanted, but they were there, as real as her desire now to leave. She moved toward the edge of the bed and he stopped her, holding her arm.

"I didn't mean to invade your feelings. It's just been such a long time since I've shared my life with anyone in any meaningful way. Gabrielle was my life."

"I can't," she repeated. "It's not something I talk about much." This time she sat up and wrapped a towel around herself, looking for her cigarettes. Then stopped when she realized this was probably a non-smoking home. The air did smell very clean and the ocean air only added to it.

He didn't try to stop her this time and sat up as well, pulling a pair of terry shorts on. "Let's let it go and just relax. How about some coffee?" He was out of bed and down the hall to the big kitchen that looked out on the sand, hustling the coffee pot and grinding the beans. She joined him as the aroma began to invade and her empty stomach growled, at which they both laughed. With large mugs of black coffee with plenty of sugar, they sat on his terrace and the cold wind of the ocean blew her hair back. He caressed her head almost as he'd hold a child's and said, "Let's get something to eat and then get you home."

As they piled into his car she asked him, "You never mention your wife. Are you still married?" He didn't respond until he parked in front of Norm's, one of a bunch of a SoCal franchise that, depending on where you lived, had the seediest clientele or some of the upwardly mobile and the very upscale.

"No, not married anymore. Gwen is down in Cabo this time of year and everywhere else in Europe for the spring, and...," he sighed, "and I think she is looking at Alaska for the dead of summer and then back down to Cabo St. Lucas for winter." They exited the car together. "She didn't want to try. Didn't want the marriage anymore, didn't want me anymore. The hard part? I suspect she didn't want another child with me." He pocketed his keys. "Oh, what the hell, it's time to be philosophical. How do pancakes sound to you?" She laughed, surprised at the abruptness.

And they laughed their way through some pancakes at

Norms, the all-night diner chain with the cracked and split leatherette booths and the filthy carpeting that never gets cleaned. This one was in Costa Mesa and he easily whisked her back to Long Beach from there. "Promise me you will let me take you out to dinner."

And she agreed. The black moment had passed. She would be okay if he didn't ask her to share Stella.

Trouble at Home

"This guy's going to bring me some kind of ball?" Nugent was slurping his Cheerios and grating Molly's nerves. She slid into bed at 1:00 and found herself wide-awake at 6:30, and it was a Saturday. At least Esther was busy in the laundry room with the week's bedding.

Nugent's sullen and accusatory remarks were not lost on her. He'd be the one to tell Javier and needle her this way with the message that he was not going to be impressed with some damn squash ball. In the last few months, he made snide remarks about "weed" and LaSheed, and she knew he was too aware of her lapses. Through her hazy six months of booze and pot she watched his quiet reproaches and now he passed one remark after another.

"Did you drink any beer last night, Molly?" His smile faded to a smirk.

"No, and what is all this attitude?" She handed him a napkin for his milk-dribbled chin, and he took it and wiped.

"I'm gonna tell." He gave her the singsong threat.

She sipped her coffee and half listened to him, thinking instead of the way she froze Michael out when he tried for an intimacy far greater than her body. And as quickly as she thought about it, she wanted to know bad enough to talk to Dr. Suarez. Because she could see she was too close to holding him away to make real sense of it, learn from it. Nugent began with the slurping again, clearly with an agenda in mind. She glared at him but he didn't stop. Instead he got up, pushed his chair away from the table without pushing it back in. His pajamas were slung low on his hips and she realized that lately, so were his jeans, so low that his underwear was easily discernible, label and all.   There was something in the way he moved, less like a boy and more like the gangsta rapper he was trying more and more to emulate. He left the room and she could hear the television click on. The sound wasn't Bugs Bunny; instead he was watching MTV high up on the cable where he could get music/video rap.

Molly got up and poured herself another cup of coffee and slipped a slice of bread into the toaster. She peeked around the corner into the living room to see bouncing booties of substantially endowed young black girls, with bootie every other suggestive word. The boy's mouth hung open as it once did for Kobe Bryant and Shaq O'Neal. A knock on the door and the entry of a boy she vaguely knew surprised her but not Nugent. He slipped off the floor onto the sofa and the other boy joined him, without an acknowledgement of Molly. She would have lied if she said she didn't feel threatened by this boy, maybe two years older than Nugent and with fiercely angry eyes. He even went as far as to appraise her. Her temper flared.

"Who are you?" He ignored her and she grabbed his arm, forcing him to look at her. He tried to pull away but she held fast to his sinewy yet muscular arm. "I said, who you are and what are you doing in my house?

"This your house?" He snickered and looked closely at Nugent who was expressionless. "This ain't your house. You don't own shit."

Before Molly had time to register shock she saw the boy move up and around the sofa as a much stronger and larger hand held him. Javier said slowly. "Get out." The boy left and as he did Nugent began to protest.

"What's up? He's my friend. That a problem, me having a friend?" He said it all in a voice Molly had not recognized before. It sounded coldly deliberate and very much like the boy he called his friend.

Javier sat Nugent down. "He lives on Magnolia? Who is his father? His mother? His family?"

"He don't need no father. I don't have a father. Why do you want to know? You don't live here."

Javier slowly pointed his finger at Nugent. "And soon maybe you won't live here either?"

"You think you're so big." His attention was now on Molly.

"All you do is drug up and drink beer. That's how you got to the hospital." Molly could hear the other boy's taunt in this last piece of dialog.

"You're right. That was all very true. And a lot has changed since then. But this is still my house and a home for you." She lit a cigarette, then thought better of it and stubbed it out. Maybe this could be the last cigarette for sure because it tasted funny. "Now tell me about this boy. Is he the reason you got into trouble at school, making noise during class, fights on the playground?"

Nugent sniffed and sat silent, his arms folded onto themselves. His pajamas hitched up on his hips. "What difference does it make?"

Javier reached over and put an arm around the back of the sofa where the boy sat so that it almost embraced Nugent and Molly. And with a warm smile on his face he asked Nugent, "What difference do you think it makes?" The boy looked at him for a long minute and then away and down.

"All the bigger kids play basketball. Ramon and Emanuel, they're too busy to mess with me. And you're going to send me back when I get too big because I'll be trouble then, that's why."

Molly and Javier moved closer to the boy so that they were all squeezed into one half of the sofa. "No," they both said in unison and then smiled at one another over his head. "No one is sending you anywhere."

Sundays

Nugent was outside. Molly could hear him shouting to Ramon, whom he re-friended. He always shouted when he was excited about something. She was glad to see him filling out. To be sure, he'd stay tall and stringy, it was in his nature, and his metabolism kept him that way. But there was a new element about Nugent now. He was happy, he felt comfortable making noise, something no one considered unusual for an almost eleven year old, but not this boy. Molly remembered the day that Foster Care brought him to her. Was it almost nine months ago? He spoke not at all. She asked him his name and after a long silence, the social worker answered for him. His eyes darted all over the living room. She put out cookies and lemonade and expected he'd swallow them whole. Instead he had to be handed a cookie and asked if he wanted more. Each time, he'd nod an emphatic yes, eyes as big as the cookies themselves. And the same for the lemonade. Only after she poured a second glass and he'd gulped that down, did he finally manage a "Thank you," and that was only after the social worker spoke harshly to him. "What you say when someone gives you something, boy?" He looked furtively from the big and imposing woman to a smiling Molly and locked into her gaze. She saw his body relax, his shoulders un-hunch, and she reached out to touch his scrabbly shock of dark hair that was cut for efficiency's sake and not style. His instinct was to flinch and she quickly withdrew her hand, understanding how wounded he was.

Molly crushed the half-smoked cigarette; the taste was flat and hot. She took a sip of lemonade, and continued to fold the laundry, pulling the next item, a pillowcase, out of the laundry basket. She folded it and placed it on top of a stack of sheets. The sweet smell of the soap clung to the dried clothing, reminding her of the only pleasant thing about Sunday afternoons in New York. She hated Sundays because Esther always planned out chores for Molly. After all, she'd say, that's not our Sabbath. And so while Molly's brother, Tory, played outside on the sidewalk, Molly and Esther attended to the laundry or the week's cooking and cleaning of their second floor front apartment of three bedrooms, living, dining room and kitchen. Molly couldn't recall exactly when the Sunday schedule began; it seemed she always worked and Tory had always played. Esther was careful to plan the chores around her husband Sam's trip to the baths. On those rare days when he stayed at home he might have rescued his daughter from the drudgery.

Molly lit another cigarette and pushed open the broken screen door to stand on the porch where she could remember her father and watch Nugent. She could see him now from the porch, hair grown in, long and silky and dark, trying to emulate Ramon on a skate board he treated like gold because Ramon gave it to him.

Without the benefit of drugs and beer to blur her edges, Molly was left alone with the memories of her father and mother and Tory. Sometimes, like today, they were half pleasant, while other times they left her raw with unresolved angers.

"Taking a break?" Esther nudged out the door, forcing Molly to move further onto the porch. "Close the door or the flies will get in." She motioned to Molly to push the door in place.

Molly looked at her mother in her pink tee shirt, white summer slacks and sneakers. She would be happier and certainly more appropriately dressed for Florida. "The few flies in California are not around this time of year. This is winter, and when they do come around they don't go inside. No one stays inside. Didn't you bring a long-sleeved sweater with you? This isn't Florida, you know."

Esther leaned against the railing and looked out over the abundant leaves on the fichus trees which she frequently compared to the limp excuse of one she kept in her New York apartment. "Don't you worry about me, Miss Smarty. I'm fine." A well-timed shiver finished her sentence and Molly struggled not to laugh at her. "I noticed you're not smoking as much. That's good. You'll be healthier and save some money too."

Molly waited for something stronger than amusement to feel

but there was nothing forthcoming, nothing she could use to poke fun.

"I'm glad you're worried about my health and my financial status, Mom." She waited for whatever onslaught of advice laced with criticism came, feeling they were inevitably next on her mother's agenda. Esther was noticeably moping about the apartment for the entire weekend, with something on her mind.

"I used to like the weekends in New York. When you and Tory were away in school, your father and I going out to Jones Beach sometimes just for the ride, but we always walked on the beach. I miss that." Without taking a breath she continued. "He was a good man, and worked hard, maybe too hard. But when we went out to Jones Beach, it was different. I think I pretended to myself that we took some wide-body plane over oceans and time to an exotic place and now we were there and on vacation." She stopped herself and said, ruefully, "Foolish."

"Did you pretend? It's funny how you and Dad never did any of that. Never took a vacation. I think the only time you ever left New York City was when you visited Tory or me when we were in school. Big deal. I was at Boston College and so was Tory. Too bad Dad didn't get to come out here when I was at UCLA." They were both quiet and she knew their thoughts went to her father's last illness, his heart too weak for him to fly to her graduation.

"Big deal? It was a big deal for us to see our children settled into their lives. At least that's what we thought at the time. Who knew?" She exhaled a breath that was unmistakable disappointment in her daughter.

Molly didn't have to hear the words to know what she referred to. Who knew I'd leave to live out here? Not get married to Stanley whatshisface? Not marry the doctor? Not buy the house in the Boston suburbs.

She turned toward her mother and said, "I never loved Stan. He was a nice guy I went to concerts with." She picked at a scab still forming on her arm. "Besides, he was too old for me." She half smiled. "He would have been too old for me if I was his high school teacher. He was born old."

Esther's words came fiercely from her. "Instead you have what? What's so great about your life? This Javier, Molly, what could you be thinking? He's the choice you made. I won't even say it, I won't even consider it a question to ask that this man should compare. That this life could ever compare."

Nugent was out of her range of sight, so Molly bent over the porch to catch a glimpse of him with the skateboard on the steep drive that led to the street. "Hey Nuge!" His head swiveled and his hand went up in acknowledgement. Funny, she thought, how he and I communicate in this minimalist fashion.

Esther caught her smile. "What could be funny? My concern for you? You think that this life with this man is what we raised you for? Him with his drugs and drinking, and you living that kind of life too? What did you expect to happen?"

Molly knew this was coming, was in fact waiting for it all these days since the moment she saw Esther standing in the door of the hospital room. She found herself nervously scratching her arms, ripping the skin with her nails.

"Stop that." Her mother reached out and placed a hand on her daughter's arm. "What is all this abuse of your body? What do you think we did to you to make you this way? Because I know as sure as I am standing right here, that you blame me for all of it."

"Just shut up. Just leave me alone for Christ's sake." Molly swung around to face her mother, shrugging her protective hand and its gesture off. "Don't mother me now after all these years. It's a little too late. Why not Stan? Why Javier? Maybe Javier is the best I can do. Maybe he's what I've always wanted. A guy who knows how to make a girl happy." She watched as her mother cringed at her remark. "He's the father of my baby whose mother was not drinking or on drugs at any time during the pregnancy or after."

Esther was rigid in anger; she could see that plain enough. "You didn't want Stan because I did. You did it to spite me. You would be sitting pretty right now, just think. Your baby could be alive, the one you had with him. It's a judgment."

Molly started down the stairs to put an end to it. "No more. You've been bursting to tell me what you think. Now you have. Now it's been said. So I won't have to hear it again. Because *I won't hear it again.*"

Regrets

The silence between Molly and Esther was deafening. What was just days felt like weeks to Molly. If Nugent noticed, he played his part well and offered big, innocent eyes. But every once in a while, she caught him spying on first one and then the other of them. Now they were alone in the house.

"So?" Molly moved the curtain back to look down the block, watching for Nugent's bus where it turned onto their street. She hesitated, not sure whether to pursue the discussion, yet something in Esther's voice prodded her to elicit more.

Esther turned the brisket in the large Dutch oven and continued the slow browning process to further tenderize the meat. Molly admitted to herself that she would miss Esther's cooking when she left. "Yes, so."

"So," Esther began again. "If I wanted to feel sorry for myself and have issues," she said, emphasizing the last word, "and go to therapy where someone convinced me I was mushugge." Esther paused, Molly knew, for full effect.

"Well?" Molly was not going to touch the subject of her therapy. But she pushed her mother to finish what she started.

"Well, enough. Maybe I'm all wrong, but it's not a bad idea to think that God sometimes makes mistakes." Her mother went on quickly. " Maybe His mistake was to give you Stella to begin with. Or to take her away from you. Or an even bigger mistake, to send you to that place where you got that Nugent."

Molly felt her face grow hot. "He's not *that* Nugent, Ma. Here we go again. And that place was Foster Care. It's not a mistake, or if it is, it's a lucky one because Nugent is with me instead of one of several kids all placed together with people who use the system and get paid, and don't feed the kids, or worse, abuse them. Maybe it's not a mistake that he got me and I got him, and we can be something good to one another."

Esther turned a hard glare at her daughter. "Very good for you to say now, but I got your letter saying how Foster Care money pays for the increased rent."

"You're right. What can I possibly say? I did say that and it was true at the time. But something happened along the way the last nine months or so. He needs me and I need his needing me."

Esther turned the meat over to even the browning. She had a small can of stewed tomatoes ready to pour over the meat and combine with its own juices. She didn't look up, didn't answer and Molly knew she wasn't speaking because she couldn't. She looked at her mother's back and saw an old woman, worn down by her own disappointments, and suddenly felt younger, felt the possibilities that lay before her for life, for someone who might occupy that life with her. What did Esther have now?

"Mom, that's the kind of thing therapy does. It helps you come to terms with your past and get rid of all the bitterness before it destroys you." She got closer and saw tears at the corner of her mother's eyes.

And in the telling of all this to her mother she reasoned it out for herself as well. Maybe she'd have something worthwhile to say to Suarez or at N.A. meetings for a change.

Holy Redeemer

The hot Santa Ana winds were blowing the dry brush around the entrance to Holy Redeemer Cemetery. It was a seedy place in a seedy part of the L.A. town of Inglewood. The heavy wrought-iron gate was cracked open just enough for an adult to slide through. Molly glanced around for some kind of attendant, and spied a small stone-looking cottage more appropriate to Scotland than Inglewood.

"Come on Nuge." She gently pulled his hand as she easily passed through the opening. Esther, right behind her, was screwing her neck every which way, unaccustomed as she was to a Christian, and Catholic at that, cemetery. Molly wondered what her mother expected, the pope or a bishop in full white and red regalia? Javier was just behind her mother and moved the massive gate open for his easier passage.

Molly was grateful for the second time today. That there might be someone who could direct them to the plot, and when she accepted Javier's offer to drive them once he knew they were set on visiting the grave. *Otherwise we'd still be stuck on the damn freeway taking two buses from Long Beach to LA.* She envisioned the tired, hungry and bored boy and the equally tired and frazzled older woman whose fuse, she knew, was remarkably short. She looked at Esther, who removed her light cardigan, the winds stoking, and though dry, were nearing 90. It struck her to see the pale and thin arms of her mother. Always throughout the last few weeks, she pitted her memory of the robust mother in her late forties with this woman reaching toward elderly.

"Go see if there's a man in there." Esther was gesticulating toward the building with her remarks thrown over her shoulder in Javier's direction. And Javier dutifully trotted off and peeked in one of the cottage windows when the door did not open.

"For Christ's sake, Mom. Stop treating him like he's your goddamned lackey."

Esther had a fixed surprise to her brows. "What's lackey?" She fussed with the absurd ruffle on her cream-colored blouse.

"Servant, Mom. Servant."

Molly looked at Javier, just out of earshot. He was calm, polite, even warm toward Esther, reminding Molly, "Querida, she is your mother."

"I just meant he should be the one to look for the attendant. He's the man here."

Molly groaned. Between the two of them all she got these days was a lesson in who was who.

Javier turned at the sound of a person walking down the hill, a man in what Molly thought of as landscaper's clothes, already bleached from the sun, hanging loosely and soft from countless washings.

Molly, Nugent and her mother came up to Javier as he inquired, "We are looking for Stella Morris." The name of her baby spoken stung her heart the way the hard, hot winds were stinging her skin. Now it became too real for her. Again. She stifled a desire to scream out, she felt her heart pound against what Esther referred to as her skinny breast. She could not trust herself to speak. Mercifully she felt her mother's hand clench her own. It was the right touch, this hard, tight hold Esther used. It was what she needed, to stay standing. She knew her feelings were opening up, and hoped the pain would abate, get easier, this day. As long as Esther or Javier became her legs, her core, held her up.

The man looked sandy, his hair bleached out years ago from the constant sun and salt air. He pointed to a directory, a book left on a podium for people such as them, to peruse and research to find the name and the location of the person they needed to find.

Because it was something to do, Molly almost rushed to it, quickly reading down the list of names. Manera, McMahon, Moriarity, Morris. Molly found a stack of notepaper and cheap little pencils meant to jot down the location. She wrote down a long number beginning with a letter, **J577990434** and consulted the map next to the book, tracing down the list to the Js and then over to areas that started with 5 until she located the plot. Javier looked at the map and then the terrain to gauge where the two most resembled one another. He took Molly's hand and led her and the others toward a long dirt path leading uphill and away from the front of the cemetery. Molly tried to remember all of this, did she really walk up this way on that day? They must have driven up some other road, a hearse could never fit up this path. Yet the tread of tires pressed into the fresh reddened, dusty path belied the presence of cars, maybe a funeral at a gravesite, now. She hoped not, *I don't want to live someone else's sorrow.* She looked back to see how Esther and Nugent were faring. The boy's eyes told her he knew what this was all about.

"Here, you'll fall." Esther took his hand and was walking at a pace to match his. The boy seemed fine with the arrangement.

"How far Molly?" Esther was out of breath already. She started to trail and the boy was moving in front of her. Javier slowed his pace to match theirs as they all struggled a little up the hill to a Cyprus tree, its branches swept out in large, grand gestures as though pointing at something in the distance. Molly remembered the tree and approached it now more slowly, feeling the sweat under her arms drying from the unceasing hot wind blowing and kicking up dust.

"Here. She's here." She gestured to a small stone, a pure white, her name inscribed:

Stella Morris
Born   April 15, 1993
Died   June 11, 1993
The Angel has gone home
May her soul rest in everlasting peace

Molly legs were as though she was given an epidural; there was a general numbness, yet they functioned. She dropped to her knees to hide her face from all of them, wishing now she could be alone with her baby. Her face was wet again like it was for days after Stella died, when in her unconscious grief, she had no sense of her unremitting crying. This time her feelings were keener.

"Baby, baby. Stella." She whispered and found she was rocking back and forth, back and forth, almost as though she were holding her baby once again. Javier's strong and warm hand rested on her shoulder, and he knelt next to her. She watched as he made the sign of the cross and prayed, his lips moving silently.

"I'm okay." She stood up and to one side, looking out at the freeway that divided the cemetery from the next town, and she wiped her eyes with the back of her hand. She became aware of Nugent and looked down into his face. "I'm sorry. I must be scaring you. This was my little girl, here. Her name was Stella."

Nugent held her hand and patted it with his free one. "It's okay. I know who she is. Javier told me."

Molly looked around for Esther who was standing just behind Javier. Her eyes were fixed on the gravestone, and for a moment Molly didn't care that the inscription had a very Catholic sounding note to it. She didn't care that she was buried in a Catholic cemetery. But then she did care and so moved closer to her mother. "Mom, for Stella, she doesn't care where she is. You know that." She whispered so that only Esther could hear.

Esther's face was flushed from the walk up the hill. Her breathing was coming fast and Molly worried that it might have been too much. *Is her heart strong enough?*

"It's peaceful up here. That's good." Esther spoke as she looked down on the ground, searching for something. She bent down and picked something up and walked toward the very white headstone and placed three small dark stones on the small ridge, and then stood back and spoke to Javier. "It's how we do it. To let people know we were here, that we care." And then she walked away, to a bench and sat down.

Molly followed her. They were quiet, Molly reliving pieces of Stella's short life, small pieces of moments. She pulled out her wallet and found the one photo she carried, taken by Javier's cousin at Stella's christening. Stella wore a silk bonnet but her hair peeked out at the top where the bonnet's silkiness slipped off her head. Her hair looked abundant and dark, her eyes were shaped like Molly's but they were deep-set like her father's. Molly handed the photo to her mother. "Javier's mother wanted to have her photo encased in the stone, but I couldn't do it."

Esther took the photo and stared at it a long time, tracing the face with her finger. "Pretty. Like you then, when you were little. Delicate. She looks like your father."

The Locket

Rainy Friday with nothing to do, and forsworn allegiance to
N.A. to stop with the beer, and Esther nearby so she couldn't sneak
one Corona or even a cigarette which she knew was messing up her
looks, so Molly cleaned out a drawer and found the locket. She
sliced through the little groove with her fingernail to spring it open.
One side held her baby photo, curls, the obligatory bonnet, the
dimpled smile. Someone must have been tickling her because
Esther had told her once if she had told her a thousand times how
taciturn and focused and non-smiling a baby she had been. Molly
was alone. Mercifully Esther decided to take a trip down to the
bodega for some fresh vegetables and undoubtedly several large
Mexican pastries, bread-like with confectioner sugar sprinkled all
over them.

The other side of the locket held a photo of her father. How
it evoked now a memory of their lives, the Bronx, their apartment
just up from Fordham Road in typical Robert Moses style, blond
brick penitentiaries gone dark from diesel spewing out of trucks
lumbering down past the university. She held the locket open,
staring closer at the picture of her father. He looked so different
than the last time she had opened it. Was this photo of him taken
when she was thirteen at her Bat Mitsvah? He was handsome.
Couldn't be from her Bat Mitsvah. The photo was tinted or it was
that pre-war thick color that faded to an orange. He was, younger,
closer to twenty than thirty, a shock of thick wavy light brown or
blond hair. Anyway, it was lighter than she remembered she ever
saw it. It must have darkened as he grew older. Esther's hair was
that Austrian deep reddish color and it was she who insisted that was
the origin of Molly's coloring. Young Esther, a pretty woman with

green eyes sitting always at the kitchen table visiting with her sister Minna. The windows propped open with little screens, the sound of the El on Webster Avenue stopping to let the students they called 'day hops' off at Fordham Prep. The aroma of the Jewish Bakery wafting up as far as the fourth floor. Always a warm, nurturing smell.

There was, she remembered, one time when Aunt Minna and her mother could not hear Molly coming in, were unaware of her entering the apartment. The door opened into a narrow foyer and hallway that led to the living room with tall windows, and beyond to a hall and bedrooms and then finally to the dining room and kitchen.

Minna and Esther were speaking in German occasioned with Yiddish and Molly understood smatterings. "…was handsome," Minna was saying.

"What did it finally matter?" Her mother's voice, always sharp, was more so. Esther stopped when she saw Molly. "Is Toby off the stoop?"

Typical at twelve, almost thirteen years old, Molly ignored her mother as she slid her finger around the oilcloth on the kitchen table, stopping directly next to Minna, a pudgy, fair woman who wore her braids on top of her head. She pulled Molly to her and kissed her cheeks with a resounding smack. "I brought some strudel. Here." She pushed a plate and fork toward Molly whose eyes were great with anticipation and who could already taste it in her memory, the sharp, tart apple under the layer of sugar and pastry.

Esther repeated her question on the whereabouts of Toby, and Molly abruptly answered her. "He's at Warren Stein's and he said you said it was okay." This last reference was in an effort to stop the barrage of questions so that she could devote proper attention to the strudel that she swore was still warm from her aunt's oven. She quickly inhaled the pastry, and reached for another portion.

Esther brushed her hand away. "After dinner. Go. Tell Toby dinner is at six."

"Who were you talking about?" At this age, Molly's rapacious appetite was equal for Minna's strudel as it was for family gossip.

"Tell Toby." Esther was resolute as she twisted Molly

around to untie the bow on her dress, and tie again.

"Dinner is always at six. Will Poppa be here at 5:30?"

Minna beckoned Molly to her to hug her one more time. She smelled faintly of Chantilly perfume and the apples and other magical ingredients of her magical strudel.

"You haven't answered me," Molly said, pouting, her pre-teen mouth pursed in a way that left Esther further exasperated.

Now, all these years later in Long Beach, there was a hard rain and it was coming down, pounding on the roof. Molly looked out on the street to see Esther with Molly's umbrella and a bag of groceries. She traced the face of the man in the locket with her thumb and looked again. She decided it wasn't her father, that it must be some long dead relative. Maybe Minna's husband. Poor Minna, widowed so young, someday dying very old and still widowed.

She swung the long and delicate chain over her head, careful not to snag it in her hair, and finished setting the drawer in order. Pantyhose rolled up; won't be needing those for a while; socks in neat little piles. *Christ, this is nauseating. There must be a book in this house to read.*

She walked quickly to the back porch and down the stairs to intercept Esther with her heavy bag of groceries. "I thought you said it never rains here."

"No. But when it does, it pours, man it pours." She smiled to herself for remembering that old sixties song.

Esther ignored the remark. Molly knew it was her knee jerk from years of arcane and obscure allusions to history or literature or the counter-culture only a Depression era person could really feel threatened by.

They walked up the stairs, Molly ahead with the bag of food, smelling of chorizo sausage and those pastries she knew Esther would purchase. "So many people in that market this morning. I saw Carlos's wife with her youngest and it's a school day."

"She could be taking her to the doctor for something. You forget the way you have to sneak around the rigidity of school schedules." She silently remonstrated against her mother's tendency to judge, and unfavorably, when it came to Latinos.

They emptied the bag together, Esther stocking the fridge and Molly the cupboards. She turned to her mother. "That was a heavy bag for someone going out for bread."

Esther spied the locket as Molly turned back to the cupboard. "What is that?"

"Found it in the dresser. I remember getting it – a gift at my Bat Mitzvah." She continued with the chore at hand. "But it's got this photo in here," she said, opening the locket. "I thought it was Poppa, but it doesn't really look like him."

Esther was quiet for so long that Molly thought she might not have heard her. "It's not Poppa." Her voice changed, something sad yet resolute lingering on the words. She finished with the groceries, and, in typical Esther fashion, neatly folded the paper bag along its creases and placed it in the narrow cupboard made to hold cookie sheets and folded brown paper bags. "Sit down," she said as she lowered herself slowly into the kitchen chair. "There was a wrong that must be fixed now. Now is the time."

Molly was taken with the paleness of her mother's lips, the tremor when she spoke. "Mom. You're sick. Mom. Let me call 911."

Esther stopped her daughter's hand reaching for the phone that sat on the table between them. "Listen. Just listen. Maybe we were wrong, your father and I, for thinking it wouldn't matter. And I know you think me a foolish old woman given to wives' tales, but I believe, and the New York Times confirms every other day, that blood will tell. Sam was not your father."

The Aftermath

Esther began to talk, slowly, all between sips of water, her color returning, and Molly's alarm abating with each normal breath coming from her mother. Molly listened and once more saw a panorama open in front of her eyes, where she saw the movements of the woman, now 73 years old and then in 1950, a post-war 35 year old caught in the next decade and still single.

"I was in the Catskills. What a cliché when I think of it now. Because that was where we all went, and every summer, looking for something different. We looked for grass and trees, a welcomed relief from the hot concrete of the Bronx. We looked for excitement, for 'maybe I'll meet a nice doctor.' For me at that time it was maybe I'll meet a widower with small children that I could help raise, not be a burden, carry my weight. Dreams, we all had them. My friends, all like me, stuck in the types of post-war jobs that men didn't want to do and that most of us hated. Oh, I was lucky. I got a job at Esquire Magazine, of all things. Maybe it was my long red hair." Esther allowed a smile to trace across her lips, which she quickly pursed while she thought deeply of the time she was still able to dream.

"You were still young enough to do more than dream, Mom."

Esther looked deeply into her daughter's eyes, and shook her head, saying, "So, maybe that's what happened." She cleared her throat and sipped some more water. "We could use some seltzer, maybe next time I go to the bodega." She was silent for a little while and Molly felt no inclination to interrupt.

"So. Miriam, Trudy and me. We saved our money, we borrowed Uncle Sol's car for the long Labor Day weekend and we left. We brought more shoes and dresses, halter dresses that were designed to show the tanned shoulders off to good effect. I had a suitcase full and a new swimsuit. It was deep green, and with my hair. Well. I was the rage."

Molly heard a sensual, warm sound drift into her mother's voice, reminding her of the times when her mother and Aunt Minna sat alone and talked. That was the only other time she heard her mother's voice sound so musical. "Who was he, a stranger?" She could not help herself, she was compelled to ask, she needed to know. She expected consternation to creep in, she expected her mother to say 'hush,' that she would tell it in her own way. But Esther did none of these. Tears filled Esther's eyes and dropped down onto her cheeks.

"He was a handsome young waiter from Harvard, completing his pre-med. He came back from the war and went to school on the GI bill, and so he was older than the others, maybe thirty-three. His name was Bill O'Brien and he was from Boston. He noticed me the first night and he pursued me. And I believed everything he said because we both wanted it to be true. And it was true. For a little while."

Molly's sense of her mother was skewed. She fluctuated widely from the mother sitting before her, the mother she grew up with, the woman who talked to Aunt Minna. They were all different, and now they seemed to all be coming together into a woman she did not know.

"Miriam warned me, but I didn't want to hear her. I wanted to hear him." She reached her arm across the table, her fingers splaying, as if a drowning woman trying to grasp something.

"Mom, you don't have to," Molly began, as she reached out and took her mother's damp and cool hand in hers. "It's okay."

"I want to. Because here is the thing that must be said. Bill loved me. We wrote when he went back to Boston, we saw one another on weekends when I could slip away from New York. We walked together on the Harvard campus. And when I became pregnant, he wanted to marry me." Esther began to cry in earnest, with small rocking motions as if to comfort herself. "But I couldn't. He was Catholic, he was Irish. He'd have to give up his dream of becoming a doctor. What would that do to him and finally to us?" Esther got up from the table and opened the fridge for an orange. It had a thick skin and she slit it with a paring knife all around and peeled it, handing sections to Molly and keeping some for herself.

"Finally, I wrote to him and lied, saying I had miscarried. It was in the third month, at a crossroad. But I couldn't. There were doctors in the Bronx for that sort of thing. There are always doctors." She cocked her head, as though listening to some silent voice inside her. "And there was Sam. He had been there for years, waiting. First waiting for the hard times to go away, then the war. There was always something. And I was pushed to marry him, by your grandmother, then the cousins. So I went to him and I told him and he cried, and then he asked me to make him the father and not this other person. He asked me to marry him right away and he'd tell everyone you were his. And he did and you were." She sobbed. "You know how much he loved you."

Molly forced the tears down her throat. "Mom, Mom. What happened to the young man?" She could not call him otherwise. He was never her father, Sam Morris was.

"I never saw him again. We moved into another section of the Bronx. I just wrote him one more time. A long letter about the miscarriage, that it I was not harmed by it, that I was okay." She turned to Molly. "You see, I couldn't let you go. I was thirty-five. I wanted you so much, so fiercely." She squeezed Molly's hand till the circulation began to falter, till her finger tips were numb.

Molly held onto her equally tight and stood and wound herself around her mother like a carapace, like a womb, protecting her from all that happened. Her mother's hair smelled of Chanel, always near her temples.

* * *

Everything changed and not. To Molly, Esther's face did not have that closed-off look to it that she remembered. Instead, her memory of feelings that played across her mother's face only occasionally was now more the norm. But after all, she reasoned, we are the patterns we make of ourselves and those stay in place. She smiled, continuing her internal dialog, which was to say, Esther still had her bite, always would.

"That Mr. Dunn. Now where does he live?" Esther was peeling potatoes and Molly had just flopped down into a chair after the two blocks' walk from school.

"Give me a minute. How about some lemonade?" She got up and poured one for herself, gesturing to Esther to join her. Esther shook her head 'no.'

She played it out in her mind and then said, "He lives in Newport Beach, which, I am sure you can figure, is a high per capita income area."

But her mother was on it, "So, since when is that such a crime? Because, let me just say, that it doesn't hurt to have an older man who can plan for both of you." Esther paused and Molly jumped in.

"He's handsome, he's got money. But he carries a lot of emotional stuff. He lost a child."

"And you can comfort one another."

"Javier and I already have that part covered." Molly felt like she was jumping double Dutch with only one way to end it, one of them would give up. It was easier to be that one, nothing to lose and quiet to gain. Surprisingly, Esther stopped with Molly's last remark, and Molly almost wished she hadn't said it.

Revisiting

"It's been confusing for him, I know," she told Dr. Suarez. Molly was finding it uncomfortable to think of Nugent the way he was with his no-longer new friend. "But the behavior was way out of proportion to what's been happening around him. I mean, I was occasionally toking and only after he was asleep. And a beer with dinner was no big deal either."

"Molly, nothing you do with that boy is going to be insignificant. You're the only model he has for a parent. He lived with those friends of his father's at Camp Pendleton, and saw them as that, people who cared, but not parent models." He looked more steadily at her and said, "You have to take responsibility for this."

"I'm then responsible for all of it, this attitude and the language and this new friend?" She brushed away the ugly picture Nugent's friend held up to her of how he saw her, a woman alone, living in a dilapidated apartment with a foster child and an aging mother holding on to her. She shuddered and Suarez noticed,

"What are you thinking right now?" He leaned forward. "Something you didn't like."

She broke from the unpleasant reverie. "Amazing you could see I drifted. How could you know?" She answered his question before he had a chance to respond or to ask again. "Nugent's friend said some things, made me think."

Suarez waited and the stillness was discomfiting. "Perhaps if you share, it might help."

"He was more of a man than a child. That was the first thing that irritated me, looking at me like I was some female he could pursue. But when I think about it now, I was more disgusted that a kid that young should try to be a man in only that one way, sexually.

That Nugent would be influenced by him was frightening and threatening all at the same time. The boy is just now turning eleven, and to find him trying to copy that little bastard...." She thought about it some more. "And to see me through this kid's eyes. That was hardest." She ended with "I felt threatened."

"Yes, but Javier was there, you said so."

"So why should I have felt so threatened? Is that what you mean?" Molly didn't wait for an answer. "Yeah, he was there. We're a funny pair, aren't we? He's a quasi-stalker, always seems to be just around the corner and pops up when I most need him." Molly's thoughts ran to Michael Dunn and it all fit together for her. "Which means he's *not* there when I don't need him." She smiled and Suarez's brow shot up as if to ask. "Dr. Suarez, Javier is *not* around when Michael Dunn drives me home from an N.A. meeting, or like two nights ago when I had a date with him."

"This is the man you met at the hospital? I didn't realized you were seeing him. At N.A. meetings?"

She smiled a woman's smile and explained the courtship dance that Dunn was dancing all around her for what she reckoned was a month and half. "He's quietly relentless."

Suarez reached down to pull on his trouser leg, the meticulous crease, the highly polished brogues. She couldn't help but notice how like Dunn he was, and how unlike her equally neat lover, Javier, though he wore clean jeans and immaculate white tee shirts.

"How does his involvement in your life and N.A. meetings fit in with everything? You have heard it many times by now, but all counselors agree that new relationships, and especially with a recovering addict are dangerous."

"We went out on a real date two weeks ago and a few times since. Two bruised souls who each lost a child. He sees it as a link to something bigger and sees nothing wrong with me at all." She reflected for a minute. "I like his interest, it's complimentary. And yet, I find it unsettling. He wants to talk about Gabrielle. It grounds him, and I can't talk about Stella because it's all too soon. I mean I know some day I'll be able to deal with it but not yet." She took a deep breath. "He wants to order my world, make it like his, I can tell. Makes me feel claustrophobic. The language barrier that sometimes comes between Javier and me is welcomed. It gives me space where I can live alone in my thoughts. Intrusive, that's the work I was racking my brain for. Michael Dunn, handsome, accomplished, rich, is intrusive."

"Maybe he's too eager," Suarez suggested.

"I feel as though you're trying to convince me to see this through, even with all your warnings about new relationships. I feel you want me to see where it goes. I was sure you'd warn me against dating him." She said this in a tone that was without heavy accusations, yet saw Suarez's body language, just a slight shift but yet perceptible, that suggested she hit some nerve. "You think he's a Gringo like me, and that education and other cultural similarities make him a better choice than Javier. Don't you?"

"I really can't answer that question, even if I had an answer. Javier or anyone else, that's for you to say."

She held onto the thought, knowing she was right in her assessment. She mentally shrugged, *why not, he's a human, even if he's my shrink.* "The jury's out anyway. I'm not making any permanent decisions about anyone."

They were both silent now as she regrouped her thoughts that seemed to have been all over the room. "I was grateful for Javier being there when that kid came into my home. And I guess I was unsettled thinking that Nugent could be feeling all the same things. I certainly felt him judging me, just like the gangsta rapper wanna be kid."

Molly thought of how Esther came up that day from the basement laundry room and probably passed the boy as he descended the back stairs.

"Esther seems better about Nugent lately. He and Javier accept her better than I do." She laughed a short laugh at the picture this conjured. "I think their behavior is actually influencing hers. Who would have thought? I gotta hand it to her, she figured it out, that something had happened."

"Did she ask you about it?"

"Esther?" Molly laughed this time for good. "Doctor, she told *me* what happened. She spoke with Esther's inflection, "'So, that boy Damont, he's been here before. Too old for Nugent. Didn't look too happy. Did Javier throw him out?'" "Nothing gets past Esther. And while we're on the subject and for the record, she encourages Dunn. Even while she appreciates Javier's respect for her as 'the mother.' I guess she has the best of intentions."

* * *

Molly tried to read as the bus zoomed back down the freeway to the Bellflower exit. They drove past California State University – Long Beach. The trees along Bellflower all bright with leaves, the campus looked serene. For the briefest of moments she missed academic life. All the PhD infighting for turf and recognition, all the energy to discover something new, test something that was never tested before. Yet for all that, she thought more than once about going back for a PhD. Is that what you do, she wondered, to fill in the hollow space left when Stella is no longer there to nurse, to bathe, to love?

The bus turned onto Pacific Coast Highway, a few more blocks and then down Sixth Street to Magnolia. She twisted the ring on her right hand, a gift from her father when she graduated Boston College. What would he advise her now? About Javier, about Dunn? She thought she made most wise decisions with a whisper in her ear from her beloved father. She thought that she hadn't made too many wise decisions in a long time.

* * *

Her beeper buzzed and she checked the number; it was Dunn. She got off the bus and dialed his number from a phone booth. "Hey, checking up on me?" She couldn't resist.

His voice was slightly baffled: "What? Where are you? I hear a truck or something heavy."

"Wrong guess. I'm just got off the bus, almost home." She hesitated then asked, "And where are you? I can't say I hear freeway in that tightly sealed Nazi limo you drive."

"Well, you're right about the Nazi limo, as you insist on calling it. I'm on my way down to O.C. for a quick ride on a friend's new surfboard and then up to N.A. in Long Beach."

Molly could tell he was waiting for some sign of acceptance or invitation or both. So the pressure was on and the speed was ramped to move them forward and faster. "I have to stop at the nursery school to check in with the principal. I took this afternoon off for my shrink visit." She bit her lip. Too much for him to know.

But he was cool about it and ignored the reference to her visit with her therapist. "Tomorrow is better. It's Friday, and the parents get to the day care earlier. That would really be better for me."

"Why don't we go up to L.A.? I have a thing I was invited to and want to take you with me."

She wondered about the "thing." Was it one of those Hollywood parties? She already felt intimidated by all the young, hard bodies with hair down to their skinny waists.

"Okay. You've got me. What kind of thing?"

"One of the producers is having a light supper and drinks. All corporate types and most of them are recovering boozehounds anyway. It's the style now. Everyone does it."

She was truly intimidated now. What do I wear being her first thought. "Let me check with Esther. What time?"

He must have opened the window because she could hear voices surrounding him. "One burger, no fries." And then, "That will be six-fifty, please pull up to the window."

"MacDonald's?" She couldn't believe it.

"Silly girl, In-N-Out Burgers."

"Call me tonight and tell me the rest, like how I should dress and who and what are the recovering corporate types like so I can begin to feel really out of place."

He chuckled as he said, "You'll be fine, darling, just fine."

The bus stopped and she walked briskly to the apartment. Shit, Javier was outside leaning against his Camaro and talking with Carlos and Ramon. Nugent was skating loops in the middle of the road and came toward her as she approached. The boy needed a haircut and his shirt looked more than its usual grimy. She said hello to Carlos and watched him as he watched Javier's face, knowing his eyes were sparkling now that she was here. There was an expression that she saw pass Javier's face, and it reminded her of Stella's sweet infant smile. Her senses were always more awakened after a visit to Suarez and sometimes it was more than she wanted to handle.

"Javier." She took his arm. "Can you drive me to the nursery school? I'm late

for a meeting with the principal. Excuse us, Carlos." She turned to the boy to say, "Nugent, tell my mother where I've gone and I'll be back in thirty minutes."

Decisions

The seat of the Camaro was hot from sitting in the sun, and Molly's legs were sticking to the leather. "You really ought to look into buying some kind of cover." She felt fried. Javier's silence said he didn't want to hear her complaints about the free ride. A gringo boyfriend would have told her to walk. Javier let his Indian blood deliver his message for him. Or, she reasoned, maybe he knew her too well.

"The director expecting you?" Now he showed some interest. He glided to the front of the whitewashed building, shabby looking and in need of a paint job. He smoothly slid the car into neutral, the big cat of an engine purring loudly.

"I haven't had a chance to speak to Mrs. Dickenson since I started back to work, and she asked me to see her." She absent-mindedly chewed on her thumb cuticle until he gently pushed her hand away.

"Don't. It will bleed." His face was soft and receptive. He took her hand and looked at it. "Maybe you should visit Theresa for a manicure. Instead, you go to the Vietnamese." She opened her mouth to protest and he jumped in. "I know, I know, they're cheaper. But look at your nails, they look bad two days later. Go see my cousin, she always treats you right." Unspoken between them and something she could have said honestly was he treated her right, too.

"Querida." He would have pulled her toward him if he could, but the big bucket seats of his behemoth vehicle prevented him. "Come with me."

"Where?" She spoke almost absentmindedly, still thinking of her nails. "When?"

"Now, when you have finished speaking to the principal." His dark brows, she thought, so beautifully drawn. "Now," he said again, "soon."

His words captured an urgency they both knew of past times, and she felt a strong and familiar stirring. "Christ, how am I going to get through this meeting?" He laughed because she knew they'd abandon everything tonight to be together. "Let me call Mom from the phone in school".

She walked briskly into the school and quickly dialed home. Esther answered on the first ring, expectant. "Mom? Did Nugent tell you?"

Esther's voice was quiet, as though she was interrupted from some deep reverie. "He came in a short while ago. You have to see Mrs. Dickenson, the principal. Is she from Nugent's school?" It was the first time her mother spoke his name, at least to her.

"Not Nugent's. The director for the nursery school. Just some catching up to do. But I called to say not to wait dinner. I'll be out a while. Javier drove me over, and I have some errands to run."

She didn't know what she expected, a tirade of words or of silence. Esther surprised her. "Say hello. I spoke with his mother today."

"Okay." She hung up relieved and marveled that her mother spoke with Javier's.

The hall was cool and dark in contrast to the hot spring sun outside. There was a breeze floating through the opened doors of the classrooms. She click-clacked in her open-backed sandals down to the director's office, the tiny cubicle most secretaries would have rejected. Inside was Mrs. Dickenson, the same easy natured woman who held the nursery school, all its children, and all their stories in place. God, she thought, how many years has she done this? And then thought how many years she worked with her students, all those high school boys and girls, and how much she now missed them all.

Mrs. Dickenson looked up as she knocked at the door that stood almost closed.

"Come in, Molly." Her voice and presence always lent a peaceful note to Molly's often jangled nerves. But now she was off all of it, the meth, the weed, even the Corona Light with a slice of lime. "You and I have been missing one another." She patted the chair beside her, "Come and sit. How have you been?"

She told Mrs. Dickenson about her mother, that she was visiting. That it was a relief to share the burden of Nugent and the work of laundry, meals, cleaning. She felt guilty because most of it was never done as well as she should have before Esther arrived.

All the while Mrs. Dickenson nodded, and Molly had a deep impression that she knew all that Molly felt. She was the closest thing to a confessor. "So good that you have her help. You've needed that." She set aside her ever present paperwork. "How have you found being back to school with us? The children?"

"I was surprised to see Anthony Baker come out of himself and showing an interest in the activities." She thought about the boy whom she realized lived with his own mother much like Molly was back when she was doing meth.

"Anthony is now with his paternal grandmother." She sighed. "So many of these children are raised with grandparents, mostly widowed poor women who barely scrape by but they seem to find the energy to cook and clean for children with such great needs. It's what they ultimately stay alive for." She rested her thin-wristed arm on the desk. "I'm glad that you returned. That we have you for at least a little while."

It was more a question, and Molly knew it was coming. "Thank you. I like the work."

"But." Mrs. Dickenson held Molly with her warm brown eyes.

Molly became awkward. "It's true that my first love in teaching is secondary Ed."

"I am sure there's more."

"And history. I like to see them come alive when they realize that history is the key to their own futures."

"Molly. I think you are about to tell me something very good for you and not as good for me or this little pre-school. Mrs. Dickenson held Molly's hand. "So, you are going back." She stopped Molly from remonstrating. "I know you like us, you liked the smaller children. You had some adjustments to make, to figure out first. But now, you're ready?"

Molly left the building, her mood coming alive again for

Javier and less for talking about the needs of her students. As soon as he saw her he started the engine, closing the windows, setting the air conditioner on high for her.

She slid into the car blasting cool air, pushing her hair away from her forehead. She told him of Esther's comment and he filled in the gaps without being asked. "My mother called looking for you. She worries, you know."

"And she spoke to Esther?" Molly was incredulous, speechless. "That must have been something." She smiled but now he was serious.

"Your mother is not well, Querida. She needs rest."

Molly decided to leave that where it stood. Instead she took his hand away from the wheel, pressing her lips to his warm, hard and calloused hand. He turned more fully to see her face, to see the passion there.

Later she'd not remember the drive to his apartment to the farthest reaches of East Los Angeles County where the roads lay, bleached against an unforgiving sun. She remembered, however, being grateful for the air conditioner in this desert part of the county.

They were in his apartment. The shades were drawn against the hot sun. She slipped out of her dress and let it drop to the floor. Javier came to her in the same way he did in their early life together. He caressed her hair, her body, he pulled his heavy jeans off, and his shirt disappeared even sooner. They stood naked in the middle of the room, and swayed together, locked in a dance they both knew all too well. At last they lay down on his big bed of heavy and ornate, dark wood, taken from Mexico to California when his family moved.

His frequent whispered words were heavy with 'Querida' or '*muchacha apacible, muchacha dulce,*' gentle girl, sweet girl. The words she heard at the beginning when they were so enraptured with one another. And now she felt that way again. She cried, thinking of how alive she felt, and how much he still loved her after all the drugs, all the bitter memories. His lovemaking was strong as he plunged into her, exciting her over and over again. They slept with their bodies together.

"Javier?" She stirred from a deep sleep dreaming of a desert, where she stood alone with a barren mountain as a backdrop. She sat up abruptly. "What time is it?" She tried to see her watch in the darkened room. Her throat was dry, as though she had slept in sand.

His heavy arm was across her bare abdomen. "Eight o'clock. Just eight." He sat up. "We can get something to eat. You will be home by ten."

He understood her concern for Esther and Nugent "I'll call Esther. She may be worried." She reached for his phone and dialed her home number. It rang twice before Esther answered. She told her they would be back by ten, having some dinner now, she lied, everything went well at the school. This last piece said to deflect any questions that might come up if she didn't fill it all in.

Molly rested her head against his chest. He was lying back down while she spoke with her mother. *"Querida, te quiero."* He loved her, she knew.

* * *

A quick dinner of tacos with salsa verde at the best Mexican place in Duarte and they were streaming back to Long Beach. In the restaurant, they sat quietly across from one another, comfortable in their silence like the two lovers they were. He drank root beer, and she resisted the Corona and sipped a soda. They frequently smiled at one another. She felt full of life, of him. He was like a rooster, strutting his prowess among his chickens with one exception: she was the only chicken in the roost. Probably too much of a woman, even for someone like Javier. He became protective when some of the other men looked too appreciatively at her, but it made her feel good to know they thought she was pretty.

The radio played softly. It was all rap even if it was Mexican rap and it reminded her how still very young he could be. What? Three years difference between them? Was that so much? He possessed the ways of a much older man. She stopped herself with an admonishment, *Stop! You measure everything.*

"Do you think of Stella?" The music still flowed through with its deep thrusting rhythm, the equally deep voice of the man pumping out the lyric, all in Mexican so she could not know exactly what he said.

She was startled by his question, its directness. "Yes, often. But in different ways. Sometimes happy when I think of her while she lived. Sometimes sad when I think of her as she would be now, a year later." Her voice suddenly broke. "God, I loved her. Loved her."

"Is it good to think of her? Yes. It is good for us to be happy with her." It was late, his English was failing him, and he was very tired. Molly knew what he meant, told him as much and said she felt the same way.

* * *

It was after ten when she got home, and Esther was blessedly asleep. Molly tiptoed into the bedroom, hastily stripped and fell fast asleep the moment her head hit the pillow. She woke to the sound of water rushing through the pipes. The clock read 6:00, time enough to get Nugent going. She lay back against the pillows, feeling the day come alive. There was stirring in the bathroom, Esther. She hugged her pillow one more time for its comfort and slid out of bed. Her image in the mirror was one of a wild woman, hair all over the place, eyes a bit smudged, she hadn't even washed her face. Esther trod past her door and as soon as she thought the coast was clear, she entered the bathroom. The door opened on the steamy room as Molly was pulling tangles out of her hair with a large toothed comb.

"Do you work today? I forgot the schedule again." Her mother scrutinized her lithe daughter, touching her back and gently rubbing the wet off her shoulders.

"Next Friday. I'm off today. Is Nugent up?" She tightened her thin robe around her.

"I thought I heard him, but I don't think he's up yet." Esther was quiet a moment. I never heard you come in. I must have been in a deep sleep." She shook her head, as though in dismay.

Javier was right, Esther was not well. The crush of years of keeping deep secrets at bay had taken their toll. "Mom, when was the last time you saw a doctor?"

"Too long most likely. But I've never been a big believer in doctors. Take your money, get rich on you and make you sicker."

Molly heard this lament before, only with a lot more spirit and spit behind it. "But maybe it's time to see someone, just for a check-up."

Esther opened Nugent's bedroom door. "You ready for breakfast?" He nodded yes. She turned again to Molly. "Check-up? For what? What's to check?"

The coffee was dripping into the pot and the aroma was permeating all corners.

Molly knew her mother would relent about the doctor. They'd have a few more conversations about blood pressure, let's just see and who knows, maybe you need vitamins, but it would happen. She looked closely, careful not to be too obvious. Her mother's skin looked sallow, there was a wet sickness to the touch of it. She wondered about adult onset of diabetes.

Nugent ate whatever Esther gave him, and today it was toast with a poached egg. He drank his juice, grabbed his backpack and was gone by 7:30. Mother and daughter sat across the table from one another, sipping coffee without much to say. Molly was at first surprised that Esther did not grill her about Javier, the time she got home, why so late. At the same time she was gratified that Esther seemed to accept him. In such a short time, or so it seemed.

The phone rang. Esther was nearest. "Yes, she's right here, Mr. Dunn."

Dunn. She'd forgotten all about Dunn. This *was* Friday, but so early? His party in Los Angeles. Oh God. "Michael. You're the early riser." She was buying time. *Do I want to do this?*

"That's right, sweetheart. The same could be said for you. Just checking on our agenda for tonight. I will be there for you at 7:00 pm. Is that going to work?"

Molly mentally shook her head, I said yes, I can't say no now. Javier slipped into her mind, and she quickly dismissed him. "Seven is fine." Now she had to find a way around Javier. She talked a few minutes more with Dunn until he got out of freeway gridlock and he was gone.

"You going somewhere tonight?" Esther regained some of the old punch. Her eyes narrowed and Molly swore she saw it all, maybe even knew how it was going to turn out.

"I forgot the dinner party with Michael Dunn. It's up in L.A. somewhere. I think maybe Hollywood or the Valley."

Hollywood

"You look pretty." Nugent went as far as to reach out and touch the black tight-fitting dress. It clung to Molly in all the right places and she wished that Michael Dunn would be here soon so that she could dash out without fanfare and head up to L.A. She checked her makeup in the mirror in the hallway, checked too to be sure no loose threads hanging anywhere, and thanked God all over again for giving her the sense to have purchased the little black number when it was on sale at Nordstrom's last year. She thought about that now, what made her choose this dress. The price was right, that was for sure, but there was no occasion then and she could never have known there would be one now. Now she remembered, the dress fit, and felt the soft lining slide down over her head as though the fabric knew her body, her name. That day at Nordstrom's was one of the few days when the sun crept in and brought along some happiness, albeit a brief respite from the constant burden of the lingering sadness.

Esther pulled her attention away from the local Long Beach newspaper, and removed her glasses. She looked tired but her color had improved the last few days. Molly was surprised and relieved when she convinced her mother to see Dr. Webster's internist friend. Her mother complained of dizziness and rapid breathing and Molly was afraid it might be a heart problem. It was sad to see her now, so much closer to the end of her life. *And where are you?* She had no ready answer. Yet she felt a life force in her now, like she was waking from a dream.

Molly smoothed the dress down where it sat snug on her hips. "So, you like my new look, Nuge?" She hugged the boy, carefully, tentatively because he didn't like being treated like a little boy. Hugs were for kids he told her. "Yeah, but for kids you like."

She and Esther were the glue now for all of them. She thought back to Javier and her visit with him. What was she doing with Dunn? She shook her head at the thought of Javier. *I can't, I can't start again.* But wasn't that what she was doing? Dunn personified advancement, improvement. A better class of people. She chided her own prejudice. No, he had more money, not more class. He never pretended to be otherwise. She began to tick off in her mind all the good things about Michael Dunn, the nice looks, the nice home, the money, and realized that it was, after all a money class thing. He was upper middle or maybe even higher up the food chain. And, he was warm, caring, sincere. She was puzzled by his attraction to her, and when he explained using words like "east coast ways," to describe it, his words sounded shallow.

Her daydreaming came to an abrupt halt with the knock on the back door. She looked at her kitchen now with Dunn's eyes, neat but old, dilapidated, even. The furniture was Ikea that she bought when she was teaching high school, but it was dated, too young a brand for a "professional woman." She needn't have worried; his eyes saw only her, and she blushed because it was so very obvious.

"You look...." He took her hands and turned her around. She noticed her mother biting her lip from the effort not to smile too broadly. "Well. I don't need to say."

"Such a fuss, such a fuss." Esther was clucking but pleased despite it all. "The dress fits nice. Still."

Molly knew the 'still' part. Still and after having a baby, still and not so young anymore. She glanced in the mirror again and saw what he saw, still young enough, still lithe, slender, long thin legs and arms, thick long hair. No slave to fashions, independent in her hairstyle. She breathed deeply, asking herself *now who's shallow?* "Gotta go. You've got Michael's car phone number if you need me." Don't need me, she prayed. Half not thinking, she hurriedly kissed Nugent on the cheek and pressed him to her and didn't look back for a reaction, sure his wide eyes were full of emotion as they were anytime she was affectionate.

Molly looked at the darkening street. Thank God the sun retreated to the other side of the world, had sunk into a cold ocean.

She knew Javier wouldn't have thought to be here tonight. He'd have no reason to be suspicious, which was the only time he stalked her. She shook her head to escape the image of his disappointment if he saw her with Michael and couldn't wait to exit this street, and Long Beach in general, just in case.

It was as though Michael read her thoughts. The car sped away and they were on the freeway before she knew it. He reached over for her hand; his was warm.

"Tell me about the party." She let him hold her hand as she looked ahead of her to the thinning traffic below El Segundo. It got heavier near LAX. "Who is going to be there and why?"

"Let's see, like I said, some other SONY attorneys, some clients." They were in gridlock just below the El Segundo exit. He swerved off the road. "I can get there faster on surface roads."

"Who else? And why?" She really wanted to know how to act, what image she should convey with any of them. "Will you all be talking business?"

Michael pulled up to a light and looked directly at her. "Some movie people. No one big, I don't think. He picked her hand up and kissed her fingers. "You don't like surprises, do you?" His tone was soft, slightly teasing. She tried to ignore him.

"I guess it's the old control freak thing they talk about in therapy. Makes me want to assess the situation before I even get there. I worried about fitting in."

"You? A control freak? " He said it in a distracted way as he wound around cars on the four lane road.

They climbed up the canyon to a small cottage-looking gate, wisteria and bright red bougainvillea dripping off the white fence. Cars were being parked by Latino valets in red vests. Michael handed his keys and ten dollars to a young man. "Don't bury me guys, okay?" He said it in rapid Spanish and the valets nodded. That would buy them a few beers.

The sounds emanating from the house were mingled with a steady rap beat, surprisingly quieter than the voices. She heard snatches of conversation as she walked in and was thankful that everyone was too busy drinking their wine or vodka to look too closely. There were some older men who stopped long enough to appraise the both of them. They responded with "Michael" and a nod. There were pockets of people in groups, some all men, some all women, some of both. It seemed that Michael took her hand instinctively when the men appraised her and she was at once endeared toward him, protective. They joined a group of people he obviously knew well.

"Glen, you talking that Bogie shit again? Damn, can you give it a rest?"

Glen was about two inches shorter than Michael, who was six feet some inches tall. Glen was somewhat thick around the middle, with a big cigar in between his chubby fingers. "Look, I gave up tennis, I told you, sos I could get some *real* exercise on the golf courses." He laughed broadly and they all joined him. He smiled at her and took her hand.

"No drink for you? Maria!" A woman stood near his elbow, and Molly told her a Sprite with ice in a quieter tone that only Maria heard. They could all think she was drinking gin. Michael ordered the same, and began a nonstop bantering with Glen. The others took turns making fun of his golf game. As the crowd moved to the next group, Michael introduced Molly to Glen. Glen's eyes subtly measured the relationship between her and Dunn and asked her, "You in the business?"

"Not yet, maybe someday." She said it to be mysterious, to belong. "Right now I'm planning to go back to teaching. High school. In the 'hood. Long Beach."

"No. You shittin' me? " He turned quickly toward Dunn. "What a waste of talent in the 'hood, though."

"The kids don't think so." Michael said this while twirling the ice around in his drink. "You remember those movies a few years ago about dedicated teachers. Everything from *Blackboard Jungle* to William Hurt in the school for the deaf kids. Did a great job."

"New England somewhere." Glen said, finally lighting his cigar. "That one was filmed there." His eyes lit up. "You're from back east. Right?"

Before she had time to speak, he went on to the next subject, some contract he needed to get signed by Tuesday or else. Molly excused herself, and Maria, ever watchful, looked toward the hallway where Molly found a bathroom. She felt some stares from a gaggle of women who looked more like the wives. Not older than she was, in fact many were younger, but wary of her. You could always tell.

The back of the house was shaped like a one-story ranch; the hallway was long with high windows on each wall where lights shone in. Molly found a door opening into a large bathroom. There was a woman in a silvery dress crunching her auburn curls and tossing it back from her face. She looked quizzically at Molly.

"You're Michael's friend." There was more she didn't say. It could have been anything from "lucky you, too bad for you or fuck you."

"And you are?" She got the impression that hardball was the game around here.

"Mrs. Glen." She tamed a wayward curl from alongside her face.

"That looked nice, you should leave it." Molly had no idea why she suggested something so personal to a woman she didn't know.

Mrs. Glen looked at her more closely and Molly had the impression that she wanted to find her glasses so that she could see Molly more clearly. The hardness that first held her face intact receded; the softness made her look older. She was still watching Molly from the mirror and absentmindedly tugged her skin slightly at the temple, taking five years with her as she did.

"We're one of those couples that last forever. But with this bunch it's a friggin' game. There's always another tight body, tighter than yours." She sighed. "Shit, we all have to die. Right?"

Molly looked around the room. Mrs. Glen said, "The 'loo' is behind that door there. Mind if I stay in here?"

"No problem." Molly stepped into the bathroom, closed the door and sat down. She also lit up a cigarette. "You mind if I smoke?" she thought to ask.

"Only if you have one for me too."

Molly exited the bathroom, washed her hands with the lilac-perfumed soap and wiped her hands on the light lavender plush towel that felt more like velvet than cotton. She handed Mrs. Glen a cigarette, one of the three left in her purse. She hated this game of trying to quit every other month.

"Funny, I am called Mrs. Glen most of the time. We're Glen and Sheila Abramowitz. When I saw you come in, I figured you still smoked. Hypnosis, patches, every friggin, thing and I still crave the nicotine. Those bastards in tobacco knew what they were doing when they grew this stuff." She hesitated before she spoke again, blowing smoke out a sliding glass door which she opened to a crack. "Don't want Glen to give me a hard time about it. But hell, I could always say it was you, couldn't I?" She gave Molly a conspiratorial look and laughed.

"Sure. Use me. We'll most likely never meet again." She walked back to the toilet and dropped the cigarette in; it fizzled and died and she flushed it. "You're from back east, I heard Glen say. Now I hear it, the accent. Do you miss it?" She didn't wait for an answer. "I do, sometimes. I was happier there. Hell, I was younger too. Ever notice how young they all look out here? The clothes, the tans, the massages and salons. It all comes to that. Of course the tans are fake bakes." She rattled on, half speaking to herself.

"Is everything all right?" Molly stood near her, Sheila sitting on a chair in front of a little makeup table filled with cut crystal perfume bottles.

Sheila shook her head. "I don't want to be mean. You should probably know if you don't already. You're still in the running, you know? You still have the look about you, fresh. Well, hold on to it, honey because it fucking fades. And Dunn will too. They all do, they fucking fade into the fucking sunset." She pulled violently from the cigarette as though it offered oxygen instead of poison. The smoke billowed about her as she spoke. Molly thought Sheila decided finally, not to hide the telltale aroma of smoke should Mr. Glen confront her.

She continued, "Dunn, he's different, lost that child, his whole life. Changed him. Until then, he did his share of running wild." Sheila smiled some secret smile and ran her finger lovingly along her lower lip. "But you mark my words, he will keep moving, like a fucking shark. Hell, he's dating you, isn't he? And you're what? Maybe almost ten years younger than him?" She pushed off the chair and picked up her empty glass. "Time for a refill."

Molly hastened back down the hall. Sheila was nowhere ahead of her and must have loped along on her five feet nine inches of longer legs. The living room was quieter now, some of the crowd was out near the pool keeping warm under heating units. The remaining group was mostly the corporate crowd with their wives. They were laughing as Molly sat down next to Dunn who commandeered a love seat. The wives exchanged some looks but Molly didn't care. Dunn was drinking something, not Sprite, that lent an air of relaxation to him.

"Yeah, Jerry had his hands full when the Japanese showed up," Dunn was saying. "You could see Yakamoto fuming in his particular way, and you knew Jerry was losing ground fast. But damn, the guy pulled it out of the water and saved the day, and our asses up there on Washington Boulevard." He gulped a swallow of whatever and reached across Molly to place the glass on the table. His hand slid across her lap as he drew back.

"You'll have to tell me your brand of Seven-Up." She said it low but didn't try to hide it from them. There were some eyebrows raised but Dunn was smiling comfortably. He laid his arm around her bare shoulders.

"What you all think of my girl? Isn't she something?" He used his finger to make suggestive circles on her shoulder which titillated her but she stopped him.

"How did you meet, dear?" A much older woman dressed in a St. John knit outfit that set her husband back at least three thousand. Her heavy bracelets clinked together on her bony arm as she raised her glass of tan liquid.

"Molly and I were both at St Mary's for some tests when we met." Dunn may have been drinking but he was definitely not off his game. "Christine, are you planning to play in that golf tournament out in Palm Desert again?" Dunn quickly interjected before one question led to another.

"Michael and I go to some of the same N.A. meetings. It's what you could say sustains us." She sipped some of his drink and found it was pure vodka. No one spoke and all of them took a sip from their particular brand of medicine or poison or both.

Conversation turned to golf again and to N.A., which one or the other of them had attended alone or as couples. Dunn wasn't kidding when he said it was a damned status symbol among the rich and shallow. As soon as she thought of them that way she regretted it because she knew there was tragedy in everyone's choice to abuse drugs or drink whether they sat under a crystal chandelier in Beverly Hills or an overhead light bulb in Long Beach.

The party trailed off into some sobering up with heavy hors

d'oeuvres and Dunn seemed more in charge of himself as they left. Yet Molly moved ahead of him to the valet to snag the keys. She was grateful that he didn't object.

"Okay if I snooze a moment before we take off?" He settled in the passenger seat for a nap.

"Just a rest and then give me directions to the apartment near SONY." He rested his head against her arm and she smoothed his temples with her fingers.

"You do want to stay up here with me, don't you?" His light blue eyes were hard to say no to, and he was endearing himself to her. She thought a moment about Sheila's remarks.

"I'll just step out of the car for a moment for some fresh air." He was already gone, so she slipped out of the driver's seat and dropped his car keys into her purse. She walked around the lower part of the estate. The grounds were casual in an off-hand way. The landscaping, she knew, must have cost a bundle to effect. All of this opulence didn't set her teeth on edge. She wondered why she didn't care as much as she should. Maybe it was something that Sheila said, that she still had time. But for what? To snag a guy like Dunn? And keep him? Would that be easy or was that the real challenge? She walked along a path and heard Glen's voice.

"Where's our golden boy?" He was smoking another of his Cuban cigars.

"Is that what he is? Golden? He's sleeping it off."

"Surely not the booze. He didn't have that much." He was frank in his look at her. It was as naked a physical wanting as any she had ever seen. No wonder Mrs. Glen wasn't doing so well.

"Not the booze. Maybe it's his particular circle of hell he lives in that is draining him."

She didn't avert her eyes from Glen, and her unspoken answer was 'go look somewhere else.' "I talked some to Sheila tonight," she said.

Glen was nonplussed. "Good. She could use a friend." He looked more closely at her. "What's so funny?"

"A friend? Do you people really make friends all that easily?" She started back to the car, wanting to be there when Dunn awoke. "And do you all *stay* friends too? She didn't wait for an answer. "It was nice meeting you."

"No, it wasn't. You couldn't wait to get out of here from the moment you arrived. So don't give me pleasantries." His voice was gruff and he coughed.

"Gloves off? You're right. I don't belong here, if that's what you are referring to. And that's really okay for me. You and those like you don't really give a fuck what someone like me thinks. But somehow, right now that's not true. Not this time."

"And you find that funny? Because I see you smile. So it's funny." He moved closer. "I'd like to know what's so funny, maybe you could spend some time with me and tell me."

"I'll tell you something. I lost my baby. She died when she was only three months old. She was the most beautiful thing that ever happened to me. She made me a better person from the very first sign of her in my belly. I heard the sounds of some kids here in a room down the hall near the bathroom. They must be yours and Sheila's. You're a busy guy, so time with them is precious." She didn't bother to register his response, but realized she said so much to him and yet had refused to share the same with Michael. Glen threw the cigar into the grass and stepped on it, "Yeah, you're right. I am too busy."

Molly walked fast down the hill to the car and Dunn opened his eyes as she sat down. "Well, refreshed and ready to go?" She started the car and he gave her the directions to the corporate apartment. He was fully recovered, so it must have been only the one drink. The apartment was a close drive down the 405 freeway from the canyon, and the traffic was late-night light. Inside the apartment was posh, yet cold and sterile, unlived in. It was decorated in all the right shades of beige and white and sand and yellow. Dunn had talked a great deal as they drove, sharing his own impression of the various party goers. He had a realistic picture of them, yet was compassionate about their problems which he ticked off for longer than she cared to hear.

"How about Glen and Mrs. Glen? What's their deal?" She waited as he thought, she supposed, how to answer her, how to handle that. They arrived at the apartment and conversation was placed on hold as she entered the garage using his pass, found the company's parking space, and then took an elevator to the penthouse.

He was quiet, and she realized thoughtful, as they settled in to the living room where fake champagne was chilling. Always prepared, she thought, a regular boy scout.

He made no pretension otherwise when he sat close, fondled her hair, caressed her face with his lips, and did all the wonderful things he did to drive her mildly mad. Before long they were in the bedroom under some very soft Egyptian cotton sheets with dimmed lights and soft music coming from somewhere, everywhere. And Molly succumbed to it all, from softness to a frenzied hunger that didn't seem to ever satisfy. Later she realized even Dunn noticed.

Michael fell asleep, but she was restless and tiptoed around the apartment, scrambled some eggs and made some coffee. Michael appeared in the doorway as she was sliding the eggs onto two plates. He poured the coffee.

"You didn't like those people did you?" He sat across from her and she saw his jaw set, unsure if it was her not liking his friends or his mind on some deal.

"They're okay, I guess." He was quiet so she ventured. "It's always amazed me how hard the laid back L.A. people work. I guess that's a misconception among us transplants."

"Were they just not kind to you? I thought they tried to be accommodating. Certainly Glen...," he trailed off.

"Well, he's the host." She didn't know where this was going, but didn't like it. "His wife is nice enough. You knew her well?"

"How do you mean?"

Molly put her fork down, sipped some of the coffee and added more sweetener and sipped again. "We both *know* how. You knew her well." She stood up and moved her plate to the sink and ran some cold water on it. She put her hands up in a 'stop' gesture.

"Let's start again. No, not crazy about the friends and won't itemize just now. Way too late and for some reason we're both on edge. I can't speak for you, but I can tell you I am, and it has to do with putting that much energy out for an evening that held so much promise. Now, I'm going to tell you what else I see. Glen is a predator, and I don't think you should call him a friend."

"I was afraid of this." Michael seemed to be trying for some Zen-centering exercise to avoid an argument. She saw deep breathing. "So he made a pass? He was probably drunk."

"Very sober, and very deliberate. Or, is that some game you all play? Everybody is fair game?"

"Molly." He got up out of his chair and held her for a good long while. She loosened her resolve. "I care for you. It happened too quickly maybe, and I can't tell you other than to say I want you in my life. I come alive, really alive when I am with you. All that fake shit, it just stands out even more, and I guess it was an experiment. I had to see you in it to gauge."

"So, a test? Did I pass?"

He hugged her again. "Pass? You have it all wrong. I'm the one in the hot seat. Do I pass the genuine test? Am I like them? Tell me."

She ignored his questions. "How about poor old Esther and the half-Mexican, half-black kid? They're not just colorful fixtures in a room, or props on a set. They come with the package. They're part of me."

"And you're all real. I had a mother, she drank herself to death. And I have a father who plays golf out in Palm Springs and hires women for…everything. I don't have anyone else. You ask me what attracted me to you. It was you at first, then it was Esther and the boy and the way you are with them."

She saw tears in his eyes and wondered whether Sheila's cautionary tale was something to heed. Whether she was his idea of real for now, until she got to be ten years older, whether he would end up like his father. She was in uncharted water.

"I'm tired and so are you." She hugged him back, fiercely. "Let's get some sleep."

* * *

"You're restless." Michael's concern was nice, but it only rattled her instead of acting as a balm over her nerves.

"Just tired." She tried to sound grateful for his attention but was sure she fell short.

Sleep, it turned out, didn't make it any better. Something was needling Molly, causing a disquiet that she felt early in her withdrawal. She closed her eyes behind her sunglasses and affected a dozing to keep dialog down while her mind buzzed with snatches of things she planned to do today because it was Saturday and there were always things to be done when she got back to Long Beach. Her mind went back to the sudsy bath she luxuriated in earlier this morning. While it loosened her tensed muscles, it had done little for her tensed mind.

"Fuck it. Can't even rest in gridlock." She raised a questioning eyebrow at Michael whether she could use his car phone. He nodded yes, and she rang Esther.

"Hi, Mom. Michael and I are just below LAX, which normally is not far away, but it's the weekend, and that means we're locked in bumper to bumper traffic. Seems like everyone wants to get down to the beaches." She looked at her watch. "Should be home by 1:00 the latest." She looked over at Michael, who nodded in agreement with her estimated time of arrival.

Michael switched the radio off when she hung up. "Everything all right on the home front?" He too seemed weary. "I was hoping we could do lunch before you headed home. Maybe stop in Hermosa. Not that far?" He raised a questioning brow. "Won't take that long?"

"I'd love to but," she said, sighing deeply. "I have a ton of stuff to do in preparation for Monday." She quickly went on, to forestall his objections about time enough. "I have Nugent's homework to get settled, and I'm going in Monday to meet the new vice-principal and get ready for teachers in-service." She realized she hadn't told Michael about the call from Cabrillo asking her to meet with the new Vice Principal at Cabrillo, so she told him now. "It looks like I'll be back teaching high school." She brought him up to date about Amy Sargent. "She replaces that dirt bag, Robert I told you about."

Isn't this a bit soon? I mean don't you think going back would be better if you took another three months, started in the New Year?"

"I really can't scrape through this way. Nugent is eating up my budget in three days." She didn't say that she did not want Esther's money. Her mother's health was not as good as she had hoped. No, Esther needed everything she had to pay for her medication and for any other contingencies that might have to be planned. She didn't say any of this because she knew he wouldn't relate, couldn't relate to her life.

"Can I help?" His remark took her off guard. He must have sensed this because he explained. "I mean you could call it a loan or something, anything that would make the transition easier for you."

"God, Michael. You are too good." She fidgeted with her

sunglasses, cleaning them with a tissue and jamming them onto her face again. "No, it's best this way. I can slide in and it's good that I am helping Cabrillo because the sub is so old. That poor old woman they replaced me with is about ninety-two, so I'll be doing them a favor. And that's the way I want it to seem, that I am helping the administration out, instead of the other way around."

They sat quietly, each lost in their own thoughts.

"I'm finding this hard to believe," Michael said after a while. "But I think you are trying to say something more to me here. It's last night, but something else too, isn't it?" His voice almost broke, and her heart felt much the same.

"Come on, Dunn, there's lots of them out there. I'm not so damn unique. Hell, someone younger, not so burdened would…"

He cut in. "Don't patronize me. Please, don't do that."

They stopped again, the traffic not even inching forward. He put the car in Park and opened the windows to allow some of the salt air to flow through it. "I think we could be good for one another. It's a mutual need fulfilled, not just one of us."

"Just hear yourself. We have dated and bedded down how many times? How can you jump ahead to where I think you are going?" She tried to reach his hand but he had gone all rigid on her. "I think we both need a break. Maybe look at this again some other time."

"You're always so restless. Your mind is always running ahead." Michael's concern was nice but it only rattled her instead of acting as a balm.

"Just tired." She tried to sound grateful for his attention but was certain she fell short.

"Sure." The traffic began to crawl forward again. He put the car in Drive and swerved through the traffic, wildly passing and just missing the truck on the left, and a little Miata on the right that was barely visible.

"Are you crazy? You'll get us killed." Molly was frightened by this unmeasured and unreliable side of him. He slowed down with the traffic that began to flow again.

"Michael, let's stop in Hermosa." She knew she owed him more than what she had said so far.

And so they stopped in Hermosa, and she called Esther and told her she'd be having lunch out and not to keep anything warm for her. They stepped into a Mexican restaurant. "It's nice," he said. "You'll like it. Upscale but Mexicans like it, upscale Mexicans." He almost acted drunk.

They ordered lemonade from a girl with an expression as sour as the lemons that were squeezed for their drinks. Molly figured she was pissed because they didn't ordered some overpriced frozen slurpee tequila drink, so their bill, and her tip, would be small. She was aware of Michael watching her twisting the paper from the straw, and self-consciously dropped it. She opened her mouth to speak and he beat her to the punch.

"Look, we're both too old to act this way. It's part my fault for not saying exactly what's on my mind. Is that the way Javier does it, tells you exactly, no nice foreplay language? I think I may have loved you from the first day. It happens, never felt it before and don't think I have enough years to feel it again. I love you. I want to be with you, help you with that crazy mother and that freaked out little orphan. I love them, too. What's it been? Four months, maybe five?" He sipped his drink. She didn't interrupt.

"Molly, you know you are very beautiful. The sad, sorrowful hazel eyes, more like the Atlantic than the Pacific, huh? That skinny waif looking figure that is remarkable to me, never a sign that you carried your wonderful baby. Well that's part of the attraction but when I saw you at St. Mary's your hair was scraggly from sleeping on it for what? A few days? You were wearing that god-awful hospital ensemble but even then you looked great. Don't stop me now, I'm on a roll here. It was the city smart-ass way about you, the no-nonsense attitude that grabbed me. I knew you were smart, educated, I knew you were Jewish or some combination thereof and I was fascinated by it all. When you were with me and gave me glimpses of your mind, I was actually thankful. No one in L.A. does that. That's gotta be an east coast thing."

"It's the Irish in me." She smiled at him and pulled the last of her cigarettes from his shirt pocket and lit and inhaled.

"Irish?" No way. I guessed at something. So you're happy-ass Irish. Who would have thought that history is in your woodpile?"

"My mother was not married to my father. Happy-ass? Never heard that expression before. The man, the very sweet man that raised me, who took me to the dentist and who even poured hydrogen peroxide on my scraped knees, Sam Morris, he wasn't the man who made me genetically prone to the grape. That man was a nice young pre-med from Boston who loved Esther and if he had known me, well, he might have even loved me." She shared the cigarette with Dunn. "Michael. You're someone I could love, hell I probably do love you. But..."

"Here it comes." He said it wryly, less a sob and more of a self-flagellating sigh.

"But, I have a life that doesn't have room in it for you and me. Together we are good but very needy."

"I'm putting a hold on things. I won't take no for an answer right now, but I won't push for any kind of yes." He smiled a wonderfully white smile against his tanned face.

The pressure was off. They ate their carnitas wrapped in freshly made corn tortillas. She even joked that these were nowhere near as good as the ones that Javier's Tia Consuelo made.

He dropped her at the curb, and she stood and extended her hand to him through the open window, and he extended his and they both smiled, a little sadly.

He said nothing for a long time. "Lady, I'll always keep an eye out for you in case things change, you change. Your mind, that is."

Back to Cabrillo High School

Trudging up the Cabrillo High School steps Molly felt beads of sweat trickling down her sides. Christ, even after all that industrial strength antiperspirant. Nervousness, that's what it was. She held her top away from her body and fanned herself, hoping to dry some of the wetness. Thank God I wore black, no one can me sweating.

The front office was a- buzz with coordinators, planners, a teacher, teacher aides, truant kids and several of the school counselors. No one looked up, no curious stares. She began to relax.

Molly stood in a line that dawdled along, glancing at her watch every few seconds, waiting to speak with the only receptionist. The woman made short work of two students, one with a phony written excuse for yesterday's absence and the other requesting permission to leave early with just a verbal approval from his mother.

"She ain't home now if you planning on calling her." The boy was tall, baseball cap on backward, pants down to where you could see the Jocky label on his scotch plaid boxers.

The receptionist was a woman mid-forties, pretty but carrying twenty extra pounds. Her hair was blondish streaks and brown at the roots. She was not fooled by the student and took him in, cap to toes. His name was Jerome Harris which he repeated for her. Her eyes narrowed as he spoke and he stopped when she held up her hand. "Regulations say students cannot leave without written permission and a reason why you are needed at home. That's true for any minor."

"Sheet, I ain't no miner. Do I look like a miner to you?" You see a shovel in my hands? His grin betrayed his false sounding innocence. Molly guessed he knew he lost the battle so was trying to have fun with it.

"Next." The receptionist waved her arm like a magic wand to indicate she had moved on.

Molly finally stood in front of her.

"Emma Morris. I have an appointment with Mrs. Sargent." She is the new Vice- Principal she thought, the one who took Robert Polesky's job after he got caught with one of the female students after hours. Stupid, she shook her head in wonder, a bar down the street and an underage Latina companion. Bad for Robert, bad for the girl, good for the school to be rid of him.

The receptionist was new too, efficient, brisk and full of energy and Molly hoped for the sake of the kids and the Vice Principal that she'd stay that way and not quit.

She did not look directly at Molly as she shuffled through a pile of papers. "Mrs. Sargent asked for you to take a seat. She'll be here in a few minutes."

Molly found a chair out of the way and close to the door to Robert's former office. She meandered through her mind, tried to arrange her thoughts, what she would say. She was hopeful when she called and Sargent said she'd be glad to meet with her. A light touch on her shoulder brought her back.

"I'm Amy Sargent. Come on in."

Sargent was short, maybe five feet two at most and stocky with an abundance of thick dark hair. There was a Latina lilt to her words which Molly guessed made English her second language and Sargent the last name of the gringo she married.

They took seats at a little round table across from one another in her office. Sargent looked at her and there was a moment of strange silence between them.

"Lots of changes here in the last nine months."

Sargent opened a file in front of her. "Mrs. Schmidt took over your class while you were on leave."

"It was good that the school found someone." Molly voice sounded feeble.

"Yes, well, she is a retiree and substitute so we haven't really seen her much, what with sick days, and finally, last week, she called to say that we should continue with her substitute. It seems she was not well enough for a full time commitment." Molly interpreted her words as "too old." Sargent settled her files by neatly tapping the edges together.

"I called to ask to sub for her if she needed someone."

Amy Sargent closed the file and hesitated. "You know the paper work around here is monumental. I am thinking we might save a few trees if we just had you reinstated if that is something you can do."

Molly felt reservations. They wanted reassurance.

Sargent leaned forward her arms resting on the little table. "I have a responsibility to these kids. I know some of the staff here may look dilapidated, but they don't come in here after a brawl, all black and blue, arms in slings. They're usually sober."

She wasn't making it easy.   Molly's voice choked somewhere in the back of her throat.

"I lost my baby, she died, and I lost…" Molly inclined her head to wipe her face.

Sargent waited. "I don't want to be the badass. We really want the Molly Morris who started work here a few years back. Are you that person?" She flicked her hand when Molly started to say that her teaching methods were somewhat unorthodox and left of conventional.

Sargent continued, her brow knit into a crease. "I have to have the person who shows up on time, teaches the curriculum, fills out reports and keeps the kids from taking over the class. I have to judge whether you are capable to hold it together, that you are no less than the least model person. Because at the end you were below par, coming in sleepy, frenetic the rest of the day, hopped up on meth, once it kicked in." She stopped mid-sentence.

Molly wanted to retch; the picture was even more than ugly. She saw herself as the others must have seen her. Could she face them?   She managed to speak, "I'm sober and I want to teach again."

They talked further about beginning with the fall semester coming up. Mrs. Schmidt had already said she was quitting. Sargent stood first and offered her hand. "You'll have to be here through August for teacher conferences."

Molly entered the hall and heard her name called. "Hey, you back?" It was Tom Kelly, one of her few friends, his barrel belly was gone. "Yup, he saw where she looked. Doc said, lose it or we'll be dropping you below the green." He hesitated then gingerly hugged her and left it for her to tell him what she would.

"You look well. Start back in August." Reinstated, she thought, in the thick of having to prove I won't fall down.

New Beginnings

Molly sat down hard on the sand. She was walking ahead of Esther and Javier, keeping an eye on Nugent when everything started to whirl and, with the dizziness, came a wave of nausea.

"Did you trip?" Esther reached her first. Her mother's cool hand pressed her shoulder where a moment before the sun was frying her skin.

Molly reached for her straw bag to dab some sun block. "It was just out of the blue. Where's Nugent?" She saw a speck way ahead and could picture him thinking about his friends, his basketball game, his skateboard. Everything except what was happening here. "Javier, please call him back."

She stood with little help from Esther who was hovering. "Mom, I'm fine. I'm not going to fall again. Really." She dusted the sand off her shorts and her legs and looked ahead to see Javier and Nugent closer now and throwing a Frisbee. "It might be that flu everyone has been getting. Starts with no warning." That seemed to mollify Esther for the moment.

She walked more slowly so that her mother could keep up and stopped every so often to look at the ocean, but really so her mother could rest.

"Let's sit here for a while." She spread a beach towel on the sand and they faced the wind and wonderful roar of the Pacific. Way out boys in their black rubber suits were sitting on their surfboards, talking and absorbing "the source" as they called it. For a moment she was happy to know that young people felt an absolute concern for the ocean's health.

"Aunt Minna used to have dizzy spells." Esther was adjusting her straw hat and slathering sun block on her freckled arms. Her skin was that of a typical redhead, someone who should always wear long sleeves. Molly told her so and straightened her mother's sweater around her shoulders. Esther continued, "I guess you could say Minna had a lot of spells of one kind or another."

"Can't believe you almost made a joke, Mom, and at your sister's expense." Molly poured little puddles of sand from her hand and smiled. She tried to picture Minna, what she looked like ten years later. "She knew about the man from the Catskills, didn't she?" She still couldn't refer to him as her father. "I remember something, hearing you two talking one day."

"She knew, your uncle knew, that's all." Esther sat up a little. "It was better that way, and how Sam wanted it. Esther looked out at the water. "Peaceful. That's why they called it the Pacific." She looked at Molly from under the brim of her hat. "So. You and Javier? And this party on Saturday? The occasion again for this is?"

"Lots of questions." Esther opened her mouth to protest Molly's reticence, but Molly satisfied her mother's preoccupation with her daughter's life by finally explaining, "Javier's cousin Theresa, you know, the one you met? She always says that any excuse for a party is good enough for the Gutierrez family." This is one of those occasions. Javier is joining his brother's business as a partner. So, a celebration. There will be food, lots of family. You'll love it."

She settled back, still a little nauseous, and looked out at the surfers. They must have found a suitable wave because they were all up on their boards and now were moving fast, pulled by the force beneath them. They were like ballet dancers, performing their exercise routines at the bar; arms and legs in position, guiding the long boards with their bodies, beautiful and slim like dancers, graceful.

* * *

The little Toyota zipped along the freeway at a nice pace. Good. No traffic, no gridlock. Molly timed her visit to Dr. Suarez right this time. And no damn bus to take. Javier's cousin sold the car to her with a profit for him and a family price for her. Javier insisted on paying him what he could get from a stranger, and Molly stepped in to accept a steep discount with payments over time. She guessed that Javier wasn't too pleased because he saw it as what family does for family. Javier Simonized the dark blue car until it looked like a mirror. She told him she felt like a citizen again. Her mother looked confused, but Javier knew and laughed.

She was early for her appointment with Suarez, sat and grabbed one of his magazines. Along with the dog-eared requisite New Yorker from three seasons ago were some of Suarez's professional journals. She scanned the covers and found one with a study of Foster Care adolescent boys, and quickly flipped it open to read. Not surprisingly the article listed unfavorable outcomes for boys adopted at later ages. Her real fear was Nugent witnessing all her use of alcohol and drugs, whether there was some lasting bad effect. She tried to rationalize and bantered back and forth in her mind that her cleaned up life was the example he saw now. The door opened and she looked up. "I'm early."

"So you say." Always the shrink, she thought. Waiting for me to fill in for him than for him to offer the reasons.

"It helps when you have a car, you know?" She must have smiled because his expression was light. He must be tired of hearing her bitter complaints about taking a bus.

"What took me an hour is now only fifteen fucking minutes." She saw the light go out of his eyes, remembering his remarks that her profanity was a childish tact she used to shock. She changed her delivery. "Sorry, momentary relapse. I'll have to get my teacher language in place before next week." She followed him into the office and settled onto the couch, kicked off her sandals and tucked her legs under her.

Dr. Suarez's expectant look, raised eyebrow, had become the signal for them to begin.

Molly smiled at his intense and serious look. "You remind me of my mother." Today she felt good, hopeful, the air was crisp outside, late spring and the next round of impatiens, bougainvillea, and birds of paradise jumping out everywhere. Most of all the clean smell of the air, her favorite time of year because fall lasted until Spring came around again.

"How do I remind you of your mother?" Dr. Suarez crossed his legs neatly at the ankle, looking more like a girl getting ready for her high school photo, sitting up in front, legs exposed, so trying to look graceful.

"You and my mother always have more questions for me than I have answers. She always wants to trim up the corners of my life for me. She asks about what will happen now between me and Javier, how about Nugent, what about going back to work, the list is endless."

"Are you ready to go back to work?" Suarez's tone was back to shrink mode, but it was less bothersome to her now.

He must have sensed that she was aware of what she termed his "starter sentences," to get conversation flowing from the patient.

"Guess I fell into my own trap this time. Why don't you just tell me whatever you want me to know?"

She breathed deeply, a little intimidated at the thought of work. "Met the new vice-principal and I'm starting back as a sub next week, and then full time after Labor Day." Her mind raced ahead to the halls full of high school students, jostling one another, calling out names they made up to ridicule one another, high fiving, back slapping, making cool suggestive remarks when a pretty girl brushed past. "I missed it." She cleared her throat and repeated, "I missed it, seeing it all from the clean and sober side."

"How does this work for the day care and the principal there with the pre-school children?" He tapped his pen against his thigh as though to keep her focused and with him.

"Mrs. Dickinson understood about my leaving them." Molly knew she was being pointedly dismissive about her time at the nursery school. "Maybe I learned something about my high school students, watching the preschoolers. Maybe where many of them came from."

Her voiced trailed off. "But inside I was always seeing Stella at day care, what she would be like at three years, four years."

He waited and she felt the pressure to make the connection, no matter how painful it might be.

"Bitter sweet was seeing her in all those little kids and then missing what will never be." She brushed an imaginary speck of lint off her skirt and fell into her silent world where Stella never spoke, but surely continued to dwell.

"And the pressures of work? Your mother?" He finally interrupted her reverie.

Molly looked down at her nails, newly manicured by

Theresa's manicurist. She thought about the heap of a car she used to drive.

"I don't know any more than anyone how to predict. Just doing small steps here, not miracles."

"Is there anything else? About being reinstated?"

"Must be a real relief for that old lady, past ninety. Don't think she's used to the kids in our part of town.

"Seems like a corner is being turned, Molly. Any slips with the beer or anything else?"

Molly thought about it, "I crave the buzz and every once in a while a taste of oblivion. It gets less but doesn't seem to go away. Yet." She found herself reaching in her purse for her cigarettes, reassuring herself that at least nicotine wasn't barred from her list of pleasures. They were not there and a panic began to rise in her throat. Stupid, silly. She left them in the car.

"I'm trying to stop smoking. Christ, that's harder. Yes, I make it to N.A." She leaned forward toward where he sat. "N.A. is humiliation and sometimes, when it's not hell to be there, it's boring. And, in case you're not up on things, it's a sure fire place to connect for drugs."

He was silent.

"Surely you know that. Let me tell you. I accidentally showed up at meeting at a different place one night, a school that looked more like a prison. Had to be built in the twenties. Big red brick building, like a fortress. Well, I went in and followed the pasted up arrows to a second floor. Bunch of women my age and some older. A support group for family of the druggies and alcoholics. Turns out they were mothers of the sad sons and daughters who were such a big disappointment, the way they turned out. I listened to these women and could not help noticing how their eyes shone when they spoke of poor Meredith or Thomas falling off the wagon. Again. Understand?"

"What's your point?"

"Their kids' addictions gave them something to do. After all, the mothers and other relatives would not have their little get together without the errant child, if the child got healthy, got clean, got sober. Would they?"

"You don't see anything in what you describe as worthwhile, maybe helpful to these mothers and other family members?"

Molly shrugged, shoulders pointing way up, "Maybe."

They listened to the whooshing sound of cars in the street, for a moment lost in their own thoughts.

"I may get to experience it all myself someday, as a mother." She spoke, "I'm pregnant."

She started to bite her nails and stopped, admiring her manicure, again.

"Do you have more to say?"

"Maybe I'm internalizing your voice because I always hear a 'but' with everything you say, even when you don't say it. I don't want to lose the party atmosphere I was generating here for myself. But since I'm not sure whether its Javier's or Michael's baby I'm having, life continues to be in turmoil."

Suarez's face was the mask she came to know, no emotion, nothing. But there was some nervous energy in him, she could feel it. "You're a smart woman, you know there's DNA testing."

"Not sure I want to know. I stopped seeing Michael Dunn."

"And, you have already planned to marry, haven't you?"

"Yes. I want to. This time.

"You say no one knows? Your mother?"

"Better this way." Molly became more deliberate in her tone, her words measured. "This is the best way for me, for all of us."

"If the baby is Javier's, but if not..." Suarez didn't finish his sentence.

"Then, I will tell him. He knew I was seeing someone so it wouldn't be too big a surprise." She tried to imagine how Javier would handle what had to feel like the consummate insult to a Latino.

They talked for a while, Suarez reminding her that she was not a recovering addict the last time she carried a baby, and that she had to be careful not to relapse. Molly realized life had not simplified, that it wasn't going to be any less complex.

Molly left Suarez's office feeling less than satisfied. If she hadn't been over all this in her mind a dozen times, it wouldn't bother her so much. She still didn't have an answer, whether her choice was the best one.

She stopped at the phone in the lobby and called home.

"Hey, Nuge, put my mom on, will you?"

"You almost home? Esther is not here now."

"She's not there? Whose taking care of you?"

"She left a note. Went to the cemetery with Javier's mother."

Esther frequented the gravesite often, and when Molly couldn't take her, Javier's mother or one of his aunts was there to oblige. Molly had watched her the few times Esther relented and took the trip into Inglewood. *I guess that's typical of older people, but it's forced the reality on me in a different way.* Today she had told Suarez, "My sorrow is not some abstract thing, but in making it solid, real, it's also finite, and I can see where it will diminish over time." And at the same time, Molly saw how it brought comfort to her mother to think back fondly on all the family she had loved and that preceded her out of this life to the final point.

Nugent's voice came between her thoughts and his need to be supervised. "I'm going down to Ramon's in a minute. Javier said I should. Just dropped my backpack here."

She was relieved, he'd be with his friend and Ramon's mother was there, too.

Molly left the office-building lobby, almost walked across the busy boulevard to the bus stop before she realized her car was waiting for her in the parking lot. She parked in a lower level where her car was spared the early afternoon sun, and she opened the windows to let the air cool the interior before she started the air conditioner. What would she do? Having spoken the words to someone, she had solidified the baby's mystery. She had counted back from probable conceptions for both Javier and Dunn to find there was no way she could say without testing.

She left the lot and slid onto the freeway. The little car purred along the road. She was grateful for the time alone that it gave her, away from her mother and Nugent, time to think.

As she approached her apartment, she saw him with his friend. He was balancing on one side of his board and as quickly flipped it over and into his hand.

"Ola, Molly." He was still the little boy, though he was growing fast. "Javier said he could take me to the barber. He'll be here later." He touched her arm as he spoke. More often now, he showed affection. She knew he thought he was one of the lucky ones; the couple who knew his father had been good to him. She hugged him quickly lest his friends catch a glimpse. Javier's machismo and that of Ramon and the rest of the boys in this 'hood colored his life, and hers.

She smiled as she walked up the back steps, huffing a little, a picture in her mind of this zany family. An older Jewish woman, a daughter who was half Irish, the bi-racial foster kid and her Latino lover, almost husband.

It was a lot like the South Bronx after all.

Renee Ebert was born in Philadelphia and realized her dream to live in and experience California in the early nineties. She graduated UCLA in 1996 and took part in writing groups in Los Angeles, Orange County and Santa Cruz. She lives with her husband in Pennsylvania.

Made in the USA
Lexington, KY
15 June 2017